P9-DFX-981

Banana Kiss

BANANA KISS

BONNIE ROZANSKI

The Porcupine's Quill

Library and Archives Canada Cataloguing in Publication

Rozanski, Bonnie, 1948–
Banana Kiss / Bonnie Rozanski.

ISBN-13: 978-0-88984-276-2.--
ISBN-10: 0-88984-276-0

I. Title.

PS8635.O96B35 2005   C813'.6   C2005-903427-0

Copyright © Bonnie Rozanski, 2005.

1   2   3   4   ·   07   06   05

Published by The Porcupine's Quill, 68 Main St, Erin, Ontario NOB 1TO.
http://www.sentex.net/~pql

Readied for the press by John Metcalf.
Copy edited by Doris Cowan.

All rights reserved. No reproduction without prior written permission of the
publisher except brief passages in reviews. Requests for photocopying or other
reprographic copying must be directed to Access Copyright.

Represented in Canada by the Literary Press Group.
Trade orders are available from University of Toronto Press.

We acknowledge the support of the Ontario Arts Council and the Canada
Council for the Arts for our publishing program. The financial support of the
Government of Canada through the Book Publishing Industry Development
Program is also gratefully acknowledged. Thanks, also, to the Government
of Ontario through the Ontario Media Development Corporation's Ontario
Book Initiative.

Canada Council
for the Arts

Conseil des Arts
du Canada

ONTARIO ARTS COUNCIL
CONSEIL DES ARTS DE L'ONTARIO

In Loving Memory of my Mother and Father

Chapter One

I am strapped to the bed. The voices are telling me I've been bad again.

Some of them come periodically from a certain white-coated individual who tells me that the other voices don't really exist. But all the other voices tell me not to believe Whitecoat. So who are you to believe?

Whitecoat tells me my latest MRI shows my auditory cortex lights up when I hear those non-voices. He is there, and hears no such voices. Proof, he says that they are illusions: they are in my head. I ask again so who are you to believe – this figment who says he alone exists? Greedy, the rest of the voices say. He's trying to dominate everything.

I feel the unpleasant sensation of that prick in my arm, but tell myself I can't be sure it's real. That makes it less real, but just as unpleasant. I turn around to see the needle withdrawing. A bulky new whitecoat smiles at me. He's got a dark brown face with a missing tooth on the upper left side. On his coat pocket, it says Alex.

'Hello, Robin,' this Alex says. 'You'll be yourself in a minute. Don't worry.'

I'm not worrying. I was myself before he jabbed me in the arm.

The room seems to shift a few degrees, nothing very significant, just enough to give me another perspective on the matter. Alex stands there, off kilter. Now I am more myself, but he is unbalanced. My head hurts, but the voices seem lower. Alex is still here. Maybe this proves he is real.

'Feelin' better?' he asks.

'Than what?' I reply, trying to sit up.

He smiles, the missing tooth showing. 'Guess I can untie you. You have your meds. You're as sane as you'll ever be.' He unbuckles the leather straps.

'Who asked you?' I say, rubbing my wrists. 'I like my voices. They keep me company. Besides, on this stuff, I feel like shit.'

'Well, that's the trade-off,' he says, edging toward the door. 'Clozaril cuts your dopamine way down. But, hey, it ain't so bad. Thorazine was much worse. Be glad it's 2005.'

He's almost out the door.

'You're new, aren't you?' I ask, trying to make contact, I guess.

He stands in the doorway, wagging his head. Something about him reminds me of my mother. 'Now, Robin,' he says sadly. 'You know me. I'm Alex. I give you your evening meds.'

Yes, of course. Alex. A voice sings in the background, Alex Alex Bo-balex Banana-fana-fo Falex Mi-my-mo Malex Alex.

Dinner is downstairs in the dining room. I make my way up the hall, down the stairs, quarter turn and down some more stairs, quarter turn and straight down the hall. My wrists still hurt.

I can hear voices coming out of open double doors. Not my voices, I think. Whitecoat's voices. Real voices, he says. Like there's any difference. But right now, my body flush with Clozaril, my own voices a low background hum, these stand out, and I almost agree with him. Take away the sprightliness, the brightliness, and this is real. Whitecoat's world.

I'm on new-generation meds, as Alex says. I walk normal, not like the older schizes, who did the Thorazine shuffle. Thorazine soaked up *all* their dopamine.

Suddenly, I'm here, midway between the double doors, looking in. Blazing with light in the threshold, I'm a heavenly figure outlined against a background of green cement hallway and cracked linoleum. I squint to see the lower life forms inside. From the shadows of the dining room, Roz is waving to me from over her meat loaf. I walk in, through the double doors, silhouette blazing, and grab a plastic tray. The lady in the hairnet, upper arms swinging back and forth like Jell-O, holds a plate of brown goop over the counter. Two sad string beans standing in for vegetables say, This is real. Enjoy. I take the plate without comment and saunter over toward Roz, who, chewing, follows my every move. I sit down across from her.

'So?' she says.

'So,' I say.

The answer doesn't satisfy her. 'You okay?' she goes.

'As sane as I'll ever be. I'm full of Clozaril.'

'I heard they had to strap you down.'

I shrug. My memory isn't so good lately. One of the lower voices tells me that several whitecoats were interfering with the will of God, and God was displeased. In the light of current reality, it doesn't seem as compelling a reason as it seemed earlier. I don't answer Roz or the voice. Sometimes not answering is answering.

Roz is busy forking the congealed brown goop over to the side of her plate, revealing a grainy, liver-coloured slab.

'Mmm,' she goes.

I put my fork down, push away the plate. Who needs it? I've been gaining weight, anyway, even though I hardly eat. It's the meds, they say. Some people gain twenty pounds a year. Interesting concept, eating nothing and gaining weight. Something from nothing. Only one being I know has that power. I look over at Roz, who keeps eating, unawares. For a schizophrenic, she is downright dull. I pick up my spoon in disgust and lance my Jell-O. She's lucky I don't send down a thunderbolt right onto her stupid head.

'Penrose thinks the answer to consciousness is in quantum theory.'

'Penrose, Penrose,' Roz replies.

'Roger Penrose. Famous physicist/philosopher.' I stuff my mouth full of Jell-O, to make her wait for the rest. I can see Roz's watery blue eyes briefly inquiring, before she loses interest and goes for another string bean.

'Quantum theory,' I say. 'Quantum weirdness,' I add. 'Quantum shrewdness.' I'm on a roll. 'Quantum lewdness.'

'Stop it. Stop it. Stop it,' Roz says, getting into the rhythm.

One more is in order. 'Quantum uncertainty. Subatomic particles can exist anywhere, everywhere, nowhere. Until they are observed, they are nowhere.'

'So what do I care where they are?' Roz replies politely.

Why should I dignify that response? I, who create the particles by observing them. I, who out of nothing make something. I stuff the rest of the Jell-O into my mouth and stand up, a ray of light emanating from my brow.

Meanwhile, Roz is choking on the string bean. Cutting around the table, I give her a whack on the back.

'Rest in peace,' I say.

The next morning, Whitecoat is there before I am, of course, reclining in his leather armchair, turned toward the window as usual. I am expected to come in and sit patiently on a small, hard seat till he chooses to grace me with his attention. I study his brown tweed back, the top of his grey head, picturing the white shirt and cashmere bow tie, the triangle of grey beard trimmed carefully around thin, expressionless lips. Those curious, soulful eyes.

There. Whitecoat swivels, shirt crisply ironed, bow tie aligned, beard groomed, mouth a horizontal line, but the eyes – the eyes, all black and scolding, are giving it all away.

'Robin, you gave Martin a black eye, and bit him on the arm. He had to sedate you and to restrain you.' He leans toward me from behind the big, shiny desk, with his trademark earnest look. 'Martin didn't want to do that to you. You forced him to. Do you understand that?'

Do I understand that? I mean who does he think he's talking to?

The other voices shout at him. It's Martin's fault, they say.

'He undresses me with his eyes,' I tell him.

'That's not real, Robin. It's all in your mind.'

I shrug. 'What's in my mind is what there is.'

Whitecoat brings his hands together in front of him, stubby little fingers braided into a steeple. 'We've been through this many times, Robin. You are not God.'

'Not being God yourself, Whitecoat, you wouldn't know.' Honestly, arguing with him is ludicrous. I could crush people like him with my shoe, if I chose. Nevertheless, I compose myself. The Bible got it wrong; I am not vengeful.

'Roger Penrose,' I explain patiently, 'says brains select what to attend to from chaos, and therefore create what there is to attend to. The tree in the forest. Without the observer, it wouldn't exist. Right? But here's where Roger goes one better. There must exist an observer to observe her own existence. And what is that?' My voice grows perceptibly louder. 'What is that observing her own existence, Dr Whitecoat?' I pause for the effect, watching him. Whitecoat's fingers twitch within their steeple, giving me the impression one of them wants to poke me in the eye.

'Consciousness, that's what.' I sit back on my hard, small chair, omnipotent.

'My name is Dr Mankiewicz, Robin. And even if that's true, it has no bearing on your case. Every one of us is conscious. If observing the world created the world, that would only prove everyone is God.'

There really is no reason to talk to this little man. Whitecoat can't see where you use logic and where you don't. He pushes everything too far. It's in the knowing that you know how far to go. Of course, not everyone can be God. That would make no one God. Silly little man.

The other voices shout at him, saying insulting things, but I simply get up and, with great composure, walk out.

I walk up the winding stairs from the lobby to the living quarters, open my unlocked door and plunk myself down on the bed. Beverly's bed is empty, as usual. She's the social one. I don't see her from one minute to the other, not that I care. I have enough people in me to converse with whenever I like. The Clozaril doesn't make them disappear; it just shuts them down a little in volume. It's good if I want to read. Otherwise, they keep commenting on the writing. You know, characterization is a bit weak, boy, could this person use a course in punctuation! It takes all the spontaneity out of a story.

I seem to remember, five, oh, ten years ago, getting lost in a book. Those years when I was small enough to just crawl in under the pages with the characters. But no more. Those were the years when I was like anybody else. Excuse me, *thought* I was like anybody else. Obviously, I had powers I didn't know I had. Those powers, scrunched up tightly like the extra six dimensions, they were there, all right, but I, whoever that is, wasn't aware. The age of innocence. Reading Edith Wharton was being there, dressed to the nineteenth-century nines.

It was sometime after that that space expanded and all hell broke loose. The extra six dimensions unfurled inside me, expanding my consciousness. No longer could I fit myself into tiny enclosed places like 1870 New York. People say I went crazy, but, of course, they would think that. Be real, they say. Keep those two feet firmly planted on the ground. Don't run away with yourself. For heaven's sake, Robin, get a grip!

But they're seeing things in those same old, same old three dimensions. Now, imagine looking at that same scene, but with six more axes. What? No, of course you can't. So, don't talk to me about reality.

I plump my pillow, as much as a fibrefill pillow can be plumped. It's almost a case in contradiction, fibrefill and plump. I throw myself backward onto its hard plumpness, a mushroom cloud of fibredust rising into the air, and stare at the ceiling. My usual mid-morning convention. The voices are readying themselves. Most are complimentary, flattering, even sycophantic. It's a pleasure to listen.

Your Holiness, they may say. Your Femininity, your Omnipotence. Sometimes they trash Beverly. They tell me she's sloppy and dead, and I should take her pillow. Most of the time they say nasty, uncouth things about Whitecoat, things that make me laugh. Only occasionally do they tell me to lie in wait for the orderly and bite him. I usually have enough fortitude to see these voices for what they are: devils, and of no consequence. Yesterday, I was low blood sugar or otherwise downish, and lashed out at Martin. I wasn't Myself. In the long run, though, it improves their dispositions if I let them run amok a bit. Amok a bit.

Still, there is something about Martin that makes me hate him, no matter what he does. He looks at me when I don't want him to, undresses me with his eyes. Not that it is physical, mind you. He doesn't actually pull the clothes off me with his gaze. He's looking underneath, creating a new software version of Robin Farber: Robin 6.3, or the Human Genome 2005. But is it real? If he pictures me with three breasts and two belly buttons, does that mean I have three breasts and two belly buttons? Robin 6.3 does. The million-dollar question is what she has to do with me.

Anyway, it freaks me out. Martin tells me he's doing nothing, that it's all in my mind, but, of course, what's in my mind is what there is.

Mom and Howard came last week. They took me out to eat, but were really put out with me for something I said. I don't even know what. No, I can't remember. No, I don't, and don't tell me that I do.

During salad, Howard broached my coming home. Something he said above the noise of all the rest of the voices, something like the insurance only pays so much, and there are other mouths to feed. Right, like what other mouths? Melissa is out of the house. Billy is a parakeet. How much does a bag of seed cost?

Mom tried to shush him but not hard enough. We tried it before, she said. Two, three times. She needs the care. You aren't helping, Howard. Why don't you go out and take a brisk walk, Howard? Howard, dear, just for a few minutes. The people are all looking at us, and I want her to calm down. Thank you, Howard.

The door suddenly opens wide, banging into the wall. Beverly stands there, all four foot eight of her, frizzy hair and big ass. Apparently, she is not dead, and it's a good thing I didn't touch her pillow. She clumps in, picks up the same *Vogue* magazine she's been reading for a month, and falls onto her bed in a kind of twisting motion.

'Five point seven,' I say. 'You'll have to do better than that if you want to beat the Russians.'

She looks at me as if she's going to cry. But that's the way she always looks, so I don't comment. Beverly is Beverly. Is Beverly. What can I say that would make her any less Beverly?

Finally, she puts down the magazine. She has not even turned the page. At this rate, she'll be reading this same magazine for the rest of her life. How long can a magazine last if you never finish the page? Like the limits we used to learn about in math class. If a tortoise crawls one foot, then half a foot, then half of half of the foot, and so on, halving the distance he has to go each time, how long will it take that poky tortoise to cross the room?

It will never cross the fucking room, says one of the more uncouth of my voices. Never, never, never. Okay, I tell it in the privacy of my head. You're right, but I don't want to hear that language again, do you hear?

Fortunately, I am God, so the voices do not rule me. I rule them. It's an important distinction. Beverly's voices are very loud and intrusive. Sometimes I think even I can hear them, they're that loud. They tell her to do all sorts of bad things like throwing herself out the window. That's why Whitecoat keeps her on such a high dosage, to shut them down. Unfortunately, it kind of damps down the rest of her brain, too. Anyway, the windows are all nailed shut.

'Heard they had to put you in restraints,' Beverly says suddenly.

I turn toward her, surprised. We don't talk much, usually. 'Yeah,' I say.

'Are they upping your meds?'

'Not yet. Whitecoat's trying reason first.'

Beverly laughs, another rare occurrence. 'Is it working?'

'You don't reason with God,' I respond.

'So they say,' she replies, and picks up the magazine from the floor. I watch her looking at the exact same spot on the page for the next four minutes until I grow sleepy and doze off.

'Afternoon meds!' a voice from above announces. I open my eyes to see Martin, leaning over me, peeping at me with one good eye. The left one is black and nearly closed. There's a bandage on his arm. Despite the damage I caused him, I can see that he is undressing me again with his eyes. I want to bite him someplace where it will really hurt.

I jump up, almost butting him in the head.

'Damn it, Robin. You'll kill me yet.'

'Stop undressing me with your eyes or I will.'

He extends the little paper cup with two pills. 'You make this all up in your head. And don't threaten me. Don't make me tell Dr Mankiewicz you're causing trouble again.'

Don't make him. He has a point, actually. If what I pay attention to is what I create, I make him do it. I make it up. I make the whole thing up.

'I've decided to forgive you,' I say.

On his way out, Martin laughs and shakes his head.

I glance over at Beverly's empty bed, panning around the room. Gone. Maybe I made her disappear.

My father was a sailor. He was on leave in Quebec when he met my mother twenty-five years ago and married her before the leave was up. Mother told Melissa and me he stayed in the navy for the next three years, then gave it up, after I was born. He tried getting work in the navy ship-yard, and stuck with it for a year before the symptoms struck. That's what Mother says, anyway. Before the symptoms struck.

Then he was in and out of the hospital before he came home one day and hung himself from a light fixture in the basement. I was only a year and a half, but I can picture the whole thing, and then he came back to me several times and we've had whole conversations about why he did it. He told me nothing in life was real enough for him. He told me the physical body of someone, the phenotype, is just the manifestation of his genes, the genotype. What is real? he would ask. Is it the physical existence of something or is it the coding of it that tells how to build it? The ship or the blueprint? The existence or the knowledge? Maybe, he said, existence is less than we think it is, and knowledge, the code of it, is all there is. He wanted to prove it, needed to prove it in a scientific way. So, he gave his genes to me, and made sure his body was good and dead. Now, he says it was the best thing he ever did. He proved that it is the code, not the body that is real. The concept of the person, not the person. The soul, really. I don't see him much, but I hear him sometimes in my head. He comes and goes, still a sailor in his soul.

I never tell Mother about how we meet. She's never forgiven him for what she calls ruining her life. Never mind that she gave birth to two delightful children, one of whom is All-Knowing. Mother says I got his genes, not hers. Melissa has hers. I know she never liked me as much as Melissa, who has her genes. Who cares? I got his.

'Chicken,' Roz says. 'I think it's chicken.'

I am sitting across from her some hours later. The noise level in Berkshire's main dining room is setting new records. Several seriously disturbed individuals moan and cry, pots clang, plastic knives crack under the pressure of slicing old, dry meat. Voices within and without heads add to the cacophony. I briefly picture an alternative universe, complete with darkened restaurant, candlelight and music. Should I zap this world and start again? Most likely it would all turn out the same or worse.

'It's either chicken or it's not chicken,' I say. 'Thinking it's chicken doesn't make it chicken.'

'See?' she says, uncovering it from the yellow congealed sauce. 'It's white.'

'Does it have a wing?'

Roz looks closely at the thing that she has uncovered and shrugs, begins to eat it, anyway.

'Well?' I ask, unwilling to commit myself to this piece of white something that has no recognizable parts.

'Eat it,' she says.

'You're not my mother.' I take a spoon and push away all the sauce, wiping it down with a waxy napkin until it's completely naked. The unidentified potentially flying object has no traces of wing, leg or hoof. What other parts can an animal have? Skin. I find some of this, which bears no witness, but soon, toward the back, I find the half-quill of a feather.

'Chicken,' I say and begin to eat.

Then this guy comes over. I've seen him plenty of times. He's not so tall, but cute. Tan hair so straight it kind of sticks up all over. Kind of high-bridged nose, good chin. Pale. None of us get out much. Anyway, he comes over, sits down across from us, as if he does this all the time. He takes a look at the mystery meat on my plate, which I have practically dissected.

'What is it?' he asks.

Before I can say anything, Roz says, 'Chicken.'

He looks at it doubtfully, asks Roz, who is smiling openly at him despite a full mouth, 'You want to taste mine?'

'Sure.' She takes a little bite of his. A minute passes, and she is not dead. He is satisfied, and begins to eat.

'Name?' I ask.

'Derek.'

Derek Derek Bo-berrick Banana-fana-fo Ferek Mi-my-mo Merrick Derek, a voice sings.

'Diagnosis?'

'"Manic Depressive" is what they have on the chart.'

'You've seen your chart?' Roz asks.

'I can read upside down from five feet away.'

'With paranoid tendencies, I bet,' I add.

Derek shrugs. 'Lots of tendencies. You?'

'Garden variety schizophrenic,' I say. 'With ubiquitous tendencies.'

He puts his fork down and reaches over the table. I wipe my hand on my waxy, sauce-covered napkin, and extend a greasy hand. 'Robin.'

'Nice to meet you,' Derek says, reaching for his napkin first. We shake hands, from either side of the napkin, dancers at a Jewish Orthodox wedding.

'Roz,' Roz says, but no one is paying any attention.

There's something in the way Derek Derek Bo-berrick looks at me. It's not like Martin, who looks AT you, burrowing deeper into you than you want anyone to go. It's not like Mother who looks at you with this overwhelming compassion that makes your heart hurt. It's not like Howard who doesn't want to hear or see too much. And it's not like Roz or Beverly who aren't entirely there. Not too hot and not too cold, not too hard and not too soft. It's just right. Whoosh, I don't know if I ever felt this before. I'm not in Kansas any more.

I look back. He smiles. I smile. Something transmits between us telepathically. Connection, current, contact.

One of my voices begins to give a compulsive play-by-play. Good vibes. He's not looking away. Steady, steady. We may be losing him, folks. Robin, Robin, do something!

'Been here long?' I ask.

'Since July. I'm just coming off a manic episode. Dr Mankiewicz has been working with me, getting my head together. For a while there, I thought I was all-powerful!'

This is all very familiar. He cuts a very small piece of white meat, laughs inappropriately, puts it in his mouth and chews. Above the mouth, his eyes are still singing to me.

Roz spears a string bean and sticks it in her mouth. 'See?' she says. 'The string beans are all right to eat.' Obviously, she's making a play for Derek, offering herself as his own private food-taster. But it's not going to work. She's using the wrong frequency. He's not receiving. His receiver is full up with me. Ten-ten on your dial. All music all the time.

Howard called me today, at least I think he did. It could have been in my head, but Howard has never appeared there. He's real, in the sense of being colourless and stolid, completely unethereal. He's like the bits and pieces of real life all stuck together: tall but lumpy, round-shouldered, face like a potato. If Howard had never existed, no one would have dreamed him up.

He says Mother wants me to come home for Thanksgiving, and he wants me to try staying a month. He's sure I can do it. Why would I want to endure in Berkshire if I can enjoy at home with my loved ones?

Loved ones, I say. Did I say it out loud? I don't know. He got miffed, as usual, with me. Not that he actually ever says anything negative. He just slows his speech down to glacier speed, slower and slower as if he's talking to a demented idiot, which, come to think of it, he may think I am. Which just goes to show you, of course, that he can't see the forest for the trees. The tree in the forest, does it make a noise? Not for Howard, that's for sure. He only sees what is there, what is assuredly and *a priori* there, solid and obvious, physical, something his senses can't miss. He never makes anything up – it's got to be already there for him to see it. Someone else has to create it first so that it is there. Someone else has to conceive it, chop down the tree, hew it into boards and nail it together first, before Howard can even allow that there is a thing in front of his eyes. And it must be a thing – a single, physical, red, green, big, little, hard, soft, undeniable *thing*. Patterns of things – they whiz right past him. Ideas, concepts, Platonic absolutes, not a clue. It's got to be hard-wired in Howard's brain for it to register.

I've tried to talk to him, to explain to him that the things he sees and hears are no more real than the things that I see and hear. And mine are so much more interesting. I carefully edit my conversation to filter out all references to God. He really doesn't like that. That really turns him off, especially when I blurt out that I create the world by looking. Then he abruptly turns away and says VERY SLOWLY he'll see me next week. This is a guy who can't deal with reality, believe me. What a jerk. I can't see what Mother ever saw in him.

Mother, another story. When she was young, she was someone else entirely. She ran away with a man she hardly knew. She won a beauty contest and played the violin. But now Mother is Mrs Howard Applebaum, and all she wants is for me to be normal. Last week, for instance, she takes me aside, asks me how I'm doing.

'Ask the doctor,' I say.

'I'm asking you,' she says.

'You don't want to hear what I have to say.'

'Oh, Robin,' she says, really, really disappointed. 'All I want is for you to talk to me.'

As I said, God is not vengeful. So, I try to talk to her. I tell her about the extra six dimensions that used to be all scrunched up until space expanded inside me. How subatomic particles can exist anywhere, everywhere, nowhere; that, until I observe them, they are nowhere. Sometime in the middle, her eyes glaze over. She turns toward the window and stands there, probably not even listening. So, I break off and ask her if she really thinks there is something out there. That she hears.

'Oh, Robin,' she says. You'd think my name was O'Robin, she says that so much. 'I guess I'll talk to Dr Mankiewicz.' Then she goes out.

See, I could make them do as I wished, but I won't do that. I create a world almost full up with determinism, but leave the top bit unfilled, for free will. Some people will then go on and on about the world being half-full, and the others will go on and on about it being half-empty, but that's their choice. There's got to be that little bit, maybe not even half, maybe a fraction of a fraction, that is void, so that people can fill it as they choose. What's the point, otherwise?

A few days later, Whitecoat swivels in his leather recliner to face me.

'Robin, your mother and stepfather have decided that it would do you some good to go home for Thanksgiving.'

Sharp, stabbing pain in my chest. 'Do I have anything to say about this?'

He smiles at me. I hate those smiles. A smile is supposed to mean happiness and joy. I don't know what Whitecoat's smiles mean.

'Go ahead,' he says. 'Say whatever you want.'

That sort of gets to me, that I can say anything I want. Before, I was going to say that I wasn't at all sure that it would do me any good to go home. I can just hear my mother sighing, 'All I want is for you to talk to me,' and Howard, the moment I try to illustrate a simple point in quantum mechanics, backing toward the doorway, telling me he'll see me later. What? Okay, you don't have to scream. I hear you. If I'm so high and mighty, why can't I just make Howard sit still and listen? Well, think about it. I left the top part empty on purpose. I gave humankind free will. And Howard would take an entire decade to start over from scratch, anyway. So, I'm pondering all this stuff, and Whitecoat is sitting there smiling at me, and now I don't have a clue.

'Fine,' I say.

'A long weekend away is a good thing. It will give you a chance to get re-acclimated to the real world. It's been a long time.'

'Whatever.'

'You'll get a good, home-cooked meal,' he coaxes.

Psychiatrists are so good at … psychology. Suddenly, I can almost smell the garlic wafting from the brown, crispy breast of my mother's turkey. Sweet potatoes with those little marshmallows, bursting with rich sweetness, sweet richness. Deep-dish apple pie with curvaceous scoops of homemade rum-raisin ice cream. My taste buds are already transporting me to a long, draped table of goodies. Then I wake up brutally to the reality of brown goop, green goop and red goop with Reddi-Wip. Why was it I didn't want to go?

The voices have started to get louder, despite the fact that I swallowed my medication about an hour ago. It should be peaking in my bloodstream, grabbing onto all my little receptors, perking up my prefrontal cortex, shutting down all that excess dopamine in my limbic system. It should be top of the morning for me, but the voices are coming on so strong I can hardly attend to Whitecoat. If I don't attend to him, maybe he'll go away.

Zap him with a thunderbolt, one says.

It was probably his idea in the first place, another volunteers.

Why would you want to stay in this place anyway?

'What?' I ask.

'As long as you take your medication and don't spit it out in the toilet – I know you do, Robin – you're about as functional as any of the patients here at Berkshire.'

'Not you,' I say to Whitecoat. 'You,' I tell the one who said it was probably his idea in the first place. It's an interesting concept. I want to hear more.

'Robin. Focus. *Focus*,' the doctorly voice says from behind the desk.

I look up to see Whitecoat, a displeased look on his face. I am not to chat with the other conversationalists in my head ON HIS TIME. Better never, but certainly not ON HIS TIME.

'I'm listening,' I say.

'If you take your medication,' he says, obviously for the second time, 'you will be ALL RIGHT. Take it slow. E-mail me how you're doing. Do you have a computer at home?'

I pondered his last phrase. 'Computer?' The thought flits through my head that I can grab the messages directly off the ether.

'Yes, computer, Robin. I know exactly what you are thinking. You CANNOT send and receive messages in your head. Erase that thought.'

Whitecoat can do it, why not me?

Beverly doesn't much care that I'm going. She says goodbye, but there's a glint in her eye that seems to be aimed at my pillow.

Roz has tears in her eyes, which she wipes with her napkin. I have to reassure her that I'll be back. I always have, I always will.

But it's Derek I don't want to leave. We're just getting started on something. Maybe it's that he's coming off the manic phase that landed him in Berkshire, and is going through a very short interval where he is balanced along the top – he calls it the escarpment – before he tips over the other side. Meanwhile, Derek's the sanest person here, Whitecoat included, but more interesting, and definitely cuter. He's afraid my going may just kick him off the ledge. I told him to hang on. I'll be back. For sure.

Howard is beeping out front, and I'm staring at my half of the room. It looks the same, with or without me. Generic white curtains, bedspread. Nothing on the walls. Easy come, easy go. And here I am all packed: my clothes, my toothbrush, my books, my life all rolled up into one suitcase. It's not much of a life, if it fits into one suitcase.

I suddenly feel panicked. I'm not going home. I am home. One foot in the room, the other in the hall.

The voices, not so complimentary, are suddenly jumping all over each other.

Stay. You know you're coming back, so why bother?

What are you doing? Are you crazy?

You'll never make it out of here.

I look up and down the corridor, searching for some reason to stay or go. A small, wide figure comes closer. White coat, burly body, sauntering toward me. I wait, one foot in, one foot out. Do I come? Do I go? Coming closer, black hair, one greenish, brownish eye, bandage on the arm. Martin. I see him. He sees me. What's he staring at, damn him? I grab my suitcase and make like a bat out of hell.

Chapter Two

The ride is long and uneventful. Howard tries to be sociable, I'll give him that.

'Your Mom sure makes a great turkey.'

'Umhmm.' I picture all my receptors grabbing onto whatever dopamine is still left in my system. Happy, happy, happy.

'We've put your room right back to the way it used to be.'

'You changed it?' I ask. The glass half-full. I do it myself.

Fake cough. 'We were using it as an office.'

'Umhmmm.'

They took your room, I hear from my head. They don't want you back.

But Howard asked me to come, I tell it.

'I'm glad you're here,' Howard says.

He said he's glad. I'm not listening to you.

You'll listen, it says.

No, I say firmly.

It's one of the devils again, always trying to bait the boss. Game of cat and mouse. Hat and house. I rummage through my bag to make sure my pills are there. Yes, one bottle, enough for four days. Derek. Derek. Bo-berrick. Banana-fana-fo Ferek. Mi-my-mo Merrick. Derek. Drown 'em out. Show 'em who's boss. Mi-my-mo Moss. Blow 'em out of the water. Banana-fana-fo Fater. Father.

Another voice, from the area behind the steering wheel. 'Earth to Robin,' Howard says.

The voice inside adds, Howard always thinks that one is so funny.

'Sorry,' I say, ignoring the inside talk. 'What?'

'I only said that Melissa is going to be there.'

'Good.'

Tell him your father's coming, too, the devil says.

'No,' I say.

'What?' Howard asks.

'Nothing.'

Tell him.

I close my eyes and try to visualize the speaker so I can shoot it down, video-game style. Pow! Pow!

Tell him. Pow! Pow!

Tell him. Pow! Pow!

The car stops in front of the house. I rush out, shooting devils in my head who won't shut up. My mother waits at the door, arms open. There is no room to either side of her. I can't cut to the right or to the left. I step into her arms.

'Robin!' O'Robin.

Tell her your father is coming, the voice repeats. I ignore it as much as I can. I knew this would happen. Why didn't Whitecoat help me, instead of coaxing me with garlicky turkey and marshmallowed sweet potatoes? So, sure, maybe my father is coming. But tell someone that, and they'll put you in restraints no sooner than you get in the door. Don't tell anyone, and you can have a happy Thanksgiving. Maybe. Don't ask. Don't tell.

Melissa is jumping up and down in the living room, waiting for her turn. It's been a long time.

Mother finally releases me to my sister.

'Robin! You're looking … good!'

Like I really believe that. Reality and illusion. Truth and lies. It's not the schiz who doesn't tell the truth. It's all the truth to us. It's the guy on the street. It's the doctor in the chair. The neighbour. The sister. Lying is knowing what's not real, and saying it anyway.

I give her a hug. I don't know. Maybe that's a lie.

She doesn't notice any of this. She's busy smoothing my hair, kissing me on the cheek, talking non-stop.

'It's been … how long has it been? Eight months? Nine, ten? I can't keep track of it.'

I shrug. Eight, nine, ten. It's all the same to me.

'Sorry I never got to visit you in Berkshire. You know, it's *such* a long drive. And I've been working around the clock.' She pauses, such a little pause, but here it comes, here it comes. 'Oh,' she says casually, 'Max sends his love.'

'Sure, sure.'

The voice says, sure Max sends his love. Who do you believe?

Max Max. Bo-bax. Banana-fana-fo Fax. Mi-my-mo Max. Max.

Howard comes from behind, carrying my suitcase.

'I'm just going to carry this into *your* room,' he says.

He walks past me, down the hallway. I start to follow him. To hell with Melissa, who's still telling me all about her job, and the plans for the wedding, and how hard it is to work and plan at the same time. How ARE you, she finally asks, when I'm halfway down the hall.

'Fine, fine,' I say, 'I'm good,' as I disappear into my bedroom-cum-office-cum-bedroom. Well, maybe we all lie, come to think about it.

I drop my bag on the floor, plunk down on the bed and stare at the wall. Max sends his love, she says. Sends it where, I wonder. I snuffle briefly.

Max. We used to lie on this very bed, me where I am now, Max on the outside, head propped on his bent arm, glasses half-down his nose, expounding on the mysteries of the universe.

'Quarks,' he'd say, for instance. 'The smallest things we know. There are six types: up, down, charmed, strange, top and bottom.'

He'd tell me how up and down make up all the protons and neutrons in the universe. How the other four live inside particles that exist for only fractions of a second, so really they don't compare to up and down, which make all the stuff that counts. 'Wouldn't it be strange to see a charmed quark?' he'd say, and I'd laugh.

Then he'd tell me about the matching antiquarks. How, when a quark meets an antiquark, they self-destruct, expiring in a blaze of energy. They meet; they kiss,' Max would say. 'Then, phssst!'

It was the best time. Just the best time.

I miss Max so much. He would tell me things I didn't know, things I needed to know, but didn't even know that I didn't know. He was my teacher, and, once, my lover. My up-down lover. My strange, charmed lover.

And then there are leptons and muons and tauons, and anti-leptons, and anti-muons, and anti-tauons. And bosons, I almost forgot. We're all made of these things, and after a star dies or a person or an asteroid, they return to the universe to make up other things. Max would say that means we're all made of the same stuff – star stuff.

Damn. I hate when I do that. I'm not going to think about Max any more. I get up off the bed, straighten up the multicoloured patch quilt Grandma made for me a million years ago, back when Grandma was still a physical presence, and take a long look at the room. Howard was right. They did put the room back the way it was before. As best I remember it, anyway. On the wall, there's the watercolour I painted of Niagara Falls. The wallpaper is still that moss green with tan flecks, the stuff they put in after I more or less destroyed the paper with the red and yellow ducks. They put in a new tan rug to go with the flecks, but that's old news. I think that was more for the office than for me. And there's a computer. I step up to it, fondle the keys. Howard says it has internet access.

I'm armed with Whitecoat's personal e-mail address, AND Derek's. Derek says he never goes anywhere without his laptop. I've got them both squirrelled away on a piece of napkin in my suitcase. My emergency numbers. I'm going to tape the napkin to the desk with a piece of cellophane tape, so I don't lose them. Maybe I'll write it on another piece of paper, and tape that to the desk, so I can leave the napkin in the suitcase. In case I lose the first.

Such insecurity from an all-knowing Being! But a foolish consistency is the hobgoblin of little minds, and mine is not a little mind.

I open the suitcase. There it is. I copy it carefully to another piece of paper, then tape it to the desk. I turn on the computer, move my mouse to the Netscape Messenger icon and double-click. The screen shifts, then settles on a list of Howard's e-mails. I could read those e-mails, if I chose, but, hell, who wants to see the contents of Howard's consciousness?

I click on *new message*, and watch as a little window opens. On top, it says 'To:'. I type in Derek's address, careful with every period and ampersand. I move to the subject line. How can I know the subject, when I haven't written it, yet? I put in a question mark. To write or not, that is the question. I move to the big, blank body. I am poised above the keyboard, thinking of Derek.

Hello, dear, I hear.

It is hard to switch allegiances in mid-stride. This is not Derek's voice.

How soon they forget, the voice says.

Father! How could I not know that voice?

I'm just back from Mauritania. I wanted you to be the first to hear from me.

I am stupidly disappointed. I always thought, hoped, that I was the only one. Now, I hear I am only the first. There are others, I can't help thinking aloud. Of course, he hears me. It's difficult to keep secrets in one's head.

Absolutely, the voice says, no rebuke in its tone. *You can't expect to keep me to yourself.*

He shifts gears laterally. *How's your mother?*

There's no need to answer. All I have to do is think of Mother, Howard, Melissa, Billy, the whole mishpucha. He gets the picture.

Howard, Father says and laughs. We both laugh.

And Max? Father finally asks.

Max Max. Bo-bax. Banana-fana-fo Fax. Mi-my-mo Max. Max. The other voices crowd in, trying to drown out a spurt of dopamine in my temporal lobes.

He couldn't hack it, could he?

Likes Melissa better.

Max is marrying Melissa, another says in singsong.

There is a visceral feeling of pain, which seems to come from the centre of my chest. Max Max. Bo-bax.

Don't listen to them, dear. Max is history. Forget Max. Derek is now. Go for it, sweetie, and don't look back.

Thank you, Father. I won't look back.

Good, sweetie. Have to go. You know me. I can't stay too long in any one place. See you soon. Bye.

The pain is gone, but in its place is a black hole which is sucking at my heart. The rest of the voices are going at it, arguing among themselves, but it's more of a background hum. I may be the centre of their being, but they lead independent lives. Not all of what they say is meant for me. I readjust my viewpoint from the inside of my head, back to several inches in front of me: the computer screen. I see Derek's e-mail address, and a big blank page.

Max is history, I think. Derek is now. Don't look back. I begin to type.

Hey, guy! How ya doin'? I'm trying to be light and humorous, to pick up Derek's spirits, and mine along with them.

Hope you're still sitting on your escarpment, and not sliding down into the depths of despair. Me, I'm in my bedroom, which is not really my bedroom anymore. Howard's computer is sitting on my old desk, and there's all this clutter they've piled up in a corner of the room. Mother's knitting, two tennis rackets and a can of balls, some scrapbooks. What looks like the insides of a radio. It's not my room anymore. You can't go home again. Haha.

Haha. I sit there looking at the pile of clutter, smelling good smells from the kitchen, and thinking miserable thoughts. The voices are getting louder, making it hard to concentrate on writing.

He's just a shit, that Max, says the uncouth voice. Shit, shit, shit, shit. He deserves to die for what he did to you.

I don't like that language, I say. Besides, Max never really did anything. It's what he didn't do. Visit me. Write me. Remember me. Love me.

But your own sister! She's worse than Max. Shit, shit, shit, shit.

You heard what I said. You don't want to mess with me when I'm angry.

The voice has gotten louder, and isn't obeying as it usually does.

He just turned on a dime, that Max. One minute he says he loves you, the next, you're dirt. You go from being in the back seat of his car with your underpants off, to … zap them both with a thunderbolt!

He was scared, I say. He was just scared of my behaviour.

Like you weren't, the voice says. You thought you were going crazy.

I *was* going crazy.

Crazy is as crazy does, the voice says.

Suddenly, Melissa's voice is at the door. 'Robin, Mom says you need to take your pills.'

No knock, Melissa just barges in like royalty. She sees me at the computer.

'Oh?' she says, sidling around the pile of junk and looking over my shoulder at the computer screen.

Zap them with a thunderbolt, the voice says again. I say shhh, but make like I was going to say 'shit.'

Melissa is reading my e-mail to Derek. 'Who's Derek?' she asks sweetly.

She's doing it again. She's going to steal him from right under my nose.

'No!' I say.

Melissa looks at me strangely, hands me my two pills and a half glass of water.

'You don't want to tell your own sister?'

Don't tell her ANYTHING, I hear.

Shut up, I want to say, but that will just incense it more. I take the pills and water from Melissa and swallow.

'So?' she says. 'Who's Derek?'

'Just some guy I met at Berkshire.'

'Oh. Schizoid?' Melissa asks.

'The word is schizophrenic, not schizoid. Schizoid is something else. No. He's manic depressive.' Melissa never bothers to understand anything about me. It's always been that way, why should I expect anything different?

'Do you like him?' she persists. For the first time since I'm home, I really look at my sister. Bleached blond hair, translucent skin, the kind of body Max wanted from me.

'Yeah, I like him. But you wouldn't.'

She looks at me a long minute. 'How do you know?'

'I know your type,' I say.

She seems to be thinking for a second. A second at a time is all Melissa can manage. I, at least, was the bright one. 'What's my type?' she finally says.

Zap her! The voice says.

'Max,' I say.

Her eyes slowly light up with comprehension. Her mouth opens, but the words take their time. 'Robin, was it this thing with Max and me that finally drove you over the edge?' Like it's never come up before.

Max Max bo-bax. I turn back to the screen and, right in the middle of the e-mail, start to type, 'I will not covet my sister's boyfriend, I will not covet my sister's boyfriend.'

Melissa's eyes crawl from word to word. You can tell she's still working on the top part of the e-mail, the part that reads, 'Hope you're still sitting on your escarpment, and not sliding down into the depths of despair.' It takes a minute or so for her to get down to the bottom. Finally, I see her shake her head, confused. Then it dawns on her.

'I knew it! I just knew you still held that against me!'

Melissa storms out of the room, shouting, 'Mother!'

I backspace over the 'I will not covet my sister's boyfriend, I will not covet my sister's boyfriend,' and type in, 'Wish you were here. REALLY. Love, Robin.' Arrow up, up, up, up, up, and add: 'Subject: Why did I ever come?' I move the mouse over the little box that says SEND, and click. Into the ether it goes. Maybe I'll be able to pick up his response on my dental fillings during dessert.

Dinner smells, and 'Dinner' shouts waft down the hallway.

This is why I came. This is what Whitecoat seduced me with. This is what made me decide against my better judgment to come visit family during Thanksgiving. I might as well get up from my little girl's bed and make my way down the hall.

Clozaril has done its job well. The voices are sleeping. They're in hibernation, like a big bear, waiting to rouse themselves for an après-slumber meal. I tiptoe around them. Maybe I can leave them here while I go to dinner. Step out from myself and let the body partake alone. I go out into the hall.

'Robin!' I hear from Howard, as I step into the living room. I can see him beckoning to me from the dining room L. Table set for four. How intimate. Mother, Howard, Melissa, and me. Billy is in his cage, sleeping under his wing. Max sends his love. I bet.

Howard is busy sawing up the turkey. Melissa is setting down sweet potatoes on white linen. Mother is taking off her apron. I slide into place. It's never been my thing to cook, anyway. Mom's the cook, Melissa, assistant cook and waitress. Howard opens cans and bottles, and does surgery on the main dish. Me, I'm clean-up crew. It suits our talents and personalities. It's like old times, and not like old times. You can't go home again, Haha.

The image of the dining table is so primal. Salad plates interspersed between the dinner plates, napkins to the left of the dinner plate, with two forks on top; glasses, knives and spoons to the right of the dinner plate. All very orderly, logical. But where to sit down? Is the salad plate to your left or to your right? There's only this unbroken sequence of plate, fork, plate, glass, knife, spoon, plate, fork, plate, glass, knife, spoon ad infinitum. Is my fork to the left of my dinner plate, or is my fork the one that follows the salad plate to my right? Where does it all start? I watch my mother casually pick up her napkin, grab the salad tongs and drop salad on a salad plate, starting the ripple around the table. Someone made a choice; the symmetry is broken. Salad plates are to one's left, then forks and napkins, then dinner plates, glasses, knives and spoons. Hallelujah!

Melissa seems determined to be civil. Maybe Mother had something to do with that. That's fine. I'm not vengeful.

'Sweet potatoes?' she says, passing the plate toward me.

'Thanks,' I say, taking the plate and serving myself a little bit.

'White meat or dark?' Howard asks, like we haven't done this particular dialogue twenty times before.

'Dark,' Mother says.

'Dark,' Melissa says.

'White,' I say. Genes don't lie.

We pass everything around once or twice, then sit down to do some serious eating.

'Glorious, Donna,' says Howard. 'As usual.'

'The turkey came out really well,' says Melissa.

I nod, my mouth full. Better than brown goop, any day.

'So, how's your job?' Howard asks. Since I don't have a job, I figure the question's not for me.

'Work, work, work,' Melissa says. 'But good. With Christmas coming, we can hardly keep anything in stock.'

As an aside, I remind myself that Melissa is a department manager at All-mart. Women's shoes, I think. She always thought she was tough shit, even with a C average in high school. Now, she thinks she's tough shit as a department manager at All-mart. I remember reading once that mediocre minds always think they are smarter than they are. That's Melissa.

I eat all the marshmallows off the top of the sweet potatoes.

Why not? says a familiar voice. Enjoy it while you can.

I breathe a sigh of relief. Father is back. But I will have to talk to him within the confines of my head. I mustn't say anything out loud. I know what would happen, if I did.

I remember those potatoes, Father says. And the turkey. The white meat was always so juicy. Almost wish I had a body again. How's it taste?

I savour the tastes, just for him. A sweet, smooth, almost carroty taste. A savoury, juicy taste, with a strong dose of garlic. Rich, mouth-watering turkey skin, crackling in my mouth. He may not have the sense of it, but he can get the idea. The idea of sweet potatoes. No, the idea of taste. The idea of anything – is it more or less than the thing itself? Father and I have a quick conversation on this point, though no words are used. Ideas fly forth: perception, the pleasure principle, Platonic Absolutes. High in the sky, these abstractions. Lucy in the sky with diamonds. Father understands my associations. I understand his. No point in wasting words. All the time I keep eating. I take seconds; after all I'm eating for two. Father stays with me for moral support.

'Robin?' I hear all of a sudden. Mother is gazing at me with that corrugated-forehead, whatever-am-I-going-to-do-with-Robin look. Her nose wrinkles up, and her eyes get all slitty.

'Aren't you going to answer your sister?' she asks.

Uh, oh. Wasn't listening. 'Sorry, Melissa. What did you say?'

Melissa is giving Mother their secret look. The look that says, there she goes again. Only Howard is not included, as he usually isn't. Clueless, he is balancing a slice of cranberry sauce on a slab of turkey, placing peas and stuffing on top till it becomes a layer cake. Howard likes his tastes all mixed together. Now he's cutting a slice of this extravaganza, spearing it with his fork and lifting it to his mouth.

'Robin?!' Mother says, her forehead a mass of wrinkles. Uh, oh. Wasn't listening again.

'What?'

'Oh, Robin,' Mother says. O'Robin.

'I asked you whether you'd be coming to my wedding,' Melissa says, a tightness around her mouth. 'You'd,' not 'you'll.' Whether I would, not whether I will. There's a difference.

Well, too bad, I don't like the question, no matter how she parses it. I spear a piece of turkey with my fork, and put it in my mouth, chewing the required fourteen times.

Tell her to screw herself, the uncouth voice says.

You have no obligation to go, your Omnipotence, another says.

Father, are you there? I ask urgently. Father, what should I do?

You can do it, Father says. You can do anything. Tell her yes, you'll be there. Whatever happens, happens.

Fourteen, I count and put down my fork. 'No problem,' I say. I can do anything.

'You mean you'll come?' Melissa chokes.

'Of course,' I say, a light show playing in my hair. Little do they know who I am. I am magnanimous, omnipotent, forgiving. Max is dirt. But dirt is Adam, the Hebrew for dirt. If I gave them free will, they are not perfect. What can I do, except to forgive what I have created? I bow my head, give them all a beatific smile. In my head, I hear Father say, Amen.

I am in the kitchen, washing up. Father has gone again. The voices are revving up, telling dirty jokes, calling Melissa names. I shush them, a smile on my lips. After all, they are funny.

All of a sudden, I feel a buzzing in my teeth. A response from Derek.

I play back my mind tape of Whitecoat telling me I cannot receive messages in my head. What does he know? Whitecoat is the ultimate authority. What he says, goes. If he can't do it, nobody can. He doesn't need proof; he just knows. Well, the same with me, I tell myself. I surely don't need proof. I just know.

I finish soaping and rinsing a glass, careful to place it in the drain board before I answer.

Buzz, buzz, buzz. Yes?

Miss you, the voice says. I miss you, Robin. I'm falling off the escarpment, down into a deep hole.

'No, no!' I shout, loud enough for everyone to hear.

'Robin?' Mother calls. 'Is everything all right in there?'

'Yes, okay, yes,' I answer.

Mother comes in anyway, takes a dish towel, and makes like she's going to dry. Or spy. She starts a conversation, trapping me in the kitchen.

'Have you had all your medications?'

Read: you're acting crazy. Should we up your meds?

'Yes. Melissa brought it to me before dinner. Remember?'

'Yes, she did.' She is quiet for a minute, drying a dish and putting it away. As if I don't know what's on her mind. Finally, 'What was it you were yelling, Robin?'

I could tell her, but it would be wrong. 'I don't remember any yelling,' I say. Deny, deny, deny. Believe me, she doesn't want to know.

'I could swear you shouted, "No, no!" Who were you talking to?'

I soap a dish, rinse it under the running water, watching the little bubbles glide down the plate and plop into the sink.

'Mother, don't worry about me.'

'Of course, I worry about you. You're my baby.'

I'm getting this sick feeling in the pit of my stomach. Too much dessert or too much compassion, I don't know which. The feeling in my teeth is still there. Buzz, buzz, buzz. Another incoming message.

Robin, it says. Robin. The buzzing stops.

No, no, I want to shout. Don't go away. Don't give up. But Mother is there, and I can't make a scene. No, I will send him back a message, a life-affirming message. No words, just a message of life. I visualize my open arms, bringing warmth and love to the world, first, all together, then one life-form at a time. The One, then the one. Macro, then micro. Think global, act local.

31

All the while, I wash and rinse and drain. Wash, and rinse and drain. There's something comforting in the soapy slippery dish rhythm. Wash and rinse and drain. It is not what I say and do. It is what I feel and think. It is not what I seem to be. It is what I am. It is not the outside. It is the inside. Not the phenotype, but the genotype. Not what is, but what knows. Know it, Derek.

Derek. Derek. Bo-berrick. Banana-fana-fo Ferek. Mi-my-mo Merrick. Derek. Know what I know.

Mother gives me that same worried look, and says, 'Maybe all this is a bit too much for you, Robin. Why don't you just go and lie down?'

I nod and put down the sponge, wipe my hands on the cloth she is holding. I walk out of the kitchen, through the dining room, the living room, the hallway, and into whatever they call this room. About to throw myself onto the little bed, I turn instead and look at the computer. Perhaps, there is a hard copy of Derek's message.

I sit down, grab the mouse and double-click on messenger. The screen shifts, then settles on the list of Howard's e-mails. At the bottom I see one with a subject name: *Why did I ever come?* Why did I? I think, then it dawns on me in my Clozaril fog: Derek's reply.

I click on the line, and lo and behold, a message from Derek. I look at the time: while I was in the kitchen. Told ya so, Whitecoat.

Dear Robin, it says. *Despite your best wishes (thank you for your e-mail!), without you, I have fallen down the escarpment, and am sliding down into the depths of despair. It was a quick trip. Last night I was fine: balanced, and normal. Today, in the dining room, I was eating the goop we laughed about, and suddenly, I felt something in me sink. Thanksgiving! What irony!*

I just picked up my tray and left. Roz sputtered something as I got up. It was mean of me, but I didn't care. I didn't want her; I wanted you. Back in my room, I had left the laptop on messenger, just so I could see the minute you wrote. First thing I walked in the door, I saw it. Thank you! As I read it, I got a feeling of warmth and love. How did you do that? Send me more.

Love,

Derek

Underneath is my e-mail, which I read again. Not much of a message. Of course, I was interrupted and pissed off. But still, he says he got the feeling. The words he got from the internet: the *'you can't go home again, haha,'* sent in little electronic zeroes and ones. But he says he got a feeling of warmth and love. That he got from the kitchen, from me directly to him.

I click on *reply* and type and type and type, until I'm done. This message is our little history. It starts with my e-mail, continues with his, and ends with mine. Hitting reply each time, we can build up an epic: mine and yours and mine and yours, ad infinitum. Like reading the collected letters of Jean-Paul Sartre and Simone de Beauvoir.

But it doesn't include the emotion, the buzz, the feeling in our teeth. All that good stuff doesn't show up in black and white on the page. It shows up, instead, in the quantum connections between bits and pieces of the universe. Father and I through time. Derek and I through space. Anything one knows, the other knows, too. We were all born in that first moment of the Big Bang, and we're all parts of the same whole. Forever, and forever, we're all connected. Roger can tell you all about that. I'm going to sleep.

'Robin! O'Robin!'

'Your Femininity, wake up!'

The light coming in through muslin curtains says dawn. Silence, except for geese honking overhead, and dark shadows, which obscure the room.

I sit up, looking for Beverly. No Beverly. I catch sight of my suitcase in the corner, the computer on the desk. Home. I am still in yesterday's clothes, lying on top of the patchwork quilt, a pink blanket covering my legs, my evening pills plus a glass of water waiting patiently on the bed table. I feel antsy and anxious, too many voices competing for my attention. My teeth hurt.

Buzz, buzz, buzz. An incoming message. I listen with my whole being. Derek? Is it you? But I receive no words, just a feeling of misery. I throw off the pink blanket and rush to the computer, double- and quadruple-clicking the mouse. There, at the bottom of the list is another message. Subject: *When are you coming home?*

I allow myself a moment of meditation. Home. Is it here or there? Then, I click on the line and read the e-mail.

Dear Robin,

The aides got so upset that I wouldn't get up from bed, that they called Dr Mankiewicz. He wasn't pleased, I can tell you, being called on his day off, but we talked on the phone for a half-hour. I told him I wasn't suicidal, I just didn't have any appetite for life.

Mankiewicz said that I've been through this before, that I shouldn't fight it, just let it run its course. He'd tell the aide to monitor the lithium levels in my blood, and not to worry. If it got bad enough, we could always go to electroshock. I'm still on my way down, I can feel it.

Love,

Derek

I feel his misery through the ether. I've been there. Well, maybe not that low, but low. You feel slow and heavy, stuporous, grey.

I go to the computer and listen in on his consciousness. I can hear Derek's voice straight from the screen: Robin, the world is so cold. My mind is empty, hopeless, burnt out. What is the point?

I try to tell him that things are not so bad. I will come back soon. Till then, to feel our connection, our bond.

Nobody knows how I feel, he says. If things are not so bad, why do I feel like this?

I open my arms and give him a blast of joy.

Thank you, Robin, Derek says in a sleepy voice. That makes it better. I can sleep now.

I am all-seeing, all-knowing, all-feeling. Derek will be all right.

I ignore the long-suffering bedtime pills, fall back into bed, and sleep a few hours more.

In the morning, Mother comes in with a second set of pills.

'You never took your bedtime pills? 'Oh, Robin,' she says, giving me the new set and watching while I swallow them with water. I think back to Whitecoat telling me not to spit them out in the toilet. I didn't spit them out; I just didn't take them. Why should I take a drug that draws down all my powers, drains every bit of colour from the world, and leaves my brain and body operating at half-speed? Why?

Mother sits on the edge of the little bed. I can remember her doing that when I was little, singing a lullaby or reading a Little Golden Book. Hugging me before she shut off the light, back in the days of the red-and-yellow-duck wallpaper, before the six extra dimensions unfurled themselves in me, expanding my consciousness. Back when she was the mother and I was the child. Now it's reversed, but she doesn't know.

'Robin,' she says, sitting on the edge, smoothing out the patchwork quilt. 'Are you happy at Berkshire?'

'Compared to what?' I ask. I always was a smart aleck.

'Compared to ... here.'

Well, this is a toughy. If she had said, Compared to a Hollywood set or to heaven, I could have said Berkshire stinks. But compared to ... here? I don't want to hurt her feelings, but home has never been where my heart is. And right now, Berkshire is.

Why did I ever ask, 'Compared to what?' What did I *expect* her to say? I skirt the second question and answer the first. 'I'm happy at Berkshire.'

It would seem that she should be overjoyed with that, but she isn't. She sighs and looks down at her lap. 'Good,' she says finally.

Something is definitely wrong. 'Where's the problem?' I ask.

She sighs again. 'Berkshire is very expensive, Robin. And insurance only pays so much.'

Echoes of Howard. 'Insurance only pays so much, and there are other mouths to feed.' I wait for the rest, such as, 'Try staying a month. Why would you want to endure in Berkshire if you can enjoy at home with your loved ones?'

You can do it, a voice says. You can do anything.

Try harder, another says.

I ignore the lot of them. 'You want me to leave Berkshire, Mother?'

She sighs a third time.

'Stop sighing!' I yell, out of patience with everyone.

'You could try,' she suggests.

My life passes before my eyes. Melissa and I as little girls, living with Mother in a crowded flat in a seedy apartment building, our most precious possessions two bronze candelabra and Grandma's patchwork quilt. Mother always afraid of the 'criminal element' outside our door, the guys dressed in gold chains and rimless dark glasses, who smoke, inject, and sell those little bags of magic powder. I asked her one day whether we could buy some, and maybe plant it in the backyard to grow a beanstalk and find the golden goose. That was the one time she slapped me. Like it was my fault. Anyway, we got out of there as soon as she could find a ticket out. Howard.

And then, in this house for the past fifteen years, a house with wall-to-wall carpeting in a middle-class neighbourhood. Lawnmowers mowing postage stamp lawns, hedged in with little white picket fences. Father, on his way back from Nepal right after we had moved, told me it all was a comedown. Girl guides, bicycles, Howard, all a comedown. How we'd gotten all middle-class, and lost our sense of adventure. How, if he were

35

here, he'd sweep us all off to Kathmandu in a heartbeat. I reminded him that he was not here, and that Howard was a good man. Then we both laughed.

My mother's voice. 'Howard was thinking that he could take you back so you could say your goodbyes, and pack up all your things.'

'Today?' I cry.

'Well, no. It's a holiday. Maybe Monday.'

'So soon,' I say.

The voices have begun, despite the morning pills.

Don't do it!

Don't listen!

No, no, no, no, one shouts.

Suddenly, there is a buzzing in my teeth, Derek in my fillings. What is it, Derek? I ask in my head. Are you okay?

Buzz, buzz, buzz. Yes? Yes? I ask.

Don't do it, Robin, Derek says. I heard what your mother said. Please don't do it!

To be honest, I am a little surprised that what my mother has said in the privacy of our home is transmitted lickety-split to Derek's head in Berkshire. It's one thing when I send a message direct to receiver, but it's another when Derek hears everything going on around me, whether I want him to or not. I mean, sometimes you want your privacy.

Nevertheless, Derek's brain-mail has put me over the top. 'I'm sorry, Mother,' I say as graciously as I can manage. 'I can't live here. I'm not ready.'

She shakes her head, as if to say, what will I tell Howard, then lifts her face to mine, and there's a smile on it. I think she's secretly happy. She didn't want me here, either.

Chapter Three

It's Monday morning, and we are in the car, Howard driving, reversing the route we took four days ago. Howard is grumpy. Mother told him what I said, that I'm not ready. He's not a screamer, but he goes all cold when he isn't listened to, which is never, by the way.

So, we're both sitting here, Howard looking straight ahead, making absolutely sure that we don't crash into any telephone poles, and me giving all my attention to the side window. Looking in perpendicular directions gives us both privacy to sit and think. Well, it gives me privacy, anyway, because Howard is completely clueless about reading minds. As for him, I know just what he's thinking. I mean, his brain waves are practically jumping out of his head.

He's thinking, how am I going to make this month's payment, and next month's, and, on top of that, pay taxes, and Melissa's wedding? And, how it would be so much easier if Donna had just showed a little more gumption and convinced HER daughter to live with us, and, after all, schizophrenia is a chronic disease, and if Robin were to just take her medication, she could do fine living outside of an institution.

See? No one has to talk out loud, says one of the voices. You know everything they are saying and about to say.

So, what are you talking for, I ask the voice.

Houses and trees flow past the car window. Children in backpacks mass at corners, the crossing guards, powerful in their orange stripes, waving their arms to stop us and let them go. We pass a school, a parking lot, an apartment house, then pass the town boundary and reach the country. Brown fields go on for miles. Finally, we turn into Berkshire's circular driveway, and I can feel Derek's misery right away.

'You can drop me off here,' I say.

Howard stops the car and gives me a perfunctory kiss. 'It's always nice having you home,' he hints. I wave and run in, bouncing my suitcase up the steps.

Robin, Derek's voice says. Are you here?

I'm here! I shout silently.

As I pass, the receptionist waves and writes something in the big book. I am off, running up the stairs to the second floor, suitcase bobbing. Down the hall, into my room, where I leave the bag. No Beverly, like I care.

Robin! I hear again.

Coming, coming, I tell him. Just had to get rid of my suitcase.

Back down the hallway, turn, turn again. At the very end, I enter Derek's room, which is blindingly dark. I stumble across to the window and rotate the wand. Gradually, the morning sun trickles in, and I make out Derek lying there like a statue, his eyes closed. Like he didn't hear me come in, after all that calling to me in my mind. Go figure.

I check for roommates, but Derek has none: his family is rich, and can afford a private room. I go over and shake him. His lids shudder and open, eyes blank and shiny like buttons. Inside, there is a hurt that goes so deep, it blanks the mind.

'Hello, Robin,' Derek says, no smile or anything.

It's not that I don't know what it's like to be so deep in a hole, you can't pull yourself out. You're walking along, minding your own business, and suddenly out of nowhere appears this bottomless pit. You try to walk away from it, or around it. You try to find a foothold or a branch to cling to, but the pit pursues you, and, against your will, it draws you down. Like a black hole, it sucks in everything, pulling you into its insatiable orbit, sucking at you and sucking at you, with you scratching and scrambling and slipping and scurrying, getting nowhere, till you get caught at its rim and start to spiral down, down, down. And no one will ever see you again, because a black hole sucks in everything, even light. I know what it's like, once you start going down. No matter how strong a swimmer you are, you'll never save yourself. You need someone else, someone who's outside the hole with outstretched arms and a mighty hand to pull you up.

So I lean over and kiss him on the lips. All the while, I am broadcasting, love, love, from my mind to his, picturing my outstretched arms pulling Derek out of the pit. I am transmitting all right. My radio is on full blast. But I can't tell if there's a soul out there to receive on this wavelength. At first, I can't seem to get a pulse. If he's reacting to me, it's so slow I can't tell anything's happening at all. Then, slowly, I feel the pressure of his lips.

Derek makes room for me on the bed, but he is not talking. I scan his head with my superior intelligence. It's like his mind is dead. Still, he's kissing me with some feeling, a sign that the lower parts of his brain are still active. Let's give his hypothalamus a jumpstart, and that may trigger the rest. I caress his face, his throat, his chest, his stomach, each time lowering my hand.

After a few minutes, I can feel a surge of something below his waist.

'Close the door,' he growls.

I jump up and close the door.

A lot of good that will do with no locks, I hear, but can't identify the speaker. I hope it's not my father, considering what I am about to do.

I pry off my shoes, one foot after another, and step out of my pants and top before lying back down. In the meantime, Derek has managed to pull his shirt half over his head. It's stuck there, like a straitjacket. I help him disengage himself, then work on his shoes and buckle. Suddenly, he pulls me down onto him, and our bodies commune for a minute through clothes, before a sound in the hall makes us dive under the covers.

A lot of good that will do, the same voice repeats.

Shut up, I tell it, and let Derek take off my panties.

What about Max? the voice persists, trying to wreck it for me.

Part of me disconnects from the action, despite the fact that Derek is very much involved. Who is this I am fucking? I suddenly ask myself.

And how can you turn on a dime, like that? the devil asks, now that it has found a crack to widen.

Max did, I say.

But he loved you.

He didn't, really.

Maybe he does.

Shut up, shut up, shut up, I say, as Derek enters me. Leave me alone. I don't want to think. I don't want to hear. I want to feel.

We work ourselves into a lather under Derek's cover. It's only the second time I've ever done this, but my body is taking over, coming and peaking, mysteriously in sync with Derek's primal beat. My voices have disappeared, and the only sounds I hear are my own cries, and Derek's loud, penultimate grunt. Afterwards, I hold him, and he holds me, and we look into each other's eyes.

Derek's have lost their blank, glassy look, and his mouth has almost managed a smile.

'You're back,' he says.

'So are you,' I reply.

* * *

39

I have to get back before Martin comes to dispense the lunch pills, so I get up to go. In the threshold, though, I can't stop myself from turning around to admire my accomplishment. Derek is still lying on his bed with his eyes closed, but now it is with an unmistakable air of satisfaction. Like between the two of us, we broke the back of his depression.

Out of the depths of despair, and back onto the escarpment, a voice remarks.

Amen, I say.

When I get back, I find Beverly is sitting on her bed, reading her *Vogue* magazine, page 11. This is the NEXT page! We live in an expanding universe. Hallelujah!

'Congratulations,' I tell her, dropping onto my bed.

'You're here,' she says.

No one seems to have believed that I was coming back.

'Ye of so little faith,' I reply.

This is the end of our conversation. It has already gone on much longer than usual.

I haul my suitcase over to the bed and open it. On top is the napkin with the two e-mail addresses. I carefully remove it to my bookshelf. Not that I need them. Whitecoat is just downstairs, and Derek down the hall. Besides, what do I need a computer for?

I take out the clothes and put them away, then stow the bag under my bed. Home sweet home.

There's a perfunctory knock on the door, and Martin comes in, black eye and all. He looks better today, actually. The bandage is off his arm, though I can still see faint bite marks, a vaccination by my mouth. His eye is more green and purple than black. I stare at it for a few moments, unable to tear myself away from the kaleidoscopic design.

'Stop undressing me with your eyes,' Martin says with a smirk.

I put my finger down my throat like I'm throwing up. No way would I want to see what is under Martin's uniform.

'Your morning pills, Your Majesty,' Martin says, handing me a small cup with two pills and a larger one half-filled with water.

This is strange. He's never accepted me as his ruler before. The sooner they accept it, the sooner they'll get better, a voice remarks. That sounds just like Whitecoat. I hope he's not in my head, too.

I give Martin the royal half-nod and upend the little cup with the pills into my mouth. He crosses the room and goes through the same thing with

Beverly, minus the small talk. Beverly and Martin don't connect. They don't hate each other; they don't love each other. They don't anything each other. Anyway, so Martin's out the door in another minute, and I go to the bathroom and spit out the pills. It's easy. Martin's supposed to watch that I swallow, but half the time he doesn't. He waits till I put the pills in my mouth, and assumes that I swallow. Bad assumption. Haha.

I open a copy of the latest Roger Penrose. Howard got it for me when I mentioned his name. He's happy to further my education, Howard said, so I can make something of myself. I am something of myself, I tell him. How can I make anything more? At this, he looks at me blankly and tells me he'll see me later.

Martin goes out. Beverly sits there, *Vogue* open to page 11, and I stare at the first page of my book, two people pretending to read. What is Derek doing right now, I ask myself? I picture him still lying on his bed, but now with his legs crossed and a smile across his lips. Sometimes you change one thing and get disproportional effects. A butterfly flapping its wings in Brazil sets off a tornado in Texas. You know, chaos theory. Sensitive dependence on initial conditions. Little change, big impact. Be careful of the shrew you step on if you take a trip backward in time to the dinosaur era, because human beings may never evolve. I kick-start Derek's hypothalamus, and his whole mood changes. Hey there, how many doctors have tried sex therapy for depression? I picture a roster posted at the front desk: 9:00 Stretching, 9:30 Foreplay, 10:00 Kama Sutra/New Positions 10:30 Sex/Therapy. Would Freud approve?

Lunchtime. Boy, have I worked up an appetite. I leave Beverly, her head still buried in the magazine, and start the long walk to the cafeteria. Up the hall, down the stairs, quarter turn and down some more stairs, quarter turn, straight down the hall, and burst in through the double doors. I scan the room.

There he is, sitting next to Roz. For a second, I am jealous, but then I look at Derek, eating and joking, and feel a warmth and a pride for the person I have healed. Roz has nothing to do with it. He's my creation. My man. Adam. My man, Adam.

Madam, I'm Adam. Madam in Eden, I'm Adam. Able was I ere I saw Elba. I am Robin. Nibor ma I.

I cross to the counter and pick up a tray and a plate. The lady with the grandma arms dumps an ice-cream-scoopful of mashed potatoes on top of my cutlet. No green in sight: ketchup is our vegetable today, I guess.

41

I haul the tray across the room to Roz and Derek, who are in deep conversation. Another pang of jealousy explodes in my chest.

Maybe you shouldn't have left them alone over the long weekend, a voice says.

I try to ignore the comment, but it was something I might have thought of myself. As I get closer, I consider passing the two of them in a huff and sitting down at the next table with the tall guy with acne, but then I realize that Derek and I have just had intimate relations and he's laughing and cracking up at the table right in front of me, and that's where I want to be. I sit down next to him, very close.

'Hi,' I say, our bottoms practically touching.

'Hi,' he says, turning to me, his eyes alight.

'Hi,' I say again, and we both laugh. Nah, don't worry about Roz.

'Robin!' Roz shouts.

'Yeah, yeah,' I say. 'Hello.'

'How was the weekend?' Derek asks. It's the first intercourse we've had since I'm back, if you don't count what we did this morning.

'Okay.'

'Your mother didn't bug you?' Roz asks, chewing.

'Not really.'

Derek looks at me strangely, like he knows more. Of course he does. He was listening. He told me not to do it.

'Actually, my mother asked me to come home to stay for good.'

Roz gasps, choking on her cutlet.

'Don't do it,' Derek says again, a worried look in his eyes.

'I won't. I told her I wasn't ready to leave Berkshire.'

Roz is still choking. I run around the table and smack her on the back, and she spits out a half-chewed piece of whatever it is.

'Thanks,' she croaks.

'You eat too fast,' Derek says.

'Yeah.'

We go back to stuffing our mouths for a minute. When I glance over, I notice that Derek has actually cleaned his plate.

'You've got your appetite back,' I say.

Derek sighs, stretches his arms out wide and looks at me with a goofy smile. 'I feel so-o-o good!'

'Can't believe this. He was like a corpse yesterday,' Roz says.

'The accounts of my death were greatly exaggerated,' Derek jokes.

You'd never guess that here were some really sick people. Between us, the voices we hear probably outnumber the people in the room. Even Roz has caught the mood. I mean, she hasn't carried on a full conversation for a month, and here she is talking with syntax and everything. It just goes to show that even seriously demented people can have their good days. Usually, they don't all coincide, that's all.

'Whitecoat is going to fall over dead with surprise,' I say, gazing at Derek, who's still laughing.

'I wish,' Roz says.

Derek stops laughing. 'Hey, I don't like the way you guys badmouth him. Dr Mankiewicz is a great shrink.'

'He must be better with manic depressives,' I say confidentially to Roz.

'Funny. No, Dr Mankiewicz is the best. I was really flying high. Not everyone could bring me down the way he did.'

High is good, a voice says. Whitecoat just can't leave well enough alone.

'Bring you down?' Roz asks.

'I thought I could fly. If he hadn't talked me down from my parents' roof, I probably wouldn't be here.'

Maybe he *can* fly, the voice says.

'Anyway, he cured me. I'm feeling great now.'

'Cured you?' I ask. 'There's no cure.'

'Well, I'm feeling *no pain*, let me tell you,' Derek says, grinning.

That's a grin I haven't seen before: ear-to-ear, that's just reeking of endorphins. I am looking at the all-new and improved Derek. It should have thrown me a little, since I've just gotten used to the old Derek. But I'm right in sync today, dopamine-rich, flying high.

'Boy, I'd like some ice cream,' I say, for no good reason.

All three of us look over at the glass counter. Three green Jell-Os and one ancient rice pudding stare back at us.

'Want to go find some?' Derek asks, a wicked gleam in his eye.

That gleam recharges my batteries. 'Where?'

'Dairy Queen sounds good.'

'Dairy Queen?' Roz laughs. 'How're you gonna get out to go to Dairy Queen?'

'Just watch me,' Derek says, standing up. 'You coming?' he says to the two of us.

43

Freedom! shouts a voice.

'Sure,' I say.

Roz just sits there. 'No way,' she answers, hugging herself.

For a schizophrenic, she's no fun.

So, we set off alone.

Berkshire is one of those *rich-man*'s sanitariums. Our families pay for the right to have us well treated, in a low-security environment. Most of us go out on the grounds by ourselves without any obtrusive sheepdogs following us around. Of course, the gates are locked, and most of us lambs don't have a lot of initiative, so we stay inside. But given someone with a little enterprise, and the gate practically swings open of its own accord. I could have sprung it myself any time I chose, but, hey, God is everywhere.

But today is different. We walk slowly, under the trees, along the outside wall, one of us always on lookout. We get to the gate, and it's locked. There's a little guard house, but nobody's there, so Derek gives me a leg-up, and we both climb out. Just like that.

Freedom! my voice shouts again, as we saunter down the road.

Derek's face is still wearing its ear-to-ear grin, and his pocket is jingling with change he's brought to buy Dairy Queen sundaes. He grabs my hand, and gives me a giggle.

You're going to get caught, a voice calls out in sing-song. Derek seems not to hear, so I ignore it just as I ignore all my voices. Nothing can go wrong, go wrong, go wrong.

We walk and we walk. It's further than we thought. It's getting toward dusk, and, of course, neither of us has brought a jacket. I shiver, and Derek takes his hand out of mine, and puts it around my shoulders. Cold is just a state of mind, he tells me, but the arm is nice, and his smile is warmth, itself. We're just two particles, separated at birth, but reunited by destiny.

Car beams overtake us, and I do a last-minute thumb thrust. Screeching brakes, and the car stops. We run to catch up.

'Get in,' the driver says, and points to the back door. He's a middle-aged truck driver type, with a thick middle and broad shoulders.

What did Howard say the last time you hitchhiked? a voice asks.

Who cares what Howard thinks? I'm stronger than anyone. And Derek's here, too.

I climb in first, then Derek, and the guy drives away.

'Where to?' the guy asks.

'Dairy Queen,' Derek answers, jingling his change, already contemplating his banana split.

The guy laughs. 'In December? You have to be crazy to want ice cream when it's this cold.'

Derek and I look at each other and crack up. 'Yeah,' I say.

'So, where are you from?' Derek asks.

'Few miles away,' the guy says. 'You?'

'Not far,' Derek answers, the two of us shaking with laughter in the back.

'Berkshire?' the driver guesses.

We stop laughing.

'I work there,' Derek says suddenly. 'I'm a psychologist.'

'You look a little young for that,' the guy says, staring at us in the rear-view mirror. 'And you, honey?'

He's talking to me, I guess. 'Nurse,' I reply.

'Sure,' he says, looking back at the road.

'I graduated from university at fifteen,' Derek offers.

'Uh-huh,' the guy grunts.

'Number one in my class,' Derek adds.

'Well, whaddya know about that.'

So, we drive for about three more miles till the guy lets us off across the street from the Dairy Queen. 'Goodbye, and enjoy your ice cream,' is all he says. Didn't turn us in. No mugging, no raping. The guy didn't steal Derek's four dollars and ninety-two cents in change. Howard just expects the worst. He's a glass-half-empty sort of guy.

By now it's dark, so the cone on top of the Dairy Queen is all lit up with blinking lights, like an upside-down Christmas tree. Derek stares at it, and with the cone in his viewfinder, blithely proceeds across the street, right through traffic. Cars screech to a halt or swerve and miss him by a couple of inches. It doesn't matter to Derek. All-powerful. I know the feeling. So, I do the same thing: walk right through the traffic in the dark. No one can touch me. And they don't, but two cars have a fender-bender just as I step onto the sidewalk, with one old driver shaking his fist at me, as if I'm to blame. 'Not me, you!' I shout. Imagine blaming someone else for your own actions. That's the whole point of freedom – something happens, it's your own fault.

By the time I reach the window, Derek's already ordering. His sundae costs $3.99, leaving me with a grand total of ninety-three cents to spend on any item of my choice. I order a child-size cone for seventy-five cents, and give Derek the change. After all, it's his money. We sit down on a splintery bench underneath the blinking lights.

'It's nice to see you eating,' I say, in between licks.

He laughs, and I suddenly feel like I'm my mother.

'I just meant,' I add, and I know I'm blushing, 'that you used to want someone to taste all your food.'

'I'm all over that,' Derek says, spearing a banana slice with a plastic fork.

Thing is, that's the serotonin talking, but I'm not going to tell him that. I can read his mind, and I can tell you that this is not going to last. It's great while it's happening, but what goes up must come down. Someday, this bubble is going to burst, and Derek is going to be back at Berkshire, pleading with Roz to taste his food, or not eating at all, and lying all day in bed in a fetal position. I mean, I don't want to think that, because if I think it, it will absolutely come true, but I cannot help seeing what's in front of him, and that what he thinks now is not how it's going to be.

'Great,' I say.

Derek grins at me and offers me the last banana slice, impaled on the plastic fork. I take it in my mouth and offer him one-half, just sticking out of my lips. We kiss, like Lady and the Tramp, over a banana slice.

I throw the plastic fork and laminated foam bowl that cannot-be-destroyed into the garbage can. The night is young. We could paint the town red on eighteen cents, or go back to Berkshire. The choice is ours. I'm shivering from the ice cream, so Derek puts his arm around me, but it doesn't help much, even though cold is a state of mind.

'I'm cold.'

'Seems warm to me,' he says, taking his arm away. He looks around aimlessly for a minute, then jumps up. 'C'mon. Let's walk around. It'll get you warm.'

So we get up and walk around the little town. There's the Dairy Queen, a hardware store, a gas station, and a Loblaw's. A block away, there's a liquor store and a pizza parlour. Beyond that, there are a few streets of clapboard houses.

'Nice town,' Derek says.

I look at him like he's crazy, which, of course, he is.

'Nice town to settle down in, I mean. We could buy a house and have some kids.'

'You proposing?'

Derek looks at me blankly, then moves on according to whatever logic is currently in his head.

'I could get a job.'

I really don't want to burst his bubble. 'Where?' I ask.

He looks around quickly, settles on the hardware store. 'There, for instance. I could save up and buy the place. Rename it Wineker's.' That's his name, Derek Wineker, so it's not *that* crazy.

'Sounds good to me,' I say.

We keep walking, while Derek gives me a long-winded story about his father, and how he always wanted to own his own business and call it Wineker's. About his mother who was up and down, like him, and when she was up, she was very, very up, and when she was down, she was terrible. About the dog he never had, and the horseshoe crab that died when it ventured under the electric heater. And how he's all ready to go back to school, and how he's going to be a psychologist, and get a job at Berkshire, and work under Mankiewicz.

All this time, we're walking out of town, the wrong way if we're ever going to make it back to where we started out. And it's getting colder, and colder, and darker and darker. And, finally, I've just had it. Ever since we finished the ice cream, the voices haven't shut up, offering comments on everything Derek says, on the cold and the dark, everything and nothing. That it's no better out here, and Derek is acting crazy, and he's talking too much and too fast. They tell me to give myself up, because they're coming to get me, anyway. Go back, they say, where it's warm and soft. They tell me to take care of Derek, because he's going someplace fast and furious, and no one can stay there long.

I grab Derek's shoulder and try to make him turn around, back toward the intersection of Dairy Queen, hardware store, gas station, and Loblaw's. But Derek won't turn until he grabs me and pulls me against him, lips to lips, chest to chest, genitals to genitals. We stand like that for a couple of minutes in the dark, him groping under my sweatshirt, until he's somehow had his fill, and then he runs ahead.

Now we are heading back toward the Dairy Queen, Derek way up in front, hypnotized by the blinking lights atop the artificial cone. I can hear the lights calling to him in code, blink-blink-blinkety-blink, blink-blink-blinkety-blink. Above the lights blinks the Milky Way, in sync with the cone: blink-blink-blinkety-blink, blink-blink-blinkety-blink. Come to me, come to me, come to me, come to me.

This beauty of the universe seduces both of us, but I won't let it keep me enthralled. I shout at him that we only have eighteen cents, and we can't buy much with that, but he keeps on running. I'm a block back, gasping for breath, trying to catch up, when I see Derek start to climb the Dairy Queen.

He shouts back, 'Hey, Robin, you ever do any cone climbing?'

By the time I'm almost there, he's already on the roof. I call to him, but he's not listening. Suddenly, he's got one hand hooked around the cone and he's scaling the side, not easy at a forty-five-degree angle going the wrong way. The wind has come up, so every syllable I shout gets blown back in my face.

I send him a message through the ether: Come down, Derek. You don't have to prove anything. Come down, and I'll have your children and we'll buy you a hardware store. Come down and all is forgiven. C-O-M-E-D-O-W-N-D-E-R-E-K. For a moment, it looks as if the message has been received. Derek stops climbing, gives me a bright smile and grabs a lower handhold alongside a string of lights. Then, no, no, I cry. I see it happening before it happens. 'Grab hold,' I shout out loud, but the wind blows the words right back.

I send out protective thoughts to soften his fall, but, of course, it happens as I saw it, because I saw it. In slow motion, I see the string of lights strip off the cone, light by light by light. Derek's hand disconnects, his foot slips off into thin air, and his body drops, first ricocheting off the word 'Dairy', then bouncing off the ground. I run to him, and he opens his eyes sleepily. 'Robin,' he says, before closing them again.

The only one in the Dairy Queen is a gangly teenage boy in a white Dixie cup hat, who charges out, then stands there staring, a chocolate ice cream cone in his hand. 'Ambulance,' I have to tell him, before he runs back in. I can see him making a call from a phone behind the soft ice cream machine. I cradle Derek's head in my lap and wait.

Derek opens his eyes again, a goofy smile on his face. 'Hey,' he says.

Five minutes later, an ambulance arrives, and a whitecoat lowers Derek onto a stretcher and starts to close the doors.

'I'm coming, too,' I insist.

'Relative?' he asks.

'Sister,' I reply.

So, the whitecoat lets me sit in the back with the paramedic. Lying is when you know it's not real, but you do it anyway, because anything else takes too long.

'Your brother is a very lucky boy,' the paramedic says, his hands feeling progressively down his neck and back. 'Concussion and a broken arm is all. Could be much, much worse.'

He looks at me, then at Derek, his face registering that we look nothing alike. Of course not. If we did, the two of us would never be attracted to each other. Opposites attract; likes repel. Ewwww! The thought of kissing my own brother grosses me out. Though I don't have a brother. But he doesn't know that.

'What was he doing, anyway?' the paramedic is saying.

'Cone climbing.'

'Excuse me?'

'Cone climbing. It's big in Europe.'

That shuts him up, but nature abhors a vacuum, and all the other voices rush in to fill the space.

You saw it happen. You made it happen.

Your fault, your responsibility.

Derek had the freedom to do as he wished, I tell them.

Ask Derek if he chose to fall. Ask Derek if he wants psychosis.

To prevent it, or fix it, would cancel human freedom, I say. I cannot intervene.

Then you are not all-powerful.

So be it, I answer, and that's the last thing I remember.

All I can do is move my head; something is holding down the rest of me. I turn my head just as a brown hand gives me a shot in the arm.

'You'll be all right, girl. Just give it a few minutes.' The whitecoat withdraws the needle and places it in a stainless steel container out of sight. I hear the *clunk* where plastic hits the metal.

'Heard you was fighting again. Now, why'd you go and do something like that?' He grins at me, like we're the best of friends.

'You're new, aren't you?' I slur, but he shakes his head at me, the grin replaced by a tsk-tsk.

'I'm Alex. Don't you know me, Robin? I give you your evening meds.'

Some events slowly come back to me. Returning to Berkshire. Under the covers in Derek's room. Lunch. I had this odd dream about going out for ice cream.

49

I turn my head to look, first at the clock, then at Beverly's bed. The clock says ten o'clock; the bed is empty.

Alex says, 'Beverly's beddin' down somewhere else, Robin. She says she can't sleep with you cryin' and screamin' like that.'

'Like what?' My voice has risen to a fever pitch.

'Like you doin' right now.'

'Can't remember. What hap ... happened?'

'You was kickin' and bitin' like nobody's business. No one could make you leave the hospital.'

'The hospital?' I cry.

'You remember going A W O L with Derek two days ago?'

Memory is very hazy. I remember walking under the trees. 'No.'

'Then you don't remember Derek falling off the roof of a Dairy Queen?'

'No!' I shout. A slow-motion vision of Derek falling off a monstrous, sparkling ice-cream cone unreels in my mind, a movie without title, time or place.

'I guess not, then.'

'Where's Derek? Is he okay?'

'He's in the hospital, recovering. Martin was there and says he'll be all right. Problem is, you didn't want to leave him. You were a real spitfire, I hear. Aide had to sedate you to move you. Probably it was the sedation that disrupted your memory.'

Maybe so. Bits and pieces, but I can't get it to come together.

'Anyway, you've got a special session with Dr Mankiewicz tomorrow morning, early.'

'Aren ... aren ... you ...' My mouth won't cooperate, so I give up. Who cares, anyway?

'Take it easy, Robin. Jes' take it easy. I'll come back soon and take the restraints off.'

'Now,' I say.

'Soon.'

Alex wheels out the cart, leaving me alone with my thoughts. My mind seems to have slowed down to a dirge, the synapses shuffling, not firing. They don't have to restrain me. I probably couldn't get off the bed, anyway.

I stare at the cracks in the ceiling. I know these cracks. There's the one that looks like a spider web, and over there, the Big Dipper. I bet I could find all the constellations in this ceiling, if I try. Cassiopeia over there: it looks like a chair, that's how I know. Orion's belt. Ursa Minor, Little Bear. It's all here. My sky.

And there are the cries in the night. There's the new girl, with the periodic howl, like a wolf, against a white noise background of snores and sobs, whines and wails. Sometimes you hear the shriek of wheels speeding down the hall, then low voices, punctuated by a loud scream. At night you wonder why you're here. I wait for a half-hour, an hour, watching, listening, before I hear soft footsteps. Time is relative: who knows how long it is before Alex comes back in?

'Feelin' better?' he asks when he finally he walks in. I can't see him, but I can hear his voice approaching in the dark.

'Yeah.'

I sense someone undoing the restraints on my legs.

'Still okay?' Alex asks before he unties my hands. He remembers what I do to Martin.

'Yeah.'

'Always in trouble,' Alex chides, loosening the ties on my hands.

'So what?' I say, rubbing my wrists.

'Gotta lotta hostility.'

'Says who?' I retort. You've got to understand, I'm not at my best, all doped up and slowed down. You slow omniscience down to absolute zero, and you've got a lot of nothing.

He laughs. 'See ya tomorrow evening. Don't do anything I wouldn't do.'

I don't know what he would or wouldn't do, and I'm so doped up, I don't care. What happened yesterday, anyway? I ask myself, but even my thoughts are slurred. Funny, how one minute something can be so important it's worth kicking and biting for, and the next it's not even worth remembering. The voices have gone to sleep. Maybe I should, too.

I wake to honking geese and Martin in my doorway.

No 'Your Majesty', just 'Take your pills.'

He watches me as I chug them down, then makes me open my mouth to make sure I've swallowed them. No more funny stuff, he's thinking.

I have this foggy vision of kicking Martin. 'Were you there? Yesterday? In the hospital?' I ask. Quantum uncertainty. The basic limitation on our ability to predict the behaviour of an individual. I hope I didn't kick him.

'Yeah. You kicked me.' Martin rolls up his pant leg to show me a purple bruise.

'Sorry.'

He gives me a black look of hate but says nothing.

I feel bad, but, hey, I can't control the world. Quantum uncertainty. Not being able to know both speed and location of a particle at the same time. Control one, and the other is unknowable. You can't have it both ways. You can fool all the people some of the time, and some of the people all the time, but you cannot fool all the people all the time.

But none of this epistemology would have any effect on Martin. Martin hates me pure and simple because I keep hurting him. From his point of view, I do it for no reason whatsoever. That makes me evil, in his eyes. He can't understand that evil is a function of freedom. Create humans and tell them what not to do, and, well, they'll probably just go ahead and do it. Create something, and it's out of your hands. We live in an imperfect world. Bad things happen to good people. Shit happens.

But, as I said, I could explain all this stuff to Martin ad infinitum, and still he'd be saying inside him, this girl is no good, and no sense trying to make it so. I can't force him to understand.

'What happened to Derek? Alex said he fell off a roof.'

'He'll be all right. And you're due at Dr Mankiewicz's office in five minutes,' Martin snarls, looking anywhere but in my eyes. Job done, he packs up his cart, and wheels it out.

I look after him and shrug. Whitecoat in five minutes. I grab my pants from the chair, a top and underwear from the drawer and run into the bathroom. The mirror reflects hand-size bruises on my upper arms and legs: the results of kickin' and bitin' like nobody's business. I pull on my shirt and pants, burying the evidence, and four minutes later I am dressed and washed and out the door. Feeling okay. A little slow, but okay. Voices there, always there, but all that doping last night compressed them down to somewhere in my feet. I can hear them complaining, but I don't care much. I slide down the banister, something we are encouraged NOT to do, but, hey, shit happens, and find myself in front of Whitecoat's open door.

'Come in,' I hear, though I am still standing outside the door, invisible from his point of view.

Wow, that guy is almost as good as I am.

I enter. Of course, Whitecoat is facing away from me, swivelled toward the back wall.

'Sit down,' he commands.

I sit on the small, hard seat, half a foot lower than his kingship, and wait. And wait.

Five minutes later, he swivels toward me. 'Good morning, Robin.'

I hate when he does this, lording it over me. Hello, I'm the patient here. I'm the one paying your salary. If you're king, what does that make me? Exactly.

Stubby fingers, in the steeple shape on top of the desk. His eyes bore into me, a game of psychological chicken. Neither one of us blinks.

'So,' Whitecoat says finally. 'What happened the day before yesterday, Robin?'

One of the voices has woken up and asks, dumbfounded, what happened the day before yesterday?

'I don't remember,' I say.

'Well, what *do* you remember?'

'Martin says I kicked him.'

'Do you remember kicking Martin?' Whitecoat asks.

You don't need to answer any of his stupid questions, the voice says.

'No,' I say out loud.

'What is the last thing you remember, then?'

He's not on your side, the voice says.

I make a supreme effort to focus and say, 'We were all laughing ...'

'Who was laughing?' someone asks. I think it is Whitecoat, so I answer.

'Derek, Roz and me.'

'Derek was laughing?' Whitecoat asks, deadpan. 'You know, three days ago, he was extremely depressed.'

This is a tangent, but I go with the flow. 'Yes, well, I came home, and that sort of cheered him up.'

'Still ...' Whitecoat says, dubious.

Does he want you to tell him anything or not? the voice interrupts.

'Yes,' I say to both of them. 'He said he was feeling very good.'

'Hmmm. Whose idea was it to leave the premises?'

'I don't remember leaving.'

Whitecoat swivels around, like the session is over, but it's not, and this is highly unusual behaviour from him. Suddenly, he swivels back.

'I called your mother and stepfather right after Martin brought you back, Robin.'

'Oh?' I say.

'I told them that you and Derek had run away, and that Derek had had an accident, and was in the hospital.'

That same vision of Derek falling goes past my eyes.

'I told them not to worry,' Whitecoat's saying, 'and that we have it all under control.'

I have this image of Howard on the telephone, listening to this, his face turning green or purple.

'Are they coming to get me?'

'No, not if you tell me what happened.'

Immense, diffuse sensation of relief.

A voice says, go on, tell him something.

But I really don't have anything to say. 'I don't remember anything,' I moan.

'You don't remember jumping the gate?'

'No,' I answer.

He tries another tack. 'How did you and Derek get over to the Dairy Queen?'

'I don't remember,' I say again.

Whitecoat shakes his head, like he's frustrated that he can't get me to perjure myself.

'Robin,' he says. 'If you don't let us help you, there's really nothing we can do for you here at Berkshire.'

'You're going to kick me out?' I ask.

What does he expect from a schizophrenic, sanity? someone asks.

'No, I certainly don't want to. But drugs can do just so much if you can't talk to me.'

'So, I'm catatonic.'

'No, you are NOT catatonic. This is not part of your psychosis. You are just not cooperating.'

'I can't help it.'

'You can,' says Whitecoat.

You can't, says the voice.

Two to one in favour of *can't*, says another.

'Why did Derek climb the cone?' Whitecoat interrupts.

Climb the cone! Before my eyes, I can see the lights popping off the cone, pop-pop-pop-pop, and Derek spiralling down. 'Hey,' he says, his eyelids fluttering.

'I don't know.' Did it really happen? Whitecoat always seems to think I can distinguish between what things happened and what didn't, but when I tell him what I hear and see, he says they're not real. So, why tell him now?

To me, it's all real, and if he didn't tell me different, I'd have no problem with any of it. *Possible* is a type of real. *Could be* is real. What I hear is real, no doubt about it. If it's conceivable, it's real. But Whitecoat thinks there are some things that are real, and some things that are not, and that he knows better than anyone else.

But quantum things can be here or there, or even here AND there, a combination of possibles, existing in the realm of the very small, but *real*. We simpletons try to pin a thing down, measure it so small that it can't escape, make it 'fess up to being here OR there, make it give up every claim to its freedom. But who says *that's* real? You've cornered it and compressed it, and stuck it in a little box. It's no longer what it really was. It's no longer real. It's simplified and ideal. Now we can conceive of it, measure it, hold it, know it. But it's no longer real.

'You're only asking me what happened because you don't know,' I end up muttering. 'If you knew, you wouldn't need to ask me. Nothing happened! Anything happened! Derek fell off a ladder. Martin bumped his leg on a chair! You can't know anything, because you weren't there. Only I know, but I don't remember, so it didn't happen!'

I am getting myself into a lather, not a good thing when you are talking to the All High Commissioner of Berkshire.

'Robin, calm down. We have what Derek told us.'

I don't know how I feel about Derek knowing what happened, and not me. There's already a pecking order in institutions with manic-depressives one rung closer to *sanity* than schizophrenics. It makes me distrust Derek.

'Good,' I finally say. 'So you don't need to know anything from me.'

'We want your side of it.'

Yeah, play one crazy off another, a voice says.

When someone wants the schizophrenic's side of it, another laughs, you can bet he doesn't have anything else.

'So, what did he say?' I ask after a moment.

I can make out just the slightest shake of his head before Whitecoat answers. 'Derek says he did it because it was there.'

Everybody laughs except Whitecoat. But Whitecoat is not amused.

He swivels backward toward the wall, and now I can see that his swivelling is all a defence. He needs to save face, and so he turns his face away. Poor guy. We get to cry and scream, and all he gets to do is swivel toward the wall.

Suddenly, his voice booms, 'Thank you, Robin. You can go back to your room now. When you remember more, we will talk.'

'Am I being punished?'

'Of course not. We're a hospital, not a prison,' Whitecoat's voice says from behind the chair..

I stand up from my small, hard seat, and head for the door. Whitecoat seems a little depressed today. Maybe he should talk to someone.

I'm in the arts and craft room, making a fucking teapot. They call this rehabilitation.

Derek's back from the hospital. His arm is still in a cast, but he's okay, except that he's depressed again. Falling from the roof must have taken the edge off of his mania, and then whatever was left, Whitecoat drained out of him with medications. I'll tell you, I just don't understand this obsession with *bringing him down*. What's wrong with a little bit of mania?

Anyway, Whitecoat's been working on Derek, trying to stabilize him. But stabilizing Derek is like trying to balance him on the head of a pin. It's totally impossible. So, now Whitecoat's upped his lithium and added an antidepressant to the cocktail. Sounds funny, cocktail. Like they're having parties here. No parties. Most people here are just trying to achieve some degree of normality.

But I say haha to normality, and today, managed to spit out my pills, because the whitecoat-on-call forgot to check inside my mouth. The run-off of my toilet must be creating a lot of chubby, normal fish. Fat, stupid fish who do what they're told, and can't feel much of anything. From Derek's toilet, we get the party fish. But, of course, Derek doesn't spit out his pills. Down deep, Derek's a really nice guy, who'd never spit out his pills. If he weren't manic-depressive, he'd be no fun at all.

Normal, who's normal? Well, Howard of course. And Mother, she's gotten to be disgustingly normal. She's got a new collection of, would you believe, teapots. That's why I'm making this. Fill up another space in her dining-room hutch. And, who's left? Ah, Melissa! Melissa's our party girl. She got a bonus for Christmas and paid for her wedding dress. The wedding is in March. She says Max looks gorgeous in a tux. Bastards.

Without those fucking pills, I can actually feel something. I feel angry, but that's good. At least I feel something. It's not right that I shouldn't feel angry at Max and Melissa after all they did. Why should they get the reward and me the punishment? They planned it from the first moment, how Max was going to lead me on, and pretend to love me. It was all an act that Melissa thought Max was a geek and everything, and that she'd never go out with a guy like that in her entire life. She was leading me on, too, so I'd make plans and then, BAM! They surprise me, and kick me out of my own life. Of course I went nuts. That was part of the plan. They just don't know who they're dealing with.

An angry God. A just God. All-powerful. All-loving. They're not contradictions. Perfection contains everything. Even giving humans a portion of freedom takes nothing from myself. That's what's so hard for people to understand. Perfection can give and give and give and still be complete. My own thoughts recharge me, balance me. I am angry but I have no impulse to act, because I am balanced. Max and Melissa may go on with their lives. I will not destroy them, though, in their iniquity, they may destroy themselves. Amen and Hallelujah.

Shit, I've made two handles and no spouts. Well, we'll just make it into a sugar bowl. There. That's the shittiest sugar bowl I've ever seen. Only a mother could love this one.

This whole day has been shitty. Martin came to give us our dinnertime meds and was all ready – I could tell – to check inside my mouth. I knew it the moment he came in, so I swallowed. Sigh. I can already feel those drugs sucking off my dopamine. Sucking, sucking, sucking the synapses dry. Whitecoat seems to think it's a good trade-off: more clarity in one's thoughts, less in one's emotions. No matter that I'd vote the other way: a little mania is marvellous. Hey, don't ask me, I'm only the corpse. God, I want to feel.

And dinner was awful, as usual. Derek wasn't there: they're still giving him his meals in his room. Well, I said he was rich. Well, that's right. I don't get it either, after that story he told me about his father wanting to own his own business, but manics make up things sometimes. I saw his mother once, and she was wearing the biggest diamond I've ever seen. I think they could have pawned that diamond and bought Holt Renfrew.

So Roz and I sat there just looking at each other. I think she misses

Derek, too. Not that I can't go and visit him. No one has locks on their doors to keep people out in a lunatic asylum. Locks to keep the residents in, but never to keep people out. I could just go and see how he's doing. Roz says that Martin told her he's not so good. So, all of a sudden, without consciously willing it, I find my feet walking all by themselves toward Derek's room, and I don't try to stop them. Let them take me where they will.

The door is ajar, so I push it open: again, it is pitch black. I creep along in the darkness until I reach Derek's bed, where I just make out a featureless blob on top of scrambled covers. A blob in a fetal position. I sit down next to the blob and put my hand on top. Maybe it's an arm, a chest, a back. It doesn't matter what part, I am in physical contact and I can feel what it feels: unadulterated nothingness. A few strands of anger, but mostly nothingness, a vacuum. Somethingness flows from me to the blob, because nature abhors a vacuum, but filling a void can take an eternity. I can't help but give to this thing. It asks for nothing, but it needs so much.

'Derek,' I say.

No answer. It's alive, but on autopilot. Awake but with no moving parts.

More of me flows out, the milk of human kindness. Good thing I have an infinite supply.

Slowly, the blob relaxes out of its fetal position.

'Derek,' I say again out loud. I could say his name in my head, but words have power. Formulas of numbers may explain the universe, but formulas of words can bring a person back to life. Incantations. Derek. Derek. Bo-berrick. Banana-fana-fo Ferek. Mi-my-mo Merrick. Derek. Wake up, Derek.

I get up and twist the little button on his bedside lamp. Lamplight plays on his face for a minute before his eyelashes flutter.

'Come on, sleepyhead,' I say.

Derek yawns and stretches, opens his eyes, like he was sleeping, which I know he wasn't.

'Robin,' he says, but there's no inflection in his voice.

I'm waiting for something else, but nothing comes. The room smells of dirty underwear and old food, so I'm not surprised to see a pair of jockey shorts hanging on the arm of a chair and his untouched dinner tray on the floor.

'You can't sleep all day and not eat.' There, I sound like my mother again. I wonder momentarily if that is such a bad thing. A person needs some mothering now and again.

But neither nagging, incantations nor loving-kindness seem to have any real effect on this Derek. There's nothing between us today. It's all give and no take. The wire is cut. I go to touch him, but Derek's back all of a sudden looks very imposing, like a brick wall. His arm, encased in a plaster cast, is poking me in the ribs. 'You depressed again?' I ask, drawing my hand away.

He turns toward the wall. 'Yeah. Whitecoat says I'm going through rapid cycling.'

Rapid cycling. I have the image of Derek pedalling rapidly through a mountain pass in France. 'What's rapid cycling?' I ask.

He turns back slowly and exhales. 'Usually, the mania phase lasts weeks, even months, and the depression phase can last at least that long. In some people, the cycle gets shorter. Like several cycles a week, or even a day.'

'You were depressed four days ago, then happy, now you're depressed again today.'

I wait for a minute, but Derek's closed his eyes again. I stand there, watching the lamplight play on his hair and eyes before I finally turn to go.

'I want to kill myself,' he explodes.

'Don't say that!'

'Why?'

I don't know. Saying it makes it so.

Derek. Derek. Bo-berrick. Banana-fana-fo Ferek. Mi-my-mo Merrick. Derek.

Chapter Four

'Melissa, shut up already! I'm thinking!' I shout into the phone.

It must be a month later. I don't know. Beverly's back from the hospital. As zonked as she was after a full hypo of sedative, she got up off her bed and tried to throw herself out someone's window. Fortunately, the only window she could find that had no bars was the administrator's office on the first floor, so she didn't fall too far.

Where was I? Oh, yeah. I was saying it's a month later. It was just Christmas. Now it's February. Days just flow into one another, and I can't remember where one starts and another ends. My life has that run-on quality of one of Melissa's sentences: no punctuation, and a lot of thoughts that don't belong together all tumbling one after the other. Haha, the way Melissa talks, you'd think she's the schizophrenic one.

Anyway, heads are popping out of rooms to see who is screaming on the hall phone. It's not their business, but in Berkshire, screaming is good entertainment. I wave my hand at some of them to go back into their rooms, and ignore the rest. Some of them turn around and disappear; the rest keep staring. Really, I can't be bothered.

Meanwhile, Melissa's still going on and on. I think she's the one person in earshot who hasn't heard me tell her to shut up.

'So, are you going to be my maid of honour or not?' she asks me for the third time.

Well, okay, I did say I would, then I said I wouldn't. Third time is supposed to be a charm.

'Listen,' she goes on. 'I don't really care one way or the other, but if you aren't, Robin, I'm asking Heather, but it's not fair. She's got only a month to get a dress, and you've got the blue taffeta that mother went out and got specially for you and fitted it to you and everything. If you were going to back out, the least you could have done was to tell me earlier ... You know Heather is two sizes smaller than you are.'

'No, she isn't.'

'Yes, she is. I don't know what they're feeding you over there, Robin, but you must have put on twenty-five pounds. You better not eat anything for the next month, or you're not going to fit into the dress … which may not matter, because you won't tell me whether you're going to do it or not! … Well, are you?'

Father? I ask silently.

All this time, Father has been trying to get a word in. Now he says, Just do it, Robin. You look very nice in the blue dress.

Really? I ask. Sometimes, for the ruler of the world, I am surprisingly little-girly.

Yes. And I don't believe you gained twenty-five pounds. Anyway, you have a pretty face.

Face. What about Max? I can't help asking. How can I face him?

How can you face him? How can he face you? he says.

Two questions at once that add up to an answer: I am not to blame. Thank you, Father.

Still, I ponder facing Max. I can hardly remember what he looks like. I concentrate, picturing his face when he tried to tell me about him and Melissa. His eyes all pitying, sweat on his upper lip. And then I think of Max's curly black hair, his bedroom eyes behind the heavy black frames. Throwing his head back when he'd laugh. Jogging with his retriever. What was that dog's name, anyway?

Poodle, a voice says.

Right. He named his retriever Poodle. I'm smiling at this, until I suddenly envision Max in his tux watching Melissa in white lace glide down the aisle toward him. I see myself standing farther back, with the bridesmaids, silently pulling a knife out of the sash of my blue taffeta dress. No, no! Seeing it makes it so.

Max is history, my father is saying sternly. Don't think about him. He's nothing!

'Nothing,' I say out loud, wiping my eyes with my sleeve.

'Nothing? Robin? Are you listening to me?!' I hear from the phone.

'Shut up, Melissa. I'll do it, I'll do it. Just stop asking. You're making me crazy.'

Melissa laughs at the joke. 'Good. Because you are my sister, after all.'

I hang up. There are still umpteen people standing in their doorways.

'Get out of here!' I yell at them, shooing them with my hands, and they scatter.

I stand there, my head against the wall, forehead pressed up against cold, rough concrete. Max is history, I recite to myself. Max is history.

Father?

I can't hear him among the other voices, some of whom have taken up the mantra of 'Max is history', so I guess he's gone. Derek is now, another voice says. I turn around and head for the staircase to go outside. It's February and it's cold, but who cares, really. Maybe I'll catch pneumonia and Heather will inherit my dress. Melissa says it's two sizes too big for her, but I don't believe that. I'm not *that* fat.

Father? Yeah, he's gone.

I'm going outside without my coat to find sweet Derek. Whitecoat has him on some new concoction, so he's not so depressed now. And he's taken up smoking – Derek tells me it keeps him sane. Good luck, I say. Anyway, he's always wandering somewhere on the grounds these days, walking and smoking, smoking and walking. Yeah, think I'll go find Derek.

I jog down the staircase, my right hand gliding down the banister in a long curve to the right, then straight down till the wood spirals like a snail at the bottom, my fingers tracing the coil, faster and faster and smaller and smaller till it ends all of a sudden in the middle. I jump down from the last step and run out the door, the receptionist waving.

It's gloomy out here. The trees are bare. The sky is grey. There. I can just make out Derek's blue sweater on the far side of the lawn.

'Hey!' I yell.

He waves, starts walking back to me.

As we get closer, I see smoke escaping from a smile on Derek's face. He's glad to see me. Me, too. I feel happy being near him, and a brief vision of Max in his tux doesn't bring on the same rush of hate.

You can do it, I hear Father saying.

Yeah.

'Can I have one?' I ask, gesturing to his cigarette.

Derek reaches into his sweater and pulls out a pack of Marlboros, tamping out a cigarette. I light mine on his and inhale, and the two of us turn away from the building, walking straight across the lawn.

'You called her?'

'Yeah.'

'What did you decide?'

'I told her yes.'

'You sure?'

'No. But she's my sister.'

'What about that guy she's marrying?'

'Max.' I should say something more. 'He's just a guy.'

'I thought you liked him.'

A voice tells me Derek's jealous and watch out.

'He's a jerk,' I say.

'Good,' Derek says, and he drapes his free hand over my shoulder. I smile at him, and we keep on walking. It's cold, and grey, and all that, but I feel good. I sneak a look at Derek's face, hoping to see the smile to tell me that he feels good, too, but it's not there. He's puffing smoke like there's no tomorrow, because nicotine really helps, clogging up his receptors, fooling the body into thinking that all's right with the world. But every once in a while Derek glances at me with this phony smile, and I can tell he knows the seed of craziness is still there, planted, ready to sprout, whenever. In back of that smile, he's waiting for the next bout. The pain is still there, like the way my voices never disappear: you can shrink them, compress them, wait them out, but they're there in potential, like a spore, waiting for a good rain.

I give him my trademark blast of goodwill, and he glances my way.

'I love you,' he says.

I don't want his love this way. I don't want to make him love me. He thinks it's free will, but it's me playing with his mind.

'No, you don't,' I tell him.

Derek draws me to him, plants his lips on mine in a hot kiss, and blows smoke in my mouth. His smoke, my smoke commune until we break up, coughing and laughing.

'I do,' he says, gazing at me meaningfully.

If only Derek knew what he was dealing with. He thinks he does, but he doesn't. This is my game. He's playing by my rules. He doesn't know it, but I've got all the cards.

I put my hand to his forehead. 'You're not hot,' I say, attempting a laugh.

'Stop it, Robin. I'm serious, and you're making this into a joke. My feeling for you is not a joke,' Derek says and turns away from me.

I follow him, and put my hand on his arm. 'I'm sorry. Whitecoat says I can't deal with relationships.' Well, he didn't say that, exactly. He said I was doing my darndest not to deal with relationships.

Derek shrugs off my arm, throws his cigarette butt onto the ground, and grinds it into the dirt. 'His name is Mankiewicz,' he says and walks off.

Lest I forget, I have an appointment with the great Mankiewicz in ten minutes. Let Derek walk off. It's better that way. I walk slowly back to the building and up the stone stairs into the lobby. Berkshire is an old mansion. It's got high arched ceilings and marble floors, all a little worn, but you can imagine what it must have been like. I walk down the hall toward the open door.

'Come in, Robin,' Whitecoat says before I've gotten to the doorway.

Damn, that guy is good.

Same old, same old. I go and sit down on the little, hard seat, facing Whitecoat's back. The moment I get in here, the voices get louder. I don't like it here. It's dark with shadows, and sometimes things jump out of the corners. I'm going three times a week now, even though Howard is absolutely screaming about the cost; I can hear him from here. Well, yes, Whitecoat's giving us a special rate. I think he wants me out as much as Howard does, and thinks if he can reason me out of my craziness, I'll leave, and the famed psychiatrist can then spend his valuable time with more agreeable patients. You think? Could be. This might be a final push to get me out before Melissa's wedding.

Here he is, facing me, a smile on his thin lips.

'Well? Robin? Did you have a good morning?'

What the hell is this? Whitecoat trying to be nice. Does not compute.

I look at him with disgust and say nothing. I really don't like this guy.

He sighs and waves his stubby fingers toward the curtains. 'I could see the two of you out of my window.'

'Is it illegal for two patients to walk together outside?'

'Robin, Robin. I was just making conversation. I'm not trying to hurt you.'

Oh, yes you are, a voice says and laughs.

'Derek seems to have gotten very fond of you,' Whitecoat remarks.

He's either fishing, or Derek has told him this.

'How do you know?' I ask.

'I can see.'

Derek must have told him, someone says.

What else did Derek tell him, a voice asks.

'Feelings are stupid,' I say.

'Are they?' Whitecoat asks.

He's trying to bait you, someone says.

What else did Derek tell him, a voice asks.

'You can't see what Derek feels.'

'Derek told me himself,' Whitecoat replies.

Did he, a voice asks.

Or didn't he, another says.

This place gets me paranoid. I can't seem to keep my thoughts together. They come apart in this office. And it makes me crazy.

I concentrate real hard. 'You're not supposed to tell anyone what other patients say to you.'

'That's correct, Robin, but Derek asked me to intervene.'

Intervene? Intervene in what, a voice wonders.

My head is ready to explode. 'Stop speaking in riddles!' I shout.

'I didn't know I was,' Whitecoat says. 'Okay, I'll be very direct. I want to know if you really care for Derek.'

Do I care for him? Does it matter? And what right does Whitecoat have to ask me that?

'It's none of your business,' I say. Haha.

'Robin, we've had these talks before. Every time you find someone you care about, you shut him out. You're afraid of feeling.'

'I'm not afraid of feeling. I'm schizophrenic, or have you forgotten?'

'You're using your condition to cop out of life.'

'It's *my* life.'

It's your life, a voice repeats.

It's your world, another says.

'Remember when Derek fell off the roof of the Dairy Queen?' Whitecoat asks suddenly.

'I told you I don't remember.'

'You don't remember or you don't want to remember?'

This guy can be really annoying, a voice says. Don't talk to him.

'Did I say I didn't want to remember? I said I don't remember.'

'You felt fear and grief and affection, and it was all too much for you. So you blocked it out.'

'There was nothing to block out. I just don't feel anything for Derek.'

The guy swivels away and just as suddenly swivels back, like he's trying to compose his face. Face. I picture Max's face, with his eyes all pitying, sweat on his upper lip. Whitecoat looks me in the eye, his face composed into a bland smiley face, and changes the subject.

'Your mother called me yesterday.'

I stare back at him, silent.

'She told me that your sister will be getting married next month, and they want you to be the maid of honour.'

'Yes,' I say.

'She told me about Max.'

Max Max. Bo-bax. Banana-fana-fo Fax. Mi-my-mo Max. Max.

'I don't feel anything for Max,' I say.

'I didn't ask you,' Whitecoat answers, a little smile on his face.

'Fuck you, Whitecoat,' I say and run out.

So, I go upstairs to my room, fling open the door and throw myself onto my bed.

The voices are going berserk.

Who does he think he is, anyway, your Omnipotence? Asking you to feel, when you are above feeling.

Intervening for Derek? What did Derek tell him?

Shush, I tell them, but they go on and on, along with a couple of voices I don't recognize.

Her mother called him, one says.

What do you think she said, asked the other.

She told him about Max.

Everything? the first asks.

What's there to tell?

She's afraid of feeling.

Every time she finds someone she cares about, she shuts him out.

I'm listening, and not believing. They're talking about me, those voices.

Stop it. Do you know who you're fooling with? I ask the voices, but for the first time, they ignore me and continue chatting. This has never happened before.

I jump off the bed and run into the hall, looking for Martin. There he is, coming down the hallway with his med cart. I run to him, crying his name. He looks up, recognizes me, and places the cart between his body and this oncoming missile. Bad girl coming to hurt him again. He cowers in back of the cart, waiting for punishment.

'I'm not going to hurt you,' I pant as I reach him. 'I just want my meds.'

'Wow,' Martin says.

He doles out the pills in a little paper cup, fills another one with water, extends the two cups across the cart. I take them, upend the pills and water and swallow.

67

'This is a first,' Martin says.

'I'll try anything once,' I say, and walk back toward my room. The two gossips have faded away.

I can see Beverly through the door; she must have snuck in sometime after I ran out. She looks strange: crouched on her bed with her legs all scrunched up under her, her eyes open wide, staring at something behind the door.

I look around the room: nothing that I can see. But, of course, that doesn't mean anything. What you see and what really is there are two different things. And what Beverly sees and what I see are two really different things. I see things as they really are. She sees them as she thinks they are. Again, two different things.

Beverly's mouth is slightly open, a thin moan leaking out. She's staring in the corner at a pile of dirty clothes. We've been through this before, so I go over and pick up the clothes, sifting them through my fingers to show that they are unattached to anybody and not the skin of a hideous monster.

'Don't,' she yells.

'Don't, yourself,' I mutter. It's stupid being afraid of a pile of dirty clothes.

'No, I won't,' Beverly says, not to me.

'Then don't. See if I care,' I reply.

'You can't make me!' she shouts. The other half of the conversation I can't hear.

I scan the room, making sure that I'm not missing something. Nothing. But nothing can be something to someone else. So I go and sit next to Beverly, who looks at me with great suspicion.

'I'm your roommate,' I say.

Beverly stares at me, like I'm crazy. Well, I may be, but that's beside the point.

'Don't look at them.'

I follow her gaze to the corner. 'Who?'

Beverly grabs at me, throwing me head down on her pillow. Yes, her pillow is better than mine.

'I told you not to look at them!'

Why do I allow illness to exist? I ask myself. Give them freedom, and shit happens.

'Beverly,' I say, picking my head up from her pillow. 'It's just a pile of dirty clothes.'

'Get down!' she yells, forcing my face back down into the pillow.

'Martin!' I sputter, freeing myself. I can hear the cart just outside our door. 'Beverly's at it again!'

Martin swings in, takes one look and gets out her pills. But Beverly is a little too far gone, and won't open her mouth. He gets a hypodermic out, fills it from a little glass vial, and has me hold her down, while he injects the contents into her arm. Within a minute, Beverly relaxes, and the two of us place her lengthwise on her bed.

I'll stay with her a few minutes, then go to lunch.

You've got to understand. This is normal at Berkshire. It's not that I'm uncaring or anything, though I'm sure Whitecoat would tell you different. Hey, Whitecoat could tell you all sorts of things, but you've got to be careful not to believe all of them. He's got delusions about people. He thinks he knows what they are thinking.

I'm halfway down the hall to the lunchroom when I hear shouts. Is that Derek's voice? It's not a good sign if you can hear Derek over all that din: it would mean that he is higher than anyone else. And you know what that means.

I stand at the door, looking in. Yes, it's him, and he's shouting. Damn. The slightest thing can set him off. I could change that, of course. Make him mellower. Mellower, I like that word. Like a yellow melon. I walk toward the counter. But if I changed one thing in the world, it would set the planet off its current path, send it hurtling into the sun. No, let it be. Amen.

Grandma hands me a hamburger and fries over the glass case. Mystery meat in the shape of a familiar icon. Piece of lettuce and a cardboard tomato on the side. Yummy. I saunter over to Derek and Roz.

'Hey,' I say.

'Hello,' Roz answers.

Derek says nothing, licking ketchup off his hand.

'Hey,' I say again.

'Hey.'

His eyes look wild.

'What are you, now? High or low?' I ask.

'Mixed.'

'Can you be mixed?' Roz pipes in.

'Yeah, sometimes.'

'Doesn't it just average out?' I ask.

Derek is busy dipping one fry after another into a puddle of ketchup. 'You'd think so, wouldn't you?'

The answer, I guess, is no, but it's not worth pursuing.

'What were you yelling about before I came in?' I ask, sounding just like my mother.

The two of them look at me.

'Well?' I ask Roz.

Roz looks at Derek. 'Nothing,' she says.

'Okay,' I answer. They don't have to tell me. He's upset with me, and, as I said before, anything can set him off if the conditions are right.

'The fries weren't crisp enough?' I ask.

'Could be,' Roz answers.

Derek keeps eating the fries.

'They couldn't be too bad. You're eating them all up.'

Derek picks up his tray and stands up, walks over to the garbage pail and dumps the whole lot in, fries and all.

That shows me.

Sunday. Mother and Howard are here. Howard is looking out my window, one hand drawing back a faded curtain from a barred and bolted window. Mother is perched on my bed, gazing at me with that corrugated-forehead, whatever-am-I-going-to-do-with-Robin look.

'I told her yes,' I say.

'You're not going to change your mind again, are you Robin? The wedding is in three weeks.'

Change my mind? To whose?

'No,' I answer.

'Good,' she says, but her eyes are still squinty.

'I'm going, I'm going,' I assure her.

Mother goes over to the closet and takes out the blue taffeta, smooths the fabric admiringly.

'You'll look lovely in it.'

An image of me slipping a dagger behind the sash goes past my eyes.

'No!' I shout.

'You don't think so?' Mother asks.

Do you take this man to be your lawfully wedded husband? a voice asks.

I touch the fabric, smooth and sensuous like skin. 'I do,' I say.

Howard lets the curtain drop and walks back to us, sitting down beside Mother. 'The sky looks threatening,' he says, giving a quick glance down at his watch. I know what he means. Time to go, it's gonna snow.

'Yeah?' I wish they would just go. They always come for two hours, like a ritual, but who needs them? I mean, they don't understand me. Whitecoat understands me better than they do, and that's not much.

Three weeks to go, a voice says.

'Well, it's time,' Howard says, standing up.

Mother fingers the blue taffeta dress one last time before she returns it to its black plastic bag. 'Now, take care of yourself, Robin dear. Howard will pick you up three weeks from this Friday. Leave the dress in the garment bag,' she says, hanging it back in the closet. 'And don't forget the pantyhose and the shoes.'

'I won't,' I say, making no move to get up.

Howard bends down to give me a peck on the cheek. 'Don't do anything I wouldn't do,' he smirks.

Very funny, says a voice. Tell him you won't.

'I won't,' I answer.

Mother leans over to give me a quick hug, like she wants to and doesn't want to at the same time. 'I love you,' she says.

'I love you, too,' I say, looking at the floor.

Beverly shuffles in, ignores everybody and crosses the room to her bed.

'Is that Beverly?' Mother calls. 'We haven't seen you in so long, dear.'

No answer. Beverly falls onto her bed and closes her eyes. Mother's not going to get an answer from Beverly today, not with all that medication they're filling her with. Garbage in, garbage out. They sure have stopped her from jumping out of windows, though.

Anyway, they reassessed her at the hospital. Now she's got chronic schizo-affective disorder. If you can't change the patient, change the diagnosis.

'Time to go!' Howard sings out.

'Robin, you take care. I'll call,' Mother says. Howard is practically dragging her out, but she's standing firm.

'Bye, Beverly,' Mother calls to my dear, dead roommate, who doesn't hear or doesn't care.

'Bye, Mother,' I say and open a book.

There. She can stay if she wants to, but I don't know who she plans to talk to.

I read a few pages, then look up. I can just hear the far-off echo of Howard's voice, and the clatter of Mother's heels fading away down the hallway, like a receding train.

Clickety-clackety, clickety-clackety, clickety-clackety, whoo! whoo!

Beverly is zonked out on the bed, eyes still closed.

'You need anything?' I ask.

Her eyelashes don't even flutter in recognition. She mutters something I can't make out. 'Didn't murfinfakir. No. It hurts.'

'Whatever,' I say.

I don't think those doctors know what to do with us. They just give us drugs to shut us up.

Monday, 10:00, facing Whitecoat's back.

Why can't they lighten this place up a little? Heavy, brocade curtains that probably date from the time that the Vanderfellers lived here. Rugs so old they should be put out of their misery. Wood panelling so dark, you can't find the switch to turn on a light. Brrr. I hate coming in here. It feels like hell.

I can hear his thoughts right through his head.

'… She's distancing herself from the very people who care for her … Of course, there's the schizophrenia, genetic through her father, but most likely triggered from some stress factor … Perhaps the loss of her biological father when she was small … Or that unfortunate incident with her boyfriend …'

'Do you mean me?' I ask, as Whitecoat swivels toward me.

'Excuse me?'

'You keep saying I'm distancing myself from the very people who care for me. I'm getting tired of hearing that.'

'I didn't say anything, Robin.'

'You didn't *say* anything. But you were thinking it.'

I can tell he doesn't believe that I can read his mind, but there it is again – that flash of surprise. Even Whitecoat has to recognize that I just globbed onto what he was thinking. He can't keep going around in denial.

'I wasn't thinking anything of the sort,' he insists.

Sure. He would say that. I must be rolling my eyes, because a vertical line appears in the middle of his forehead, before he plasters it over with that bland smiley-face. He thinks I can't tell when he's annoyed, but he's like a sheet of glass to me. Never mind. Have it his way.

'You know, Robin, you think you're reading other people's minds, when, in fact, what you're doing is ascribing your thoughts to others. Other people are not thinking these thoughts. *You* are thinking them.'

He's still angry about my getting into his head. Whitecoat is way too anal. He wants to control everybody.

'Am I?'

The vertical line between his eyebrows jumps into existence. Whitecoat's thinking, I can't wait till this little shit of a girl goes back to Hamilton and stays there.

He changes the subject. Good for Whitecoat. Recognize when you're beaten.

'Robin, how do you think you will feel when your sister marries your ex-boyfriend?'

Wow. Chalk up one for Whitecoat. That one came from left field, so fast that I can't stop the wave of hate that descends on his office. Whitecoat must feel it, too: a tsunami filling the room. Must not think. Must not feel. If I did, could destroy the world.

Voices tell me to zap him with a thunderbolt. Lightning crackles. I pull the dagger from my sash.

'Robin?' I hear Whitecoat asking, like he's been repeating it for some time. 'Does this upset you?'

'Does what upset me?' I ask.

'Your sister marrying your ex-boyfriend.'

Kill them both, a voice says.

'Max? You're talking about Max? Max is history,' I say.

'So, seeing Max is not going to upset you, then?'

'No.'

'Then, why are you so angry?'

This guy is so annoying. He thinks he can read me. I run rings around him.

'I'm not angry.'

Whitecoat pauses, then continues. 'Why don't you go ahead then and describe the wedding ceremony to me. Who will be walking down the aisle first. Where you will be. Just tell me what happens.'

Sure. I can do that. I'm not angry.

'Well, Melissa will be wearing white. Mother says it's lace with a train.

I'm wearing blue taffeta with a sash.' I pause, thinking of the sash.

'Go on. Who is walking down the aisle first?'

'The bridesmaids, I think. Four, dressed in blue, holding violets.'

'Then?'

'Then the ushers. I don't know how many.'

'Okay.'

'Then me. With violets and lily of the valley.'

'Sounds pretty.'

I know he's being patronizing, but what the hell.

'Then Paul, the best man.'

'Friend of yours?' Whitecoat asks.

'Friend of Max's,' I say, and a thundercloud escapes me to sink heavily to the floor.

Whitecoat nods. 'Then?'

'Max.'

I pause, an earthquake in my heart. Max Max. Bo-bax. I see him striding down the aisle, gorgeous in his black tux, lilies of the valley in his lapel, wide smirk on his face, catching my eye for a split second and looking away.

Whitecoat is about to give me another word of encouragement, but I rush on.

'Then, Melissa with Mother and Howard.'

There, it's over in my mind, and I survived.

'And?' Whitecoat asks.

'It's over,' I say.

'It's not over,' Whitecoat insists.

Don't go there, a voice warns, but Whitecoat is waiting and I plunge on.

'And they come down and stand under the chuppah, and Max breaks the wineglass, and the rabbi says, "Do you take this man?" and "Do you take this woman?", and "to have and to hold" and all that shit, and they both say, "I do". And they kiss.'

And Robin pulls the dagger out of her blue taffeta sash and kills them both. But I don't say that. If I said that, they wouldn't let me go.

'You're okay with all this?' Whitecoat asks. 'Because you don't have to go, you know.'

Oh, yes you do, says a voice.

'Sure, sure,' I say. 'I'm okay.'

74

* * *

Tuesday morning, out on the grounds with Derek, walking and smoking.

It's a nice day for February. Cold but nice, with the sun shining, and a certain crispness in the air. It's all right for February.

Derek's all right, too. He's still holding his own, not too high and not too low. I think maybe Whitecoat has hit on the right formula, for once, with the anti-convulsants added to the lithium. Even with the drugs, though, Derek is still a handful. You do not want to make him mad, believe me. Well, he's already mad, but angry. Do not make him angry, then he's up and down all over the place. Or jealous. Just the normal human emotions seem to kick him into overdrive. So, don't. Just don't.

And sometimes it all seems too much trouble to deal with Derek. I have my own problems, though I wouldn't tell Whitecoat this, but he's right that I don't like to get too close. Too close is an already small room that's closing in on you. I'm a big person. Well, not physically, although Melissa keeps harping on my being fat, which I'm not, but I didn't mean that, anyway.

But, let's face it: I'm the ruler of this world. Le monde, c'est moi. I'm as big as the world, bigger even, because how can the creation be bigger than its creator, even in an expanding universe? Freedom doesn't weigh much. You give the world its freedom, and it expands and expands, but it's no bigger than it ever was. It always is what it is, with the potential to be bigger, like a child who grows up. It expands, but it never becomes something it didn't have in it in the first place. Q.E.D., it can never get bigger than I am. I am.

So, don't try to hem me in. Don't look into my eyes full of yourself and tell me you love me. Because most of the stuff humans call love is all about the themselves. It's not about the loved one. It's about the one who does the loving, if you want to call it that. It's about trying to own people. Or about loving and leaving. And hurting. I love the world, but I'd never try to own it. Give it space. And time. On the other hand, I'd never create something and leave it all alone. You understand what love is now?

Ergo, you keep your distance, and I'll keep mine. Walls make good neighbours.

Derek looks at his watch.

'Don't you have Dr Mankiewicz in twenty minutes?'

'Yeah.'

'He helping you any?'

I shrug. 'What am I aiming for?'

Derek laughs. He seems to think this is funny. 'Sanity?'

'The impossible dream,' I say.

'Survival?' Derek asks.

'Not enough.'

'Happiness?'

'Too much.'

'Contentment?' he asks, the expression on his face telling me that this is as far as he'll go.

'In the ballpark,' I reply.

Derek takes a long, slow drag on his Marlboro. We walk a few more paces before he says, 'Couldn't you be happy with me, Robin?'

Uh, oh. I was distracted and didn't see where this was going. The walls are closing in.

'I don't think I can love anyone, any more,' I say.

I should have known. The next question follows as night follows day. 'Did you love Max?' Derek asks.

He's so one-track. Derek's obsessed with love, the way Whitecoat's obsessed with reality. 'No,' I answer.

You did, a voice says.

Fact is, I did. Max was when I was three-dimensional and happy of it. But look what he did with my love. Threw it away. And now it's too late. You can't love in ten dimensions. Evil, the far end of chaos, exists happily in all ten. But love has no dimensions. Love is a zero point energy field. I'm too big for love.

But you did love, the voice insists.

I did love. The echo of my love still exists, a signature in the cold radiation of space. I can't erase what happened. I did love.

Derek is still looking at me, with a lovelorn look. 'You said you didn't think you could love anyone, *any more*. You must have been in love once.'

He's such a stickler. Just like Whitecoat.

'Put out your cigarette,' I command.

I pull Derek down behind a bush and distract him with sex. Men confuse sex with love, and I thoroughly confuse him. Fifteen minutes later, flushed but happy, we sit up, readjust our pants and jackets, light one cigarette between us.

Derek looks at his watch. He's good that way. When he's balanced on his escarpment, Derek is a responsible, law-abiding citizen, not like me. 'Time for your session, Robin,' he says, giving me one last hot kiss, and pushing me out of the bush.

I stumble into the building, down the hallway.

'Come!' I hear, echoes of *Star Trek*.

This time Whitecoat is facing front, waiting for me. He seems gentler somehow, like someone's grandfather. The grey beard looks less like Sigmund Freud and more like Santa Claus.

This must be a new ploy to try to soften me up. I try reading his thoughts, but they seem all fuzzy and nice. Bet he got into the Xanax.

'Tell me about your sister, Robin,' he says softly.

Oh, where oh where to begin. The thief. The evil witch. The sister from Hell.

'We never got along too well,' I say out loud.

'Why not?'

Mother always liked her better. She stole my boyfriend.

'We're very different,' I finally answer.

'Different – how?' Whitecoat croons.

'What is it with you?' I shout. 'You're not yourself today.'

He laughs, but the laugh is warm. 'Who am I, then?'

'Walter Cronkite,' I say.

Whitecoat laughs again, but I utterly refuse to like him, no matter what he does.

'Different – how?' he asks again.

Ah, this is the Whitecoat I know, the one who never gives up. Never lets you get away with anything. This is the guy.

'I forgot the question.'

I wait for the vertical line to pop up between his eyebrows, but there's no sign of it. What a mellow guy. Something is wrong. 'First, tell me why *you* are different today,' I say.

He laughs briefly, then gets serious. 'My wife had a baby last night.'

'You? You have a wife?' I ask. Will wonders never cease?

'Yes.'

'But you're so old!'

He smiles. That makes three times in the hour. 'My wife is considerably younger than I am.'

Apparently. Wow. Whitecoat human. It takes the breath away. Suddenly, I think to ask. 'Boy or girl?'

'Girl,' he says, smiling. That makes four. 'Six pounds, five ounces. Rachel Ellen.'

Rachel Ellen Mankiewicz. The name trips off the tongue.

'So,' Whitecoat's saying. 'Let's get back to business.'

Of course, business.

'How are your sister and you different?'

The question seems long ago and far away, from a distant galaxy. I let the question speed on through space till it reaches me, and then I answer.

'Melissa is all looks and no character,' I say.

'And you? What are you?'

'I'm the ruler of the universe.'

There. The vertical line between the eyebrows. Yup, this is the same guy.

'You are the smart one,' he ventures.

Mind reading again. This time he's right. 'Yes, I am. Was.'

'Still are. What happened with Max, Robin?'

Anger, anger. I'm not angry.

'The two of them lied to me. They acted like they didn't like each other, while they were fucking each other's brains out behind my back the whole time.'

Whitecoat doesn't bother to chastise me for my language, just asks, 'How do you feel about that, Robin?'

Feel. Feely. Touchy feely.

Don't tell, someone says.

'I don't know.'

'It's important for you to admit to yourself how you feel,' he adds.

The voices are having a heyday.

Feelings are for wimps, one says.

Don't feel. Don't feel.

Look what feeling got you.

'I don't feel anything,' I say.

'I don't believe that,' Whitecoat scolds.

'Don't believe it. I don't care.'

Whitecoat sits back in his chair and looks at me, a scientist observing his specimen. He waits. And waits. He's going to wait all day for all I care.

Finally, he says, 'Well, if you don't want to talk to me, we can just sit here. Mind if I finish my newspaper?'

When I still don't answer, Whitecoat picks up a newspaper from the bookshelf and begins to read. For the first time, I am angry. I mean I wasn't angry before, with all that talk of Max (oh!) and Melissa. But now I'm angry. This is my time. Howard is paying for this time.

'I want to talk,' I say.

'Good,' Whitecoat says, putting down his newspaper. 'What about?'

Be careful, a voice warns. Don't tell him anything. Or else.

This gets me more angry. How dare they order me around. I'm going to tell him something the voices would not want me to tell. I feel a little thrill, because I've never done this before.

'My father,' I say.

'Your stepfather?' Whitecoat asks, looking a little surprised.

'No. My real father.'

There's a great rush of voices in my head all of a sudden, my father's among them.

You can't tell him anything about me, Father says. He won't believe you, anyway.

Oh, I didn't realize you were there, Father.

I am. He's just giving you enough rope to hang yourself, you know.

But Whitecoat is speaking. He sees me preoccupied and says it again, and I listen, despite my father's admonition.

'Tell me about your father, Robin. I want to hear.'

I'm going away and I won't come back, Father says.

But why? I ask.

If you tell, I will never come back.

Tell what? That you killed yourself?

'Robin? What is it?' Whitecoat is asking.

Robin, Father says ominously.

'No, I can't. I'm sorry. I can't,' I say. 'He won't let me.'

'Is he talking to you now?' he asks.

Don't answer. It's me or him.

No, no, Father. I won't betray you.

I knew you wouldn't, Robin.

'No,' I finally answer. 'I'm not talking to anyone. Anyone,' I repeat and stand up.

Whitecoat seems disappointed. The vertical frown line is running all the way from his eyebrows to his hairline now. I feel bad that I ruined his day, but Father is right. Better not to talk to strangers.

Chapter Five

Two weeks to go. Had a dream last night, which I won't tell Whitecoat. Father, wearing his sailor suit, and not Howard, walked Melissa down the aisle. Whitecoat was the rabbi. Rachel Ellen Mankiewicz, in a blue taffeta dress, was watching the proceedings from the audience. Where I was, I don't know.

Roz and I are eating breakfast in the lunchroom. It's snowing outside, but Derek's out anyway, smoking. I could care less, really. He's been ragging on me so much lately, I don't give a shit any more. Do I still have feelings for Max? How do those feelings compare to mine for him? Maybe we should just elope and go off to Australia? He's sure his mother would be happy to give him her ring – with the diamond that could buy Holt Renfrew. And we could buy a ranch in Australia, complete with horses and cattle and buffalo and kangaroos. Like hell we are, I said, but Derek just stood there looking at me, like what did you say?

I told him he was getting manic, and he said, no, he just felt good, and why does everyone think that having good feelings makes him manic? Wow, he gave it to me. I guess Whitecoat must be on his tail about that, too.

So, Roz and I are eating breakfast, and in comes Derek through the doors and sits down next to me. He squashes his cigarette on the floor – we're not supposed to do this, but seeing how many squashed cigarettes are on the lunchroom floor, you'd realize that this is not something that's strictly enforced. He's got a tray full of oatmeal, toast, eggs, juice, bacon, a muffin and coffee. In fact there's so much food on the tray, that the muffin is sitting on top of the toast. Of course, anyone can see from his big appetite that he's on his way to happy land. Only Derek can't see it. Won't see it, I think, because the signs are all there, and he's got eyes.

I talked to Whitecoat yesterday about Derek. Or tried. Suddenly, Whitecoat won't tell on anyone, especially Derek. Can't betray any confidences, he says. Hello? I seem to remember when he butted into my session to ask how I felt about Derek. Anyway, I tried to tell him that Derek might be all right in his sessions – I don't know – but he sure was acting like an asshole out of them. So what do you think Whitecoat did?

He asked me how I felt about that.

'About what?' I asked.

'About the possibility of Derek getting out of control,' he said.

'Is Derek getting out of control?' I asked.

'I can't betray confidences,' he said.

The stupid jerk. You can't get a handle on him. One day he's warm and fuzzy, the next he's a cigar store Indian, all hard and cold. His mouth says one thing and his eyes another. And all the while he's asking you what you feel about this and what you feel about that, and not understanding one's basic right to privacy. My feelings are my own, not his. But he doesn't get that. The voices were all laughing and shouting and trying to get me to kill him, and it was only by the grace of myself that I didn't do it.

So, Roz and I are eating breakfast in the lunchroom. And Derek comes in with all this food and squashes his cigarette and sits down next to me. And what do you think he said?

'Will you marry me?'

Right in front of Roz and the whole lunchroom. All of a sudden, you could hear a pin drop. Roz starts to choke, and I have to run around again and clap her on the back, till she spits out this truly disgusting piece of egg and toast, all mixed up.

I come back to my seat, with quiet dignity.

Derek says, 'You want me to get on my knees?'

'No!' I practically shout. 'Don't do that!'

Of course, by this time, everyone has stopped eating and is looking at us with bated breath. And Roz has her mouth open so wide you can see her tonsils. And I'm sitting there, wondering what to say. I mean, it's not that I don't like Derek. The two of us have a lot of chemistry. I just look at him and get the hots. You know what I mean? I could fuck him till the cows come home, but marriage?

Well, of course, Melissa is marrying Max (!) in two weeks, and it would really be something if I could announce to everyone and Max (!) that I am getting married, too, but do I really want to marry anyone just to announce it to Max? And what would it be like to be married to someone who will never really be well? Someone who will always be on a roller coaster and drag me up and down with him, to the end of time.

I have responsibilities. I have to keep watch over the world. And it's not that I don't *love* Derek, although you know what I think about love.

That it's not about owning or about hurting, and most humans think it comes naturally, which it doesn't. Like, with Derek, it would be about owning, and with me, it would be about hurting, and where would that get us?

So, all this time, Roz is sitting there with her mouth open, and Derek is bouncing up and down, ready and set to kneel in front of me, and the whole lunchroom is holding its collective breath. And I want to say, 'Like hell I am,' but I'm hesitating, for some reason. Is it that I would actually like to marry this lunatic or am I afraid what he might do to himself if I say no? Is Whitecoat right in his yadayadayada that I don't know how I feel?

Yes no yes no yes no.

Finally, surprising even myself, I say, 'Yes.'

Derek lets out a triumphal scream. Roz looks like she's swallowed a horse, but I can't be bothered with her right now. She's got to learn that you don't use the same tubes for swallowing and breathing. The rest of the lunchroom cheers. Oh, myself, I think. What have I done?

The voices. They begin slowly, talking to themselves. From what I hear, they are arguing over who is the new ruler of the world. It's all a cacophony, no one listening to the other, everyone talking at once, and none of them talking to me.

Set up a new government, one says.

Who makes the rules here?

Robin is dead. Long live the new Robin.

I cannot believe what I am hearing. I'm not dead. I am that I am.

Derek starts to pull at my arms.

'Let's go, Robin. You're acting really strange. Let me take you to Dr Mankiewicz.'

I have no idea what I'm saying or what I'm doing. Derek falls down on the floor, clutching his stomach. The look on his blue face is pure surprise.

Next thing I know, Martin is here, and Derek is pinning back my arms.

'Sorry,' he says, as I feel the prick of a shot in the arm, and the room goes black.

I wake up in bed, my arms and legs pinned at four points.

Derek, looking down at me with the same lovelorn look, is saying the marriage is off, at least for the near future. That I'm not up to it.

'What happened?' I ask, but when I look into Derek's face, it all comes back to me.

Martin is standing in the corner, no black eye or bandaged arm. I remember now who I punched.

'Sorry,' I say.

A voice laughs. Shut up, I tell it, or I'll send you to hell.

Yessir, it says and laughs.

Derek is holding my hand, a sad smile on his lips. 'It's okay. You didn't break anything.'

'Does your stomach hurt?'

'Don't worry about it.'

'I didn't mean to hurt you.'

You did, the voice says.

'Shut up!' I finally shout, in exasperation.

Derek stops patting my hand.

'Not you,' I say.

'I've already given her a heavy dose,' says Martin from the corner. 'She shouldn't be acting so wacko.'

Wacko, the voice repeats.

I don't understand. The voices used to listen.

'What did I tell you?' I shout to the voice. 'To Hell!'

No, it says.

'Martin, make it shut up!'

'Uh, oh,' Martin says. 'I'm going to get Dr Mankiewicz.'

Ten minutes later, Whitecoat appears. This is a first. He's NEVER visited me in my room before.

'Robin,' he says, looking down at me. 'Who are you talking to?'

'One of them,' I say.

'One of whom?' he asks, sitting on the edge of the bed.

'The devils.'

He nods, as if he believes me. 'And what is that devil saying?' he asks.

The voice is saying, Fuck you.

'Fuck you,' I say.

Whitecoat does a double-take.

'That's what it's saying. Can't you hear it?'

Whitecoat confers with Martin for a minute, before announcing, 'I'm updating your medication.'

84

Ooh, I'm afraid, the voice says.

But I am. It's never acted so hostile before. 'Dr Mankiewicz,' I say, and Whitecoat does another double-take. I guess I've never called him that before. 'It's all your fault.'

'My fault?' he asks, very serious.

'You wanted me to feel. This is what happens when I feel.'

The next week goes by in a dull, grey fog. Whitecoat's new cocktail is working, squeezing out the very juice from life. Now I know how Derek feels, curled up in a fetal position. Hopeless, futile, without illusions. The voices are there, but so low I can ignore them. I laugh at them now, they seem so powerless. So, who is the ruler of the universe now?

But I don't believe it. I don't know what to believe any more. I'm not the ruler of the universe. I'm just a girl who spends her life in an institution. Hurrah for medication!

Derek has been coming around every day, but I can tell he thinks I'm no fun. Whitecoat hasn't treated him for the hypomania. He's not sleeping much, and keeps telling me everything will work out. Don't worry, he says, it will all work out. What a reversal.

Every other day I go see Whitecoat, who has been tinkering with my dosage. Too much, and I don't want to get out of bed; too little and the voices start getting nasty.

One week to go till Melissa's wedding. Mother has told me that if I can't make it, I can't make it. Not to worry. They'll have Heather come in her prom dress. Melissa is pissed at me in a major way, though, and just called me to say that Heather in her pink prom dress would ruin the whole effect, and if I don't pick my fat ass off of my bed and go with Howard next Friday, she will never speak to me again. Hey, is that a reward or punishment? Derek says he'd love it if I stayed here with him. I think he's still unsure of Max and whether I might punch him in the stomach, too. That's nothing. I never told him about the visions I had of stabbing the happy couple with the dagger in my sash. I know now that they were just the product of a sick mind.

Yawn. I can't go like this, that's for sure. I can barely get myself off the bed. I'm just going to have to start spitting the pills out in the toilet the way I used to do.

Oh, here's Beverly. She's a little less zombie-like today. She comes in and smiles at me. Wow, Beverly smiling. Contradiction in terms.

'Get up,' Beverly says. 'It's a nice day.'

Maybe there's something in her drug cocktail that is actually working. She's different. Whether she's Beverly, though, is something else. I have a problem with taking meds, as you probably know. I don't like the feel of it: take a pill, and some active ingredient changes who you are. Then who are you, really? It's just another way to shut us up, shut the real us up.

I struggle to sit up, and look out the window. Right she is. The sun is shining. Ouch.

Beverly picks up her magazine, a ray of sunshine illuminating the page number: 24! Was it Beverly who read those pages or did the drug cocktail read them directly? And even if she is happier, maybe she was really happier being unhappy. See, it's someone else deciding who they want you to be, a person who's more like everyone else, and then changing you into that person. How is that possible, you said? How can you change someone else, when their blueprint stays the same? Hey, they're fiddling with genetic blueprints now. They can turn people into amoebas if they want to.

'Were you outside?' I say to the person who looks like Beverly.

'Yeah,' she says, turning a page: 25!

'See Derek?'

'Yeah.'

'What's he doing?'

'Jogging around the yard.'

Not a good sign. This means his energy is way up.

'Is he smoking?'

'You think I spy on him?' Beverly asks.

I think a moment. Do I think she spies on him? 'No,' I say.

'Good,' she answers and turns a page.

'Are you really reading that?' I ask, all the while trying to determine whether this is really Beverly or her clone.

No answer. This is vintage Beverly. Maybe this is not a clone, after all.

'Are you really reading that?' I repeat.

She looks up from page 26. 'Looking at the pictures.'

'Want to take a walk?' I ask.

Nothing.

'Want to take a walk?'

Beverly looks up. 'Take your own.'

'Please.'

'I've got to finish this.'

'You don't have to finish that. You've been reading that stupid magazine for six months!'

'Shut up, Robin,' Beverly says.

End of conversation.

I pick one leg up and throw it over the edge of the bed. Then I pick up the other and do the same thing. I sit there in suspended animation for a while.

Martin appears in the doorway. 'Time for your meds.'

Turn me into an amoeba, why don't you.

Martin comes straight toward me, pours some pills into a cup, gives me some water. I upend the cup, work the pills under my tongue and take a sip of water. He looks at me with suspicion, but goes on to Beverly, then out the door. I spit the pills into my hand and stand up. No way that I am going to feel like this any more. I trudge over to the bathroom, throw the pills into the toilet and urinate on top of them. There, take that. You won't be making any more trouble now.

Wash my face, brush my teeth, everything in quarter-time. Trudge back to my side of the room and struggle into my underwear, grab a top from the drawer, a pair of wrinkled pants from the closet. I stand there for a moment, lost in a cold fog, staring at the black plastic bag that shrouds the blue taffeta dress. I bet Whitecoat doesn't realize what his prescriptions do to my life, just thinks he's purging me of hallucinations, doesn't realize that the hallucinations are what makes it all bearable. Then he goes home to his home and wife and baby. His young wife. Whitecoat probably grabs her the moment he comes in, slams the door, no, he wouldn't do that, he'd wake the baby. Grabs her, tears off her apron, and does it on the living-room floor. That's probably how they made Rachel Ellen. And comes in the next day and writes more prescriptions for the walking dead.

A look out the window shows Derek in sweat pants, jogging the perimeter of the grounds. I watch him for about ten minutes, until he picks up a towel from a chair, wipes his face, and heads back toward the building. What's Max got that he hasn't got, I ask myself. Probably nothing, except Melissa. And good riddance, I say.

A little voice coming from the vicinity of my Nikes says, listen to her now.

I drop the curtain, start the long walk to the lunchroom. I'm still waiting for my delusions, but the stuff Whitecoat's been prescribing has such a long half-life, I'll be grey and delusion-less for another week.

The same voice, hardly noticeable, says, Just in time for the wedding.

So, I'm walking down the hallway, on the last lap toward the lunchroom, when Derek comes up in back of me, like he's going to jump me from behind.

'Don't even think of it,' I say.

'How'd you know I was there?' Derek asks, coming up on one side.

'The smell,' I say, though, of course, I just know these things.

'Didn't have time to shower,' he chuckles.

'Well, just don't stand so close,' I say, giving him a push.

He laughs, half again as long as he should. 'You're such a pill these days, Robin.'

'Not any more,' I reply.

'What does that mean?'

I keep on walking.

'You're not off your medication again, are you?' Derek asks.

I give him as much of a smile as I can manage.

Derek laughs. 'You are, aren't you?' He tries to get serious, but can't. 'You know I should tell Mankiewicz, don't you?'

'But you won't.'

'I won't. If you start taking them again.'

'How will you know if I don't tell you?'

'I can tell.'

'Sure, sure,' I say as we burst into the lunchroom. Roz is already there, stuffing her face.

We cross to the counter where the grandma lady fills Derek's tray up with food. I let her dump a little mound of peas on my plate and grab a yogurt.

'Dieting? For Max?' Derek asks, eyeing my tray.

'For you,' I say quickly. You do not want to make Derek jealous. Believe me.

'I like you just the way you are,' he says.

I am dressed in wrinkled pants and an old top, my hair is all matted up, and, if Melissa is to be believed, I'm twenty-five pounds too fat. What is this guy on? Well, I know what he's on, actually, but none of that stuff should cause hallucinations.

We sit down in front of Roz, who points to the spaghetti on Derek's plate.

'Don't eat that. Mine had a fly in it.'

She thinks she's doing Derek a favour, pre-tasting his food and all that, but he waves her off. 'Extra protein,' he says, and starts eating the spaghetti.

We all laugh, even me. Maybe that means the pills are wearing off. Yesterday, I couldn't even smile. Today, things seem, all of a sudden, brighter. I begin to eat my peas, one at a time.

Derek hands me his straw. 'Hey, try this.'

I try to suck up a pea, but it gets stuck in the end. I keep sucking, but the pea just ensconces itself in the straw and sits there.

'Not supposed to be cooked,' Roz tells us.

'Yeah,' I say, and blow out. The pea lands in Derek's hair.

'Hey!' he laughs and throws a meatball at me.

I blow another pea at him.

Roz stands up and dumps her plate of uneaten spaghetti and fly onto my lap.

I have a choice, the way I see it. I could get angry that Roz has upped the ante and ruined my wrinkled pants. Or I can go with the flow. Yes no yes no yes no. Yes. Maybe I'm not really making decisions here. Maybe I always say yes. In any case, I grab the spaghetti from my lap and throw it at the tall guy at the next table, where it lands on his shoulder.

The tall guy does not look pleased. He grabs the wad of spaghetti from his shoulder and throws it back at Roz, who handily catches it with her face. Then the tall guy begins to cry and runs out of the lunchroom. Meanwhile, several other people have gotten in the act and are throwing meatballs around. The counter lady runs out in panic. Derek gets hit in the back with red Jell-O.

Oops. Martin comes in with a few of his henchmen, hypodermics at the ready. Most of the terrorists calm down, with the exception of Derek, who, laughing uproariously, throws a couple of meatball missiles at Martin's head. Martin is not amused, grabs the both of us and puts us each in solitary for an hour. Hey, it was worth it.

The next day I find out that Whitecoat is angry with both of us.

'Robin, did you start the food fight in the lunchroom?' he asks, half a minute after swivelling toward me to start the session.

'Ask Derek.'

'I'm asking you.'

Whitecoat's face looks like one of those tribal masks today: face hard, eyebrows up in the air, mouth in shouting position. It scares me. I hunker down in the little, hard seat.

'I blew a pea at Derek.'

'And what happened then?'

'Derek threw a meatball at me.'

'I see,' Whitecoat says, his pudgy hands in a steeple on the desk. 'And then?'

'I don't know. It got out of hand.'

'You bet. James Moyer won't come out of his room. The counter lady says you threw spaghetti at him.'

'Spaghetti can't hurt you,' I answer.

'And Derek is back in a depressed state,' Whitecoat says, ignoring my defence of spaghetti.

I don't give a shit about James Moyer, but this is the first I hear about Derek being depressed.

'Poor Derek,' I mumble.

Derek is such a loser, a voice says.

No, no, I tell it. Leave him alone.

Max is better, the same voice says.

'Stop that,' I say out loud.

Whitecoat stops what he is saying, something that I obviously have not been listening to.

He looks at me curiously and says, 'Robin, you have not been taking your medication, have you?'

'Yes, yes, I have,' I lie.

Whitecoat gives me another of those looks and scribbles something on a piece of paper. 'I'm writing myself a reminder to tell the aides to check that you have swallowed.'

He doesn't believe her, a voice says.

Sure he does, another says.

'And I'm going to call your mother to tell her to check as well.'

The wedding. I had almost forgotten that.

'Robin,' Whitecoat says and gives me a long pause, that means, this is important. 'I want you to listen.'

I wait, eyes down on the floor.

Finally, he says, 'Sometimes I think you don't want to get better.'

She's not trying, the first voice says.

I like her just the way she is, the second says.

'I do,' I say.

'Then why do you keep playing games with your medication?' Whitecoat asks.

See? He doesn't believe her, the first voice says.

'I don't know,' I answer.

'I think you do,' Whitecoat says.

Damn Whitecoat. Damn everyone. How would he like to live in a grey fog of nothingness? To be slow, and weak, and powerless like everybody else?

'You don't understand.'

A hint of a smile appears on Whitecoat's face. 'Then tell me what I don't understand.'

'All it does is take the colour out of everything.'

'The colour?'

'The power, the glory.'

'Your power? Your glory?'

'Yes.'

'You don't want to be just human?'

'Human is having no control. Human is being hurt.'

'Ah,' Whitecoat says. 'You'd rather be crazy than be hurt.'

Is that true? A voice asks.

Is she crazy about Max? Another asks.

Father? I ask into the blue. Are you there?

I can hear a whoosh, and Father's voice, loud and clear.

You're just too big for him to understand, Robin. Don't listen to him.

'What are you talking about?' I shout, getting up. 'It's the medicine that makes me crazy.'

Two days to go. I'm standing at the window, watching the trees blow. No Derek today. He's lying in bed.

Up till a few days ago, I was able to carry on a lively conversation with the blue taffeta dress, but no more. No voices, no colour, slow as a turtle. Whitecoat told every goddamned aide to make sure I swallow, so here I am, looking out the window, watching the trees blow. Nothing going on outside, nothing going on inside.

'Your sister is on the phone,' someone shouts from the hallway. I let the curtain fall and shuffle out into the hallway. Eventually, I reach the phone.

'Hey.'

'God, you sound bored.'

'My name is Robin.' I remember when my name was God.

'Haha. That's really funny, Robin.' A long pause. 'So, ready to be a maid of honour?'

I want to say no just to rile her, but it isn't worth it. Nothing's worth it.

'Yeah. Ready, set, and go.'

'Gee, you're a barrel of laughs today. What's wrong with your voice?'

'Nothing,' I say in a monotone.

'You sound like you're half asleep.'

I snore into the phone.

'Okay, funny girl. I get it. I get it. Anyway, we're all set. Dress, check. Tux, check. Rabbi, check. Wedding favours, hall, flowers, check, check, check.'

She goes on like this for a while. I don't know what else she says, I'm not listening. Suddenly, I hear,

'Well, do you want us to come over today or not?'

'Want who to come over?'

'Dammit, Robin. You make me say everything sixty times. Max and me, that's who. Do you want to us to come over or not?'

'Max and me?' I say.

'What? You're getting weird again, Robin. Max and me! Not Max and you. Do you want us to or not? It's really nice of Max to offer to drive all the way out there, don't you think?'

I picture the two of them in their wedding clothes, gliding through the door, wedding march playing in the background. Max Max Bo Bax. Do I want to see him? Yes no yes no yes no. Yes. I always come up with yes.

'Yes,' I say.

'Really?' The voice on the other end seems surprised. 'Well, okay, then. We'll be over sometime after lunch. We can't stay long. I've got a lot of last-minute details.'

'Sure,' I say. 'After lunch. Max and me,' but Melissa's already hung up.

I shuffle back to my room, sit down on the bed and survey the room. Two desk chairs should be enough if Beverly donates hers. I'll sit on the bed. I contemplate Max and Melissa in my room sneaking peeks at the dreary curtains and the barred windows, and decide to meet them downstairs. And change your clothes, why don't you, I tell myself.

Father? I ask, but there's no one there. Off in Madagascar or Tahiti, maybe.

Anyone? The voices are asleep or hiding. No one there. Just me. Not even my shadow.

I change into a skirt and find the sweater Max used to like, pull it on and tug it over the top of the skirt. There, cover the fat. I squeeze a gob of gel onto my palm and try to finger-style my bangs. Look in the mirror, and who do I see? No one I know. Someone trying to look like the Robin Max knew. I still have a few hours. Maybe I'll look better later. Maybe I'll look better if I don't look in the mirror.

The clock says ten, and off I go. Hickory, dickory, Doc. Whitecoat awaits.

I march straight into his office, and sit down. Whitecoat's not facing forward in his swivel chair, nor is he facing backward. He's not there. He could be hiding in the shadows or behind the curtains, but no, he walks in the door, looking crumpled, circles around his eyes.

'Sorry,' he says. 'My wife and I were up all night with the baby.'

Rachel Ellen. 'Is she sick?' I think to ask.

'Colic.'

I have no idea what colic is. 'Is that serious?'

Whitecoat gives me a weak smile. 'Just for the parents,' he says.

I think that's a joke, but it doesn't seem very funny. I smile, anyway, just in case.

'Well, down to business,' Whitecoat says, easing himself into his chair.

I suddenly have this feeling of what it must be like to be Whitecoat. It doesn't matter that he was up all night. It's always down to business: the daily fear and madness, delusions, dread, desperation, hopelessness, suicide, of schizophrenia and depression and screams in the night. Always down to business: listening and listening and listening, of being objective, of never breaking down, of never, never showing your feelings ...

'Melissa and Max are coming to visit,' I say, trying to drown out the image.

'Oh?' he asks, his hands becoming a steeple in the air before they ever hit the desk. 'When are they coming?'

'After lunch.'

'Today?'

I nod, swallowing.

Whitecoat looks at me with concern. 'Are you ready to see him?'

'Him?' I say, examining my nails.

'Max.'

'Max?'

'Robin, I know about Max. You've told me about Max.'

'Have I?' I ask with great innocence.

'Robin, if you don't want this session, I'll understand.'

'Why?'

He's getting exasperated. I can see the vertical line throbbing between his eyebrows. 'If you want to go upstairs and get dressed, for example.'

'I *am* dressed.'

'I see. Well, then, why don't we just talk about Max, today, then.'

Max Max Bo Bax. 'He's coming today.'

'You told me that already. How do you feel about that?'

Banana-fana-fo Fax. 'I don't know.'

'Why don't you imagine the conversation you're going to have with him?'

Mi-my-mo Max. MAX. 'Hello, Robin,' I begin, and look up for Whitecoat's approval.

'Go on.'

'Hello, Max.'

He's trying unsuccessfully to stifle a yawn. 'And?'

'Long time no see.'

'Robin, why don't you play Robin, and I'll play Max.'

'Okay.' I wait for a minute, then launch into it.

'Yes, Max, it's been a long time. You're looking good.'

'So are you, Robin,' says Max Whitecoat.

I ignore the fact that that is an absolutely impossible thing for Max to say, and go on, anyway. 'I see you're marrying my sister.'

'Yes. I am. Do you have any problems with that?'

I break out of character and say, 'That's something you would say, not Max.'

Whitecoat's nostrils flare in another desperate attempt to smother his yawn. 'You don't think Max cares how you feel?'

I can feel the voices mulling around, somewhere deep in my body. 'No, Max doesn't give a shit how I feel.' I change viewpoints. 'Max, you don't give a shit how I feel.'

'That's not true, Robin. I'm really sorry about how it all turned out. I didn't mean to hurt you. That's the last thing I would have wanted.'

'Sure, sure. You're only saying that because you dumped me, but now I'm going to be your sister-in-law, and you have to be all nicey-nicey.'

'You sound very angry,' says Max Whitecoat.

'Who's talking?' I ask.

'Max,' Whitecoat says.

'I *am* angry. I loved you and now I hate you, I'm so angry.'

This feels good, and the guy across the desk from me doesn't say anything. His mouth is open like he's going to say something, but nothing he says will make any difference anyway. I take a good look at him. He's got dark curly hair and black glasses, and his eyes are brown and there's sweat on his upper lip, and his mouth is open because he's laughing at me. Suddenly, I feel this rush of hatred like I never felt before.

'I hate you,' I yell. He's talking, but I'm not listening.

'I hate you.' Don't even bother talking now, because it's too late, it's too late.

'I hate you!' Each time my voice gets louder, and now it feels just great and I want to kill him, so, I stand up and lunge at this Max creature in front of me.

He grabs my wrists, and we play a little tug-of-war for a minute over the desk.

'Robin!' Max Whitecoat says, as if he's been saying it for some time. 'Enough, Robin!'

'I hate you,' I say one more time.

I'm staring out the window in my room again, waiting. Whitecoat told me that after that spectacle, young woman, I don't trust you to see your sister and your sister's fiancé alone. He's fixed things so we meet in the social worker's office, with the social worker as chaperone.

I've eaten lunch if you want to call it that. Derek wasn't there. Like I care. If he wants to curl up like one of those slugs you find under a rock every time something goes wrong, I can't help him. This is not my problem. It's his problem. Let Whitecoat help him. That's what he's there for. Let his parents help him. Just not me, because Derek isn't my problem. He's not.

Shit, they're here. The red Infiniti. It's stopping in the circular driveway. Parking at the curb, of course. Melissa always breaks the rules, and never gets called on it. Curb door opening with two legs slinking out: one, then the other, a short skirt, a blonde head. The driver's door cracking open, left Doc Martin boot coming into view, attached to a long khaki leg. Now, broad shoulders framing a head of dark hair. That face. Max.

I watch as they climb the steps to the entranceway and disappear from view. I can feel them entering the building, announcing themselves, sitting down in the overstuffed chairs in the lobby. Waiting for me. I don't want to go. I want to stay here at the window for the rest of my life.

Father? I ask, but he's not there. Please! I beg. Be here now.

And he is.

Hello, dear, he says.

Oh, Father. I don't want to go down. He's there, downstairs. I can't. Can't make myself.

Robin, dear, dear Robin. Max is not worth one hair on your sweet head.

Stay with me, Father. I'm going now.

I'm here. Go.

I cross the room to the door, checking myself in the mirror, pulling down at my bangs which have inched upward toward the top of my head. The face is the same. He'll recognize the face.

You still have a pretty face, Father says.

Out the door, slowly, carefully. Down the hallway, holding onto the wall for dear life. Down the centre stairs, right hand on the banister all the way.

'Oh, there you are, Robin,' says the receptionist. 'I was just about to send someone for you. Your sister and her husband are here.'

I hear Melissa's laugh to my left. 'Not yet he isn't.' 'Robin!' she says to me.

Max stands there in back of her, just getting up from his chair. He's looking at me, looking at me. He's thinking, who is this fat girl with Robin's face? He's thinking, how could I have made love to this girl in the back of my red Infiniti? How *could* I have?

96

Father? I ask without moving my lips.

I'm here.

I go right up to Max, brushing past my sister with her lips out-stretched, ready to kiss.

'Hello, Max.' Just as I practiced.

'Hello, Robin,' he answers, standing there, his arms at his sides. Max Max Bo-bax.

'You're looking good, Max.'

A swallow. 'You, too, Robin.'

Whitecoat was right: he said it. But what else could he say?

I put out my hand, and Max shakes it, our life forces intermingling.

The receptionist says, 'Go on down the hall to Abigail's office, Robin. She's expecting you.'

'Who is Abigail?' Melissa asks, hands on her hips.

'The social worker,' the receptionist tells her. 'You're meeting in her office.'

'Why?' Melissa demands.

The receptionist looks unhappy.

'They're worried I'll act up,' I say.

'Oh, she won't act up,' Melissa assures the receptionist. 'Max and Robin are old friends.'

That's why, Father says.

'Well,' the receptionist says. 'I'm only following orders.'

'Come on,' says Max, starting down the hall. 'It doesn't matter.'

'Well, it does,' Melissa says. 'I want a little privacy.' To the reception-ist, 'Can't we just stay here?'

'Please,' the receptionist says.

From halfway down the hallway, Max calls, 'Come on, Melissa.'

I follow him, leaving Melissa standing in the middle of the lobby. Finally, tossing her head, Melissa comes after us. We walk down the long hall to the last door, encrusted in golden letters: Abigail Weber. Max knocks.

'Come in,' a voice says, and we do.

We can hardly see her behind her desk, Abigail is so little. 'Sit down,' she says. 'Don't mind me. I'm just here as an observer.'

Observing is creating, I observe.

Max and I sit down.

'I really can't see why we need anyone to observe us,' Melissa says.

'Well, I'm sorry if you object, Miss Farber, but Dr Mankiewicz asked me to sit in.'

'You think my sister might get violent?' Melissa demands.

'Well, no. That's unlikely.'

'Please, Melissa,' Max says.

Max is getting what he deserves, Father remarks.

'Because if she does, I don't think anyone,' and here Melissa looks Abigail over from top to bottom, 'who's no more than four foot two could really do anything about it.'

'I'm four eleven,' Abigail says.

'Melissa,' I say. 'Shut up and sit down.'

'Robin!' Abigail gasps, and makes a lunge for the phone.

But Melissa sits down. She just needs a dose of her own medicine.

'Don't mind me,' Abigail says again, puts down the phone and starts doing paperwork in a big way.

The chairs we sit in are wedged into three corners of the office, so we form a triangle: Robin (A), Melissa (B), and Max (C). Max (C) has to hunch over so his head doesn't hit the bookshelf above him.

'Robin, why don't you and Max change places?' Melissa says.

We both get up, and C takes A's chair. A sits in C's chair under the bookshelf.

'Satisfied?' Max asks Melissa.

Uh oh, Father says. Trouble in paradise.

I laugh.

'What's funny?' Melissa asks.

'Nothing,' I say.

We sit in silence a minute before Melissa says, 'Max just graduated. Did you know that, Robin?'

'No,' I answer.

'Tell her,' Melissa says.

Max shrugs. 'I finished my degree in computer science.'

'That's nice,' I say. 'What school?'

'Waterloo,' he answers, not looking at me.

'Tell her the prize you got,' Melissa urges.

'Stop it, Melissa. She wouldn't care about that.'

She. He called her she, like she's not even here.

What does he think she is: crazy? a voice asks.

Crazy, the first voice agrees.

This is not going the way I thought it would. I imagined Max grabbing me, sobbing it was all a big mistake: he never wanted Melissa, never even *liked* Melissa. He didn't know how it happened; she seduced him against his will, made him think he loved her. What a fool he'd been, but now he knows! Robin, you're the only one I've *ever* wanted.

Instead, we sit in a cramped little office, triangled off against each other, making tiny-talk.

Melissa is saying something to me about the menu.

Father? I beg. Tell me what to do.

Know thyself, Father says. And then there is a whoosh, and he is gone.

I know myself now. Of course. I am stronger, bigger, far too big for this little office, far too big for Max. I'm bigger than the world. Angry I may be, but I have no impulse to act, for I am balanced on the head of a pin. Max and Melissa may go on with their lives. I will not destroy them, though, in their iniquity, they will destroy themselves. Amen and Hallelujah.

I get up with great dignity and walk out. I couldn't care less about Melissa shouting, Max swearing, and Abigail stabbing at the buttons on her phone.

Ironically, it was Max who first explained to me how I create the world.

He'd go on and on about how light is both a particle and a wave, how it has this dual nature.

How if you shine a bright light through a slit in a screen, you light up the wall in back with the brightest point in the centre and the light tapering off around the edges, just as if you'd thrown a handful of beans. Only they're photons: tiny packages of light energy. Ergo, light's a particle.

'Okay, light's a particle,' I agreed.

But if you shine that bright light on a screen with two narrow slits in it, you split the light into two streams, identical but out of phase, just like waves. As each stream meets its twin, some waves match and some mismatch. Where they match adds to light; where they mismatch cancels to dark. Their interference pattern throws stripes up on the wall. Light. Dark. Light. Dark. Ergo, light's a wave.

'One slit: light's a particle. Two slits: light's a wave. One if by sea and two if by land. Just get to the end and tell me the answer,' I said.

But something was up. I could see the old gleam in his eyes. Nothing in my right hand. Nothing in my left hand. Nothing up my sleeve.

'Let's make this easy,' Max sighed. 'Let's say we take the double-slit screen but dim the light till it's just one photon that comes out. Take one particle and aim it at the screen. What do you see?'

He thinks he can trick me, but he can't. Two slits, one slit. It doesn't matter; it's one particle. 'One little spot on the wall,' I answered.

'You'd still get the interference pattern,' Max replied, smug. He always liked to confuse me.

'Oh, that's just silly. How can one photon interfere with itself?'

He shrugged at this. 'It's as if it goes through both slits.'

'As if?' I yelled. 'Doesn't the guy know? Why doesn't he just watch where it's going?'

'If the experimenter watches the slits, the interference pattern disappears!' Max said with his Cheshire cat face. 'Just by watching it, he changes the results. If he doesn't watch, the little light particle acts like a wave, travelling through both slits and interfering with itself. The moment he looks, the wave collapses into a particle. Quantum weirdness,' he added, and then he laughed.

Last day. Mother called me to ask me what was wrong. I can still back out, she said. What is it I said to Melissa that made her come back and barricade herself in the bathroom for two hours? And Max and Melissa had a fight, and really, dear, they're getting married in three days, and what did you do to cause it?

It's not my problem, I can see that now. Give them freedom, and shit happens. It's my job to gather the ingredients, add them together with a pinch of chaos, and mix it up. I told her it was none of her business, and to let them work it out on their own.

So, then Melissa called and told me she doesn't even want me to be maid of honour, but I'm the only one with the dress, and, at this point, she'd rather have her lunatic sister in blue taffeta than Heather in her pink prom dress, because the table settings were blue and the flowers were blue, and even the cake was blue, and Heather in her pink prom dress would ruin everything!

And she said Max was very hurt that I had walked out on them like that. For her, it didn't matter, because she was used to me acting like a spoiled bitch, but Max wasn't, and here he had come all the way out to

Berkshire to make amends, and I treated him like shit. And what did I have to say for myself?

I told Melissa that shit happened, and she had to be prepared, because it would come when you least expected it. And that Max *was* shit, so it was only fair that he was treated like shit. But, after all was said and done, that I loved her, and I wished them both well.

Then when she was actually speechless, I said goodbye and hung up.

So, tomorrow morning, Howard comes to pick me up, and we'll go have a wedding.

My last talk with Whitecoat before the big event. I come in and sit down on my judgment seat. Whitecoat looks stern, playing God. Just playing, but he looks very Old Testament right now, beard and all.

'What happened yesterday, Robin?' he asks.

There are dark circles under his eyes. Rachel Ellen has been colicking again. I can see it in his face.

'What?' I ask. I really don't have much sympathy for him, anyway, what with his young wife and his grabbing her in the vestibule as soon as he comes home.

Whitecoat sighs, a good long one that ends with his bearded chin on his chest.

'Robin, tell me what happened. Please.'

Please is the magic word. Mother taught me that. 'Max was talking about me as if I weren't there.'

'And it upset you, obviously, to be treated like an object.'

'It wasn't like I thought it would be,' I say, examining the patterns on the old, worn-out rug. 'I thought Max would be happy to see me.'

'He wasn't?'

Of course Max wasn't, and he knows it. But this is just Whitecoat's way of pulling things out of me: standard psychiatrist's strategy. He asks me things he already knows. If you ask a question you don't know the answer to, you just might get an answer you don't want to hear.

'No. He just stood there, with his hands at his sides. Didn't want to touch me, I could tell. I shook hands with him.'

'I see. That hurt you.'

He's always going on about hurt. 'I'm not hurt,' I reply.

'Then why did you leave like that?' Whitecoat asks.

I laugh. I picture myself leaving and the two of them yelling and screaming. 'There's nothing either of them can do to me now.'

'They hurt you before, but they can't hurt you any more?' he translates. Standard policy, I told you. Whitecoat's just taking what I say, turning it around and sticking a question mark at the end.

'Yes.'

'But you still want to punish them?'

I shrug. 'He doesn't need me to punish him. Melissa will peck him to death.'

'Melissa will what?'

'Peck him to death. I see it now.'

'Ah,' Whitecoat says, pulling at his beard. 'Your mean henpeck.'

'Yes. Henpeck.'

Whitecoat sits there for a moment, thinking. I can hear his thoughts. He wants to know what I think of Melissa.

'I've asked you before what you think of your sister,' Whitecoat says all of a sudden. 'All you said was that you were very different. You want to elaborate?'

'You want me to tell you what I think of Melissa?' I ask.

'Yes,' he replies.

What did I tell you?

'Okay. Melissa is … a piece of shit. Dreck. Turd. Doodoo. That's what I think of Melissa.'

'Not a nice person, in other words.' There he goes again, saying it in another way.

'Not a nice person,' I echo, laughing. An idea comes to me. 'Max and Melissa. They're perfect for each other.'

Whitecoat laughs. That's very strange behaviour from him; he must be really tired.

'You'll let them inflict punishment on each other,' he says.

'Exactly.'

Whitecoat gets serious all of a sudden. 'You will let them alone, then, Robin?' He's trying to find out if I can be trusted to go to the wedding.

'So be it. So be them.'

'You'll let them be?'

'I'll let them be.'

'Good. Now, do you still want to go to the wedding?'

Do I still want to go to the wedding? I think of Max, of the blue taffeta dress, and the dream dagger I still pull out of its sash. Of being balanced on the head of a pin, self-sufficient, perfect, God-like, unfeeling. Do I still want to go to the wedding? To go or not to go. To be or not to be. Yes no yes no yes no.

'Yes,' I say.

It was really Max who got me started on the long road to omniscience. I can't deny that double-slit thing really blew the hell out of reality for me. Here I was thinking that apples are red regardless of whether I looked at them or not. Or that the tree that fell in the forest really fell, even if I wasn't there to see its huge trunk crashing down into the earth, bark flying, a sea of branches crushing innocent little rabbits and snakes. I thought that the world was independent of me. I thought it wasn't up to me to watch something in order to make it happen. Ha!

So, that was the beginning of wisdom, a hard lesson. It's up to me. It's all up to me. I didn't want this thing, but I'm all right with it now. Still, it's a big responsibility, making the world from scratch every day.

Max used to talk about this guy Wheeler who palled around with Einstein and Niels Bohr. He worked on the atomic bomb, so he really knew his stuff.

So, anyway, you look away, and light is a wave. You look at the slits, and light is a particle. This is bad enough, but then Wheeler has to go and say, wait till the electron is past the slits. Wait till it happened, already. It's done and gone, and don't you think that's the end of the story? No!

NOW go ahead and look. Poof! It's a particle. So, whatever happened didn't really happen, because the experimenter makes it a particle, even though it was a wave when it went through. Not only can he choose what happens, he chooses what already happened. Time is no object. Object is no object. Max would laugh and laugh at this. It never seemed to bother him that the world was a scaffold crumbling away under my feet.

You don't see it? You still think it's all one way: that the world is hard and real and unchanging? Think again. It's nothing at all until I look at it. Nothing at all. Just a great smoky dragon, Wheeler calls it. Smoke and mirrors. A cloud of probability. Max told me Wheeler says the universe started out all skinny and got bigger. Then it gave rise to life, then mind, then observation, and finally, by watching those first moments, the observer gives it reality. Of course, I do.

Derek has deigned to come out of his room and to join us for lunch. He looks paler than usual, pale upon pale, which is practically albino. His skin looks pale. His hair looks pale. His eyes look pale. It looks like he's been hiding from the sun his whole life.

'Hey,' he says as he sits down. On his plate he has a slice of bread and an apple.

'Dieting?' I ask.

'No,' he says. Then he looks at his plate and just sits there.

'Want me to taste the bread?' Roz asks helpfully.

Derek half-nods, and Roz takes a small bite of the bread.

'Good,' she says. 'Want me to try the apple, too?'

'Yeah,' he says and hands her the fruit.

'No problem,' Roz replies. 'It's okay.'

Derek waits the requisite five minutes to see if Roz drops dead, and when she doesn't he begins to eat.

'I only came down to say goodbye,' he finally says between bites of apple.

'I'm not going till tomorrow morning.'

'Yeah, well.' Derek, looking like he's just lost his appetite, puts the apple down, half-eaten.

'I'll be back by Tuesday the latest.'

'You never know,' he says, staring down at his tray.

I give him my trademark blast of happiness, pure energy, direct across the table, and he smiles, sort of.

'Let's take a walk after lunch,' I suggest.

He shrugs, takes a half-hearted bite of his piece of bread.

'C'mon,' I say.

'Okay,' he mumbles through another bite.

'Isn't Mankiewicz helping you?' Roz asks.

'He's trying.'

'Tell him you need prune juice.'

'I'm not constipated, Roz,' Derek says. 'I'm just what they call a non-responder.'

'You know he has a baby?' I tell them, apropos of nothing.

'Who?' Derek mutters.

'Whitecoat.'

No response.

'Mankiewicz.'

'No!' Roz exclaims. 'He's a man!'

Derek is busy playing with the crust.

'His wife had it for him.'

'Oh,' says Roz.

Derek has stopped playing with the crust and is now head down in his plate.

'C'mon,' I say. 'Let's take a walk.'

It's the blind leading the blind. Or the sick leading the dead. Maybe we can yet add up to one decent person. I stand and pull up on his arm, and Derek lets me lift him up. We dump our trays and go outside. It smells good out here: a hint of spring, maybe, but coming from far, far away like an orgasm. Derek seems a little more together the further we get from the main house.

'Tomorrow morning?' he says, pulling out a cigarette.

'Yeah. Can I have one?'

'Sure.' He lights the cigarette and gives it to me, pulls another out and lights that, too.

'Better?' I ask as we both exhale.

'Yeah. A little.'

We walk.

Halfway across the grounds, Derek stops, looks at me. 'Don't go.'

'Gotta go. I'm the only one with the dress.'

He's heard this one before, but it doesn't wash with him. 'Give the dress to someone else to wear.'

'Who? My sister doesn't know anyone size twelve.'

That baffles him for the moment, and we walk some more.

'I don't know what I'll do without you, Robin,' Derek begins again near the far wall.

'You'll be all right. You've got Mankiewicz.' I'm careful to call White-coat by his right name, just so Derek doesn't get mad. But he isn't getting much of anything today.

'I'm not in love with Mankiewicz,' he says, gazing at me with deep, bottomless eyes.

'His wife is.'

'I'm in love with you, Robin,' Derek insists.

Maybe it's time to say something back. 'Me, too,' I say.

'Sure. You're still in love with Max,' Derek says.

'I'm not, I'm not.'

We walk a few paces farther.

'I told my parents about you,' Derek says.

Watch out, a voice says.

'They said that they were sure you are a nice girl, but it was better not to get involved with anyone at Berkshire. That I'll be out soon, and I'll find someone nice at the country club.'

He's getting ready to dump you, a voice says.

'You always listen to your parents?'

'It's just that I don't have a lot of energy to fight everyone at the same time.'

We walk a few more minutes, my voices starting up big time. I can't stand much more of this.

'You're getting ready to dump me,' I say, turning back toward the building.

'No,' Derek says, following me. 'I love you. I'd never do that.'

'How could you do that to me?'

'I won't ever do that,' he says. 'I told you.'

'You will, when you leave. Your parents will make you.'

Derek gives a little honk, almost like a laugh, except that Derek's not laughing

'I'm never getting out of here,' he says and throws his arm around me.

It feels good there. 'We'll stay here together, then,' I say. 'The two of us together, forever.'

We walk a couple of paces further, when Derek suddenly moans and throws his body around mine. We stand melded together like this for a long time, I don't know how long, not doing anything, just leaning against each other; our hearts beating in tandem, boom boom boom boom, our lungs inhaling, exhaling. He's hurting: I can feel it, but I can't fix it.

'It's okay, Derek. I'll be back by Tuesday. Just hold it together till then.'

I give him a kiss on the mouth and a blast of good will, and leave him there in the yard, crying.

Chapter Six

Howard's waiting out front in the Buick. Robin, oh, Robin, he waves.

I see you already, I wave back.

He's got this big grin on his face, and a lily of the valley in the zipper tab of his parka.

Howard pops the trunk, gets out of the car, kisses me on the cheek and hoists the suitcase into the back, all with that same Melissa's-getting-married grin. In his head he's thinking, nice to have them all home again. What a nice day. Good weekend for a party. Stuff like that. Howard's basically a good guy, just transparent.

I kiss him back, hang the black plastic bag on a hook in the back seat, and get into the car.

'What a great day!' Howard is jabbering, all the time with that goofy grin.

'Nice,' I answer.

'Excited?'

Make him happy. 'Yeah,' I say.

'Melissa is waiting for you back home,' Howard says, casually.

'Yeah.' He wants me to bring it up. I'm not gonna.

A couple of minutes pass.

'You're happy for her, aren't you, Robin?'

I can see myself in Whitecoat's office.

You want me to tell you what I think of Melissa? I ask.

Yes, he replies.

Okay. Melissa is … a piece of shit. Dreck. Turd. Doodoo. That's what I think of Melissa.

'Sure,' I say out loud.

'Good,' Howard says. 'Because she loves you. She'd never want to hurt you.'

Not a nice person, I hear Whitecoat saying.

'No,' I reply.

'And neither would Max,' Howard goes on.

I can hear Whitecoat's voice, imitating Max. That's not true, Robin.

I'm really sorry about how it all turned out. I didn't mean to hurt you. That's the last thing I would have wanted.

'The last thing he would have wanted,' I repeat out loud.

'I'm glad you feel that way,' Howard says, looking straight ahead.

I stare out the window at an empty brown landscape, interrupted here and there with a patch of dirty snow.

'So you're okay with this wedding?' Howard finally asks.

You're okay with all this? I can hear Whitecoat asking. Because you don't have to go, you know.

Yes no yes no yes no.

'Yes,' I say to Howard.

Howard settles back into his seat, satisfied. He's done his job, just like Mother asked him to. Smooth things over. Make sure no one has any hurt feelings. Happy, happy, happy, happy.

Max and Melissa, I think. They're perfect for each other. I hope she pecks him to death.

Howard drives the Buick right up into the garage, and we get out, head for the back door. I can see the light on in the bathroom. A little squeal, and the light turns off. The back door opens, Mother's face appearing, big smile set against the permanent frown lines of her mouth. Happy, happy, happy, happy.

'Robin, dear!' she cries and gives me a hug and a kiss, whether I want them or not.

'You're here!' Melissa shouts from her back. I can just see a smile on her face, too. Guess we're not fighting. I kiss her, too.

'Where's Max?' I ask.

'Oh, he'll be by later,' Melissa says, standing in the doorway. 'We're going to pick up the rings.'

We've been standing there for a couple of minutes, when Howard comes up behind me with the suitcase. The two of them step aside for me, but I just stand there, staring into the dark hallway. 'So, go in already,' he says, one hand on my shoulder, pushing.

I hand off the hanger to Howard, who takes the whole shebang into the office.

'So?' Melissa says, looking at me. 'I think you lost a little weight.'

I shrug. 'I haven't been eating too well.'

'That dress better still fit you.'

Mother leads me down the hall. 'Well, let's fix that. I've got some

Entenmann's crumb cake, the one you always liked. And fresh coffee.' She bustles around here and there. 'You brought your pills, didn't you, dear?'

'In the bag.'

'Good, I wouldn't want you to run out of anything.' Read, run out of medication and go crazy.

'The shoes?' she goes on.

'In the bag.'

Mother turns off into the kitchen doorway, while Melissa leads me across to the dining-room table, covered from end to end with wedding gifts. Silver chafing dishes, pewter trays, crystal decanters that shine like cut diamonds.

'Pretty neat, huh?' She says.

'How many people are you inviting?' I can't help asking. So many gifts mean so many people. I picture a large hall stuffed like a subway car. A feeling of nausea comes over me.

Melissa is fondling a china plate. 'Three hundred.'

'Does Howard know?' I ask.

'Sure he does. He's paying.'

Mother calls from the kitchen to come have a snack, and we leave the treasure table for the kitchen table. As we come in, she's pouring two cups of coffee, cutting a piece of cake. She pushes me into a chair and says, 'Eat.'

'What about me?' Melissa is asking, standing in the middle of the kitchen floor. 'It's my wedding.'

I can't believe that Melissa is still expecting Mother to wait on her hand and foot.

'Go sit down,' Mother says and pours another cup and cuts another piece. She brings it over and sits down, herself, beaming. 'My girls.'

The kitchen is warm and smells like crumb cake and coffee. Girl chatter fills the room. Mother and a younger version of Mother, laughing, talking. Funny how I never noticed they look so much alike. Same smile, same laugh.

Look at this picture. Who does not belong? Never will belong.

Father? I ask.

No answer.

Father? I ask again, with more urgency. Where is he? Damn pills: they muffle the voices so much I can hardly hear them. He could be here, but the connection's bad.

Father?? I call as loudly as I can without moving my lips.

I hear nothing but a muddle of voices down deep. I'll just try again later when the lines are free.

I finish the crumb cake and drink the last of the coffee and get up to take them to the sink, but Mother waves me away. She can do it.

'Don't bother, sweetie,' she says and hums as she clears the dishes. I notice her forehead looks less wrinkled. Maybe she's happy, what with one daughter down, one to go.

One to go where? I think briefly of Derek, my fiancé of one hour, who told me later what his parents said about finding someone rich and normal at the country club. One to go where?

I muddle back to my office. Howard has laid the suitcase on the bed, hung the dress bag in the closet. I open the suitcase, take out the shoes and place them lovingly on the floor under the dress bag. I unzip the black plastic, revealing a slash of blue. Hello? I say, but the dress isn't talking.

The computer, however, is sitting there quietly, waiting on my every wish. Yes, someone to talk to. I sit down, fondle the mouse, move it to the Netscape Messenger icon and double-click. The screen shifts. Click on New Message, Address: Dwinek@aol.com. Subject: *Still Alive.*

Dear Derek,

Hope you're feeling better. Nothing new here. Wedding yet to start. Miss you.

Love,

Robin

I click on send, and there it goes, into the atmosphere, a heat-seeking Derek missile. As I sit there, staring at the screen, I hear a beep, and another line jumps into existence at the top. Subject: *Hello, Robin.* I double click and read,

Dear Robin,

Not feeling better. Nothing new here. Miss you. When and where the wedding?

Love,

Derek

Dear Derek, I write:

Wedding is Saturday at 5:00 p.m. at Wanamaker's in Cambridge. Having second thoughts. Cannot get in touch with my father....

I think for a moment and backspace over *rehtaf ym htiw hcuot ni teg tonnaC.* Never did tell him about that.

Father? I call. Still nothing. All I can hear is static in my feet. I'm sad, want to talk to someone who understands, and have the sudden desire to kiss Derek's left eyebrow. Instead, I write,

Just thinking how nice it would be if you were here. See you Tuesday.

Love,

Robin.

Beep! Out of my way, new message coming in. Subject: *Feeling better, already.*

Dear Robin,

Tell Max I'm coming.

Love,

Derek

I write back,

Don't be jealous, I haven't even seen Max. Anyway, you're not invited. Melissa already inviting the whole world. No more room.

Love,

Robin

Click send, and off it goes!

Beep!

Subject: *Feeling much better. Dear Robin, Then one more won't matter.*

Love, Derek

I laugh, and send one more back.

Dear Derek,

Don't know how you're going to get here, but if you can meet me out back at 4:45, I'll sneak you in the back. I'll be the one in the blue taffeta dress.

Love,

Robin.

Click and send. Then, bing bing bing, delete all the messages.

Somehow, I fell asleep. Woke up and found my pills on the bedside table with a glass of water. Good, I don't have to bother with the whole charade of pretending to swallow them. I just take the pills and flush them down the toilet, along with the water.

'Take your pills, dear?' Mother asks as I come out.

'Yeah.'

'Good,' she says and goes back into the kitchen.

The doorbell rings, and Melissa comes running.

'I'm getting it,' she shouts, almost mowing me down.

'Hi, Max,' Melissa is saying from the front door. I can hear the soft suction of lips meeting, coos, murmurs and Melissa's giggle, and I hurry back to the office.

The mirror tells me I am a horror, hair sticking this way and that, a crease on my right cheek where the pillow was. I grab my brush and fight with my hair. I lose, but at least it's all in the same direction, now. I find my blush-on and dab it on my cheeks, change my pants, grab a magazine, and saunter out to the living room. I feel good. I feel energized.

'Hi, Max,' I say, dropping onto the couch and opening to an ad on hair colouring.

Pause and, 'Hi, Robin.' I can feel his gaze on my bent head. I can hear his heart pound. I glance up to see him still looking at me.

'We've got to talk,' he says.

He wants to talk, a voice says.

My throat is dry. I shouldn't have dumped all the water into the toilet. 'Sit down,' I say, pointing to the other end of the couch. Instead, Melissa sits there.

'Melissa, this is between your sister and me,' Max says.

'I'm not going to leave the two of you alone,' Melissa replies.

'What are you worried about, Melissa?' I ask her.

A kiss for old time's sake, a voice says.

'Nothing,' Melissa says.

'For God's sake, Melissa, leave Robin and me alone.'

For God's sake, the voice says.

'There's nothing that I'm going to tell her that you don't already know.'

'Then, there's no reason I shouldn't hear,' my sister answers.

'You're crowding me. You told me you'd stop that.'

Melissa gets up reluctantly. 'Ten minutes,' she says, and goes off into the kitchen.

Kill her, the voice says.

Max sits down at the far end of the couch, and looks down at his feet. He's fiddling with his hands, and I can see that he's bitten all his nails down, just as he used to do. Part of me feels sorry for him, but it's a very small part.

'Robin,' he says. 'I'm really sorry about how it all turned out. I didn't mean to hurt you. That's the last thing I would have wanted.'

I can hear Max Whitecoat saying exactly the same thing. I didn't believe it then. I don't believe it now. So, I don't say anything at all. The last time I said something to this, I ended up trying to wring Max's throat.

'Robin?'

He's trying to get me to forgive him.

'Robin,' Max repeats.

I'm not gonna.

'Please.'

Please is the magic word. My Highness should set an example. 'Yes?' I say.

'You know I didn't mean to hurt you.'

There's sweat on his upper lip. He may not have meant to, but he didn't really care one way or the other. He just wanted Melissa.

'You told me you loved me,' I say. 'You just wanted to fuck me.'

Max does a little jerk with his head, as if I slapped him across the face. His glasses have slipped halfway down his sweaty nose, and he pushes them up with his finger.

'That particular time, yes,' he says.

'You were sleeping with Melissa all the time, weren't you?'

He shakes his head. 'Not at the beginning.'

Who does he think he is, a lawyer? a voice says. Kill him.

Don't say that, I tell it.

He did wrong. He should be punished, the voice says.

What the lord does is her own business.

'Robin, I can't help what I did,' Max says, swallowing. 'It was wrong. I was wrong. But I can't help it now. I love Melissa and she loves me. What I need to know is … can you forgive me?'

An angry God. A just God. All-powerful. All-loving. They're not contradictions. Perfection contains everything.

I look into those dark, deep eyes behind the glasses, those eyes that snared me in the first place. And I suddenly remember how it was before the six dimensions unfurled and I got too big to feel. I'm folding up: ten dimensions down to four. Kachunk. Kachunk. Like bouncing down a staircase. Kachunk. Kachunk. The big bang, backwards. Kachunk. Kachunk. Back to a zero point energy field. Kachunk. Kachunk. Kachunk. That's what love is.

'I forgive you,' I say, before everything goes dark.

* * *

I come to, listening to the worry in Mother's voice.

'What is it you said to her?'

Melissa. 'I didn't say anything! I was in the kitchen. It was Max who was with her.'

Max. 'I don't know. I don't know. I asked her to forgive me.'

'Is that all?' Mother is saying.

'Did she?' Melissa asks, her voice like chalk on a blackboard.

'Yes,' I say, opening my eyes.

'Oh, thank God!' Mother says, and touches my forehead with her lips, like she used to do when I had chicken pox or the flu. A test for temperature, more than a kiss. Worry more than love.

'What happened?' Max asks me.

I give him a weak smile, but Melissa gives him the explanation.

'She used to do this all the time, black out whenever things got too much ... or I was getting too much attention.'

'Melissa!' Mother scolds. 'She's sick.'

'Yeah,' Melissa says. 'She's sure gotten a lot of mileage out of that one.'

Meanwhile, Max is helping me to sit up, his hand under my arm, his dark eyes watching me. Something in the eyes goes directly from him to me, a wave of no dimensions, encoded so only I can understand. Yes, Max. I love you, too.

'You're all right now?' he asks, taking his arm away.

'Yes.'

'She'll be okay,' Melissa says. 'Let's go for the rings.'

Max gives me one last glance before he gets up from the couch.

'Bye,' Melissa tells us.

Mother sits down in Max's place. We hear the door open and close.

'I'm worried about you,' she says, her forehead creased again.

'I'm okay. Don't worry.'

'What's going to happen at the wedding? I don't want you fainting when Melissa says, "I do."'

'I won't.'

Mother sighs. 'You better make sure to take your pills on time.'

'I will.'

'I'm glad you forgave Max, Robin. He still loves you, you know. Like a brother. He wouldn't want anything to happen to you. Did you see how gentle he was with you when you fainted?'

Not like a brother, a voice says. You saw the way he looked at you.

Mother pats my hand, gets up and goes back down the hall.

I won't faint. Everyone else will, when Max leaves Melissa at the altar and marries me, instead. I knew it. I knew he still loved me.

That's the way it was way back when we met in high school. Max and Melissa were seniors, me a sophomore. Somehow, Max didn't notice Melissa then. Sure she was a cheerleader, and had all that blonde hair and long legs and a big chest that bounced whenever she jumped up in the air. But he didn't like those things then. He was a computer geek, one of us: the nerds, the outsiders, the outliers, who didn't fit into any standard category. He was tall and skinny and smart and wore thick glasses and threw his head back when he laughed and made puns that made us groan. He was in the chess club and the math club and couldn't write a simple sentence in English if his life depended on it. He liked me the first time he saw me, I remember. And I liked him.

Robbing, he used to call me. Robbing Fibber, like I was a thief and a liar. But the way he said it with those eyes and one corner of his mouth curled up, it was just an affectionate tease. Like calling someone 'bad' when you mean good. I asked him what his full name was. How can Max be your whole name? Is it Maximilian? Maxwell? Maximus? Maximum? That made him laugh, really laugh, throw his head back and laugh. I loved that laugh. No, he said, his parents named him Max. Just Max.

Sounds like a dog's name, I said.

His retriever's name was Poodle, he said, and that made *me* laugh. That was how it started. Because, normally, a senior doesn't go out with a sophomore. There's a strict caste system in high school, as bad as India or England. A senior who dates a sophomore drops several ranks into the untouchables. But Max didn't care for that; besides, his social ranking was already so low, it was off the charts. So, he wouldn't have thought of dating a senior, or a junior. He had to dip down lower to be acceptable to a girl. A sophomore was just about right. I was just right.

We went out for that year and half of the next one, when he went to Waterloo to study computers. His father practically made him go, told him *he* had been to Queen's, and Max was at least as smart as he had ever been, and that's where he should go. But, hey, Max was eighteen, and he was a computer whiz, who would work all hours in his room in the dark and come up with a totally new object-based application for data manipulation, or knowledge importation, or web-based graphic design. He was a natural, and he couldn't see what college was going to do for him. Why should he go someplace to learn from professors who'd ask him after class to come over to the house and fix the glitch in their own system?

Me, I urged him to go to university, but he wouldn't have it at first. And he didn't actually go anywhere till … Melissa came into the picture. I didn't know it, of course. I thought Max had finally listened to his father and me and decided to go. But it wasn't either of us; it was Melissa who convinced him. But I only found out about who it was much later.

And by that time, I guess, Melissa and he had been going to bed together for at least a year. Max had finally gone away to Waterloo, and Melissa had moved out, and it turns out they were living together, but I didn't find that out till later. By that time, I was a senior myself, and I was applying like crazy to all these Ivy League places, until …

Suddenly, I couldn't do it any more. Father had come back again and I got busy talking to him all the time. And they were talking about me on the radio, I was so famous. And I was so involved with affairs of the universe. Then, my A's became B's, became D's, then F's. And Mother got worried. And Melissa didn't want to come back home any more, because Mother kept telling her to keep it down, her sister was sick. And Howard spent more time in the office. And finally, I just couldn't get out of bed. And that was that.

Oh, and Melissa and Max came home together one day. Yeah, that was during the time I was still applying to all these schools, and suddenly they came home together, and I said, hey, I didn't know you two knew each other, and they looked at each other, a good long look, and Max took me aside and told me that he couldn't be my boyfriend any more, because he had fallen in love with Melissa.

Forget all the details. I mean, Max only met Melissa, because she introduced herself to him as Robin's big sister one day when he was buying a basketball at All-mart. He never would have known her if it wasn't for me. Except that Melissa is the type of person who would introduce herself to the Emperor of Japan if it suited her purposes. Would have said that she knew his ninja or something. So, maybe fate had a hand. Maybe it was set to happen in the first place, and it wasn't me, but Melissa who was destined to marry Max.

But, of course, that's not true, and now I know. Max is destined to marry me. He always was and he always will. Mr and Mrs Max Silverstone, that's us.

* * *

I'm wearing the short black dress that Mother bought me last month along with the blue taffeta. She wanted me to have something to wear for the rehearsal dinner other than my brown corduroy skirt and the tan sweater. She had me wash my hair, and she fixed it for me, so I'd look nice.

Mother is okay. I know I say some bad things about her, about her being such a worrier, and always looking at me so disapproving, how she's dull and middle-class and conventional, how she never should have married Howard, but it's her life, after all, no matter that Father says she's a fool. And she's kind-hearted, really. She wants the best for me, she just doesn't understand me, because I'm not at all like her. She never understood why I wanted to go to college. She never understood what I saw in Max, before Melissa took him, even though now she thinks he's the greatest thing since sliced bread. I used to love her, but I just don't feel very much for her, any more. I can't feel what I used to feel. For anyone, really.

Except Max, a voice says.

We're going to the rehearsal dinner. Melissa is running around like a lunatic, what she usually calls me. She's got her pantyhose on, and a skirt, but she decided not to wear what she planned to wear, and now she's ransacking Mother's closet for something else.

'Mother!' I can hear her from here. 'Where's your red cashmere sweater set?'

She thinks she's marrying Max, but she's not, the voice says.

Mother is running after her, and trying to make sure I don't put my head through the arm hole or some other stupid thing she thinks I just might do. And she's kind of jumping in and jumping out of the room, herding me along, so I won't make them late, even though Melissa is the one, Melissa is always the one who makes people late. Yes, yes, you remember that, don't you? The time we were going to Roger's bar mitzvah, and Melissa wouldn't come out of the bathroom and we missed the whole Torah-reading and half his bar mitzvah speech?

He's marrying you, the voice says.

There. Mother's sticking her head in again. Time to go. I'm wearing the black dress, and some old black shoes of Mother's that are too big for her, and Melissa's old suede coat that she left here because she doesn't wear it any more. I can't button it, but it looks nice anyway, unbuttoned. I didn't bring enough clothes. I forgot I'd need anything but the blue taffeta dress and shoes.

Howard's calling from the front door. Okay, already. I'm coming, I'm coming.

Mother's waiting in the back seat of the Buick; the door's open and she's motioning for me to sit down and close the door. We sit here for a few minutes, waiting for Melissa. What did I tell you?

Another five minutes, and Melissa comes running, Mother's red cashmere set under a tan sheepskin coat, paid for with All-mart money. She sits down in the front passenger seat, and turns to us as Howard revs the motor. Melissa's flushed, and her hair is coming down over one eye, but she looks happy and pretty, and starts talking a mile a minute to us in the backseat. Okay, Melissa, enjoy the anticipation, because that's all there is.

She looks at me and just sees the smile, doesn't know what the smile means.

'You'll have a good time tonight, Robin. There's an usher friend of Max's you might like.'

Who cares? a voice asks.

'I'm okay,' I say.

'I hope so,' Mother worries, trying to button up the suede coat for me.

'I'm okay,' I say again, this time aimed at Mother.

Her fingers linger on the last button before they let go. Let go, already, I want to tell her.

I have a quiet period for myself as Melissa chatters, sending Derek a message through the ether.

Don't come, Derek. I'm in love with Max, and Max is in love with me. Max and I are the ones getting married tomorrow, so don't come.

I stop transmitting, then send a postscript: But if you don't get this message and you do end up coming, I can set you up with one of the bridesmaids.

There. I could write more, but time is money, and I was taught in English to keep it terse. Anyway, whatever I say, Derek won't understand. He's going to be jealous, and you can be sure he's going to come. Whatever. I tried. Now, we can all have a good dinner, and rehearse what's supposed to happen tomorrow night.

I'm really sorry about how it all turned out, I practice telling Melissa. I didn't mean to hurt you. That's the last thing I would have wanted.

I have to do it over and over until it's right. Lying doesn't come naturally. By the end of the tenth repetition, Howard stops the car. We're here.

Melissa is the first one out, like a bat out of hell, out the door and up the steps, before Mother has even finished telling her to not drink too much tonight. I get out more sedately, as befits a new bride. Mother opens her door and smooths her skirt, fixes her hair, steps out. Each in her own way.

We go up the stairs, Howard opens one side of the double doors festooned with brass hardware, and we go in. Max and Melissa are already in the vestibule, facing each other, Melissa fixing his collar, Max flinching.

'Chapel's across the floor on your left,' Melissa says, straightening his tie. 'We'll be there in a minute.'

So, we proceed across the floor. Howard opens the door that says 'Chapel'.

Six bridesmaids and four ushers are there before us, because Melissa made us late.

'Come in, come in,' says a middle-aged man, who introduces himself as Morris.

Max and Melissa come in, and we start, Melissa and Morris pushing us through our paces. The bridesmaids go in, in some kind of complicated pattern that ends with one usher walking alone. Then me alone, then Paul alone, then Max, his parents, and Melissa with Howard and Mother. It works out all right with a little practice. Melissa seems to think I don't know how to walk. She tells me several times that I'm shuffling up the aisle and I better get with the program. I can see a few of the bridesmaids tittering behind their hands, as if that hides what they're doing. They're just like ostriches putting their heads in the sand, and supposing that they can't be seen, except that ostriches don't really do that. It's a myth.

On our third try down the aisle, I hear Father's voice.

Hello, everyone.

I am so happy you're here, I tell him. I thought you wouldn't get here in time.

Had to rush here from Shanghai, he says. Tanker sprang a leak, and there's a huge oil slick a mile off the coast of China. He pauses, and I can tell that he's watching Howard and feeling sad that he can't walk Melissa down the aisle, himself.

It doesn't matter, I tell him. She's not the one who's getting married tomorrow.

I know, he says. You don't need to tell me. Mazel tov.

'Thank you, everyone,' Morris says. 'See you tomorrow evening.'

We get to the restaurant, and Melissa seats me next to Mark. I can tell this is the usher she was telling me about, but I can't get all that excited about him. I mean, he's got red hair and freckles, and he's maybe 250 pounds. I guess that's what Melissa thinks of me. She thinks we're a match: two fat people. Put two fat people at one end, and maybe they'll hit it off. They can always talk about food, for goodness sake. So, I spend most of the meal pretending I'm listening to him talk about stereo equipment, and peeking at Max and Melissa from under my eyelashes.

Max glances at me every once in a while, showing me he hasn't forgotten me, and that he knows this whole thing's a farce, but, well, we've got to go through it, and tomorrow we'll show them. Melissa doesn't give me a glance. She's so caught up in the moment, in laughing with her friends, and playing the big shot, that she doesn't suspect a thing. Not a thing.

She can't help herself, Father is saying all of a sudden. She's dreck. Doodoo.

Actually, I'm sort of horrified by that. Melissa is his daughter, too.

Yes, but I gave my genes to you, he reminds me.

I am my father's daughter, I say, and he seems pleased.

Ah, toasts. Max's father is lifting his glass. To a beautiful couple, he says, looking at Max and Melissa. Then he goes on and on, and no one can shut him up, but then again, he is Max's father, so we all pretend we're listening while we ponder what we're going to have for dessert.

Then, not to be outdone, Howard has to stand up.

You're not her father, Father shouts. I look around, but no one seems to have heard.

For heaven's sake, I tell him. I never thought you would get so emotional about this thing. If you were alive, it would be you. Howard's just a stand-in.

He grumbles a little, asks me to order the chocolate mousse, so he can taste.

Howard says something nice but nondescript, as befits Howard.

Then, Max. Lifts his glass toward Melissa and says, 'To my beautiful wife to be. I love you so much,' clinks it against the one that Melissa is holding out to him, and drinks.

Wow, what a performance. If I didn't know better, I'd think he was sincere.

Then it all gets a little out of hand, with Melissa making a soppy, drunken speech about finding the one man in the world, and Paul raising his glass, but going teary-eyed and choking on the wine, Max's mother saying how he has always been such a good boy, and Heather telling the story of how she almost came in her pink prom dress. I could have told Heather off, that Melissa never dreamed of her coming in her pink prom dress, that she might be two sizes smaller than me, but her boobs are too small, and if what she was wearing today was any indication, her prom dress must be something to throw up over. I could have said a lot of things, but Father had come to his senses by then and told me to say nothing and act demure, that tomorrow was my wedding day.

Melissa woke up today with a hangover and wouldn't talk to anyone until noon. On the other hand, I woke up very chipper, threw my pills directly into the toilet and flushed. I knew I could do without those lousy pills. All they do is slow me down.

But today I am in control of the world. My thoughts are its command. Build it and it will come. What will be will be. I've got a feeling there's a miracle due, gonna come true, waiting for me!

Melissa can't see Max until the wedding; it's supposed to be bad luck for the bride to see the groom. That goes for both of us, but she doesn't know that. She's just come out in her old bathrobe and is pouring herself a cup of coffee.

'Robin,' she says. 'Come have a cup of coffee with me. It will help me to wake up.'

'The coffee or me?' I ask.

'Both.' She pours me a cup without asking, brings the two cups to the kitchen table.

'How'd you like Mark?' she asks, sitting down.

Melissa looks like hell. She got her hair done yesterday, but the pins are coming out. Her eyes are red and puffy. She really better get herself together or Max won't even want to pretend he's getting married to her.

'You thought that two fat people belong together?'

Melissa looks insulted. Like it's she who should feel insulted. Really.

'He's going to be a dentist,' she says. 'I don't know what you're looking for.'

Max, a voice says.

'Forget it,' I answer from inside my coffee cup. 'Just forget it.'

'Whatever.' Melissa takes a long draft of coffee.

We sit there for five minutes maybe, total silence as we drain our cups.

'What ever happened to that guy Derek?' she suddenly asks.

Oh, Shit. Derek. What am I going to tell him?

'He's still there,' I answer.

I'm really sorry about how it all turned out, Derek.

'Anything ever happen between the two of you?'

'Yeah.'

That's the last thing I would have wanted.

'Yeah?!' she says.

'Yeah.'

I didn't mean to hurt you.

'You don't seem very enthusiastic.'

'I am,' I say.

What I need to know is ... can you forgive me?'

'Hello? Hello? Anyone there?'

I look up to see Melissa's hand passing back and forth across my eyes. 'What did you say?'

'I said you're acting weird again. Have you been taking your pills?'

'Sure,' I say.

'Well, take some more. There's a funny glint in your eye, and I don't like it. I don't want anything happening tonight.'

The very day, 3:30. Melissa insisted everyone in the wedding party come by limousine, so we're all reclining against leather seats, Melissa with a glass of champagne in her hand, peering through tinted windows at the Ontario countryside. Why is this night different from all other nights? Why on all other nights do we sit; and tonight we recline?

Mother and I are already dressed, Melissa still in her jeans. She wants to dress in the bride's dressing room at Wanamaker's, reflected at every angle in a diamond of mirrors, a dozen Melissas all dressed in white Alençon lace, pearls and silk shoes.

'You took your pills, dear?' Mother asks me for the third time.

'Yes, Mother,' I say. I took them. Took them and threw them down the toilet.

Howard, in a rented tux, potato face above a starched white collar and ruffled shirt front, beams at us.

'Today's your big day!' he crows, pinching Melissa's cheek.

'Howard, please!' Melissa says, turning away.

Howard stops beaming and looks hurt. Mother pats his knee and whispers something in his ear.

Father? I ask, ignoring the live people.

I'm here. Where would you think I am?

You said you were going off to Peru.

Not till after the wedding, of course. By the way, you look lovely, Robin dear.

Thank you, Father. It's not a wedding dress, but this way we have the element of surprise.

Good idea, Robin. You always were the smart one.

We are approaching Wanamaker's. The driver pulls the limousine under the canopy and unlocks the doors. A general in gold braid stands atop the red-carpeted stairs and throws open the pearly gates.

I look around for the second limousine, carrying the Silverstones, but it's not here, yet. Howard carries the dress; I carry the shoes; Mother carries the train, and Melissa carries a small suitcase with everything else. Inside, Melissa makes a beeline for the dressing room.

Me, I go check out the dining room, a study in blue and white, blue and white. Everywhere blue and white. Thirty white-clothed tables, each with tower of blue flowers, blue ribbons on the chairs, blue party favours by each blue willow plate. No wonder Melissa said the pink prom dress would ruin everything.

When I return to the entrance hall, I can hear Melissa's voice shouting for her shoes. I look down at my hands, and lo, I am carrying one set of ivory silk shoes. Across the lobby, Mother is waving and shouting. Over here! Over here! I start to run in my blue pumps.

Melissa is still shouting from inside the dressing room when I reach Mother.

'Hush,' Mother is telling the person inside. 'Robin's bringing them.'

As I enter, I see Melissa standing on a mirrored platform in her pantyhose, a slip and one blue garter, hands on her hips.

'What were you thinking?' she asks.

'What?' I gasp, looking around. Mirrors and more mirrors. A dozen Melissas in their pantyhose and slips attack me, rip the shoes from my grasp.

'Melissa!' Mother scolds. 'She was just carrying them, for heaven's sake. She wasn't stealing them.'

Melissa puts the shoes on, to go with her pantyhose, blue garter, and slip.

'Mother, the dress.'

Mother unzips the bag, removes the dress and drapes it over her two outstretched arms like an offering.

The princess shakes her head. 'Help me into it,' she says and stands stock still so Mother can slip the dress over her head. Then she turns her back to be fastened. I sit down on an ivory silk chair off in the corner and watch Mother struggle with a mountain range of buttons.

'Ah, I almost forgot,' Mother says, going into her handbag and coming up with a blue velvet box.

'Your pearls!' Melissa squeals, kissing her.

My pearls, Father says. The ones I brought your mother from the South Pacific.

'Just for tonight,' Mother says, draping them around Melissa's neck.

You better give them back, he warns.

The two of them place the veil lightly on her blonde hair, and Mother steps back. An infinity of brides stares back at us, an endless regression extending back and back, mirror reflecting mirror reflecting mirror. A multidimensional bride.

'Lovely, just lovely,' Mother says of all the Melissas.

Melissa preens in the mirror. It's all come together, she's thinking. The blonde hair, the great body, the Alençon lace. A pause, then she thinks. The groom.

Shame on you, Melissa, Father says. You don't appreciate Max. You don't deserve him. But it doesn't matter, anyway, because he's not yours.

Howard looks in, points to his watch. 'It's twenty to five. The guests are coming.'

Then he sees Melissa and makes a low whistling noise. 'Beautiful,' Howard says, coming over to the platform and kissing her on the cheek. 'Max should always keep you on a pedestal,' he adds, as he crosses the room. Then he points to his watch again, and leaves.

Oh, no. Twenty to five. Derek. 'I'll be back,' I tell them. 'I want to see who's here.'

'Okay, dear,' Mother says. 'But not for long. The ceremony starts at five.'

I rush out. Howard was right: the guests *are* coming. I recognize some of them: Roger, Uncle Rudolph, the Persinger twins, but I stay out of sight, heading for the nearest exit, and the rear parking lot. If Derek's coming, he should be here now.

I think this is the side parking lot. More guests are just getting out of their cars: a lot of people I don't know, maybe Max's side. Some more I recognize: Great-Aunt Dora, Max's parents. I walk with my head down, hugging the building, till I reach the back. There, in the distance, I see someone. A guy with light hair. He's coming toward me, waving madly. Who would wave that madly if he weren't mad?

Yes, Father says. It's Derek.

I wave. He waves. We close the distance between us. Derek Derek Boberrick. Banana-fana-fo Ferek. Mi-my-mo Merek. Derek.

'You're here!' I say. 'I told you not to come.'

'No, you didn't. You said to meet you here at 4:45.' Derek looks at his watch. 'It's 4:45. Aren't you glad to see me?'

He looks so sweet, in his blazer and grey pants. 'I didn't know you had anything to wear,' I say.

'Is that why you didn't want me to come? You were afraid I'd show up in a running suit?'

I picture Derek coming down the aisle in his red and blue running suit. 'No ...'

'Aren't you glad to see me?' he asks again, cutting me off. Derek's operating at double time. Even I can't keep up with him today.

'Sure,' I answer.

Derek makes to kiss me, but I move my face, and he gets my ear.

'What's up?' he asks, peeved. 'You asked me to come. You want me to leave?'

I check my watch, under my eyelashes: 4:54. *I'm really sorry about how it all turned out, Derek.*

'No. Now you're here, anyway.'

'Thanks,' he says.

That's the last thing I would have wanted.

'Really. I do. But I have to sneak you in. The ceremony is starting in six minutes.'

'Okay. I've been standing here for an hour already. I'm ready to go. Hey, Robin!'

I turn and he grabs me, twists me toward him, and kisses me hard.

'Mmmm,' I can't help going. Who do I love, anyway?

'Yes!' Derek shouts, pumps his arm up and down a couple of times:

4:55.

He's cute, but he's crazy. And right now, he's more than a little happy.

'We better go in,' I say, and make toward the back exit.

Derek follows me, touching me everywhere. 'You look great. Hey, blue's your colour, girl.'

'There aren't any name tags on the chairs. You can sit anywhere. But sit in the back. That way no one will spot you.'

'What about dinner? Can't I sit down next to you then?'

I picture the head table, all done up in black tie, Derek in a red and blue running suit.

Who's he? Melissa is going to ask.

'No. I'll find you somewhere.'

'Is that why I hitchhiked forty miles? So I *can't* sit next to you?'

'I don't know.'

'You don't know?' Derek is asking, way too loudly.

We're at the exit door, and I put my index finger to my lips: 4:56. I pull Derek in the door, and usher him into the chapel, pointing to the last row. Derek shrugs and makes to sit down, then grabs me and kisses me on the mouth. Only a couple of people notice, Max's side. I rush out to the opening bars of the processional.

I cross the lobby to the dressing room: 4:58.

'Robin!' Melissa whispers. 'Where were you? You've got to go. They're starting right now! Go! Go!'

I run back to the chapel. A line of bridesmaids and ushers clog the doorway. Morris is opening the doors.

'Now,' he whispers to a group of three.

'And now!'

'You two next!'

The line of bridesmaids and ushers dwindles, then Morris looks at me, says, 'You!' And pushes me out. There I am, walking down the aisle with six hundred eyes on me, trying not to shuffle and to get with the program. I take a quick glance at the last row, and Derek is not there! Where the hell is he? The music keeps moving along, and I keep walking, staring straight ahead, like I'm supposed to, but my eyes are swivelling around as much as they can. No Derek here. No Derek there. Finally, as I close in on the front, I can see him in the first row, chatting up my aunt. He makes an okay sign to me, like this is fine, it is exactly what he should be doing, it's what I asked him to do. Damn him, but I have to keep smiling, looking straight ahead.

You're doing just fine, Robin, Father says. I don't know what Melissa was saying about you not walking right. You're terrific.

Thanks Father, I say, just as I get up to the front and turn around. I can see Max coming down the aisle with his parents in back. Melissa was right, he looks gorgeous. I give him a wink, and he winks back. Yes! Going according to plan! Except for Derek, who is winking at me, too.

The organist is playing 'Here Comes the Bride', and the whole room turns with a gasp to stare at Melissa, walking sedately down the aisle between Mother and Howard. I glance at Max's face, and it is glowing with admiration, as he gazes at the bride. Very convincing. Every beat, they come closer, until at last they stand before Max, and Melissa steps up to him, Howard and Mother turn to the side and back off to their assigned places, do-si-do your partner. The bride and groom step under the chupah; the rabbi begins to chant.

Derek is trying to catch my eye, but I've more important things to do than to spend my time connecting with Derek. This is not my destiny. My destiny is with Max, who must complete his mission first, before he abandons Melissa and merges with me. I understand; I smile and wait.

'Do you, Max, take Melissa to be your lawfully wedded wife, to have and to hold from this day forward, for better or for worse, for richer, for poorer ...'

I wonder just how far we have to go with this. At what point does it become legal?

'In sickness and in health, to love and to cherish for as long as you both shall live?'

'I do,' says Max, staring at Melissa, a half-smirk on his face.

He can't keep a straight face. Neither can I, my smile growing until it threatens to burst out in a laugh.

Robin! Father scolds. You know what you have to do.

I do, Father. I do.

'Do you, Melissa, take Max to be your lawfully wedded husband, to have and to hold from this day forward, for better or for worse, for richer, for poorer ...'

How much longer? When does it happen?

'In sickness and in health, to love and to cherish ...'

When will Max stop this charade?

'For as long as you both shall live?'

Apparently, it is up to me. I didn't realize. I've given them freedom, and I couldn't quite tell how this was going to play out, but now I see that a miracle is called for. Every thousand years, God must show some spine and perform a miracle, interfere in human existence: part the waters, send down a plague. Okay, here goes. Thunderbolt from on high.

'I do,' Melissa says.

I watch in amazement. No thunderbolt. Life goes on.

'May I please have the ring?' the rabbi is saying.

One more time, then. Zap!

I watch Paul fumble in his jacket pocket for the ring, undisturbed.

Am I not God? Of course I am. Father?

Miracles come in many forms, he says. Grab the ceremonial wineglass. Before the rabbi places it on the ground for Max to smash with his foot. Quick. Take it. Unwrap it. Smash the bowl.

I do this. I reach around, grab the glass, unwrap it from the linen napkin, and smash the top of it on the chupah pole. A jagged piece rips my palm. No matter, this seems to be working. The entire room is entranced, watching. A miracle. No one moves.

Take the glass, and slash Max's throat, Father says.

Kill him? I ask. Is it necessary?

Yes, Father says. It is necessary.

But I love him. I don't want to kill him.

Kill him, Father demands. Then yourself, and the two of you will live together in the world above. My world. Do it.

But, no, I don't want …

You don't want? You call yourself the lord of the universe? Do it!

'Yes, Father,' I say out loud. I extend the glass, the edges sharp and deadly toward Max's throat. No one moves. The rabbi's mouth is open, in mid-sentence. Max's hand, arrested in the act of placing the ring on Melissa's finger, hovers in mid-air. No one can stop me. Closer, closer, slower, slower, hold back time to do Her work.

Kill him! Father shouts.

Yes, Father.

Out of nowhere, comes a hand, knocking the glass to the carpet.

Derek stands above me, holding my cut hand. 'You're hurt,' he says as he reaches for the napkin I dropped and wraps it tenderly around my hand.

No one moves. Derek and I must exist in some alternative reality, acting between everyone else's heartbeats. Derek pulls me out of the chupah, away from Max, down the red carpet, through the double doors, across the lobby, and away from the building. We run through the parking lot, down the block, run after a bus, climb its steps, and drop into a seat.

This was a miracle, and Derek was its instrument. Why did I ever doubt myself?

Derek is flushed with excitement. We're both giggling like schoolchildren, holding hands. Derek pulls me toward him, gives me an embrace that culminates in a long, passionate kiss.

'I love you,' he whispers.

A miracle, Father says.

We look out the window of the bus, holding hands.

'What were you doing, Robin? Trying to kill Max?' Derek asks after a minute.

'He told me to,' I say.

'Who? Max?'

'Father.'

'Your father's dead. You told me that, yourself.'

I say nothing, look out the window.

'Tell me, Robin. Tell me what happened.'

'You know! You were part of the plan.'

Derek looks at me in a puzzled way. 'I was? How?'

'The instrument.'

He starts all over again. 'You meant to kill Max?'

'I told you. Father told me to.'

'Why did your father want you to kill Max?'

Should I tell him? Will he believe me? 'Perform a miracle,' I finally say.

'Perform a miracle,' Derek says, rubbing his chin. 'You expected Max to rise from the grave?'

I can't read his eyes. Is he on my side? 'No. Kill myself and be together in eternity.'

Derek does a little jump. 'Robin, have you been taking your medication?' he asks.

Damn him. Just like my mother. 'No,' I say. 'I don't need that shit.'

Derek's mind is working; I can read his thoughts right through his eyes. He's thinking how to get me back to Berkshire, the traitor.

'You decided on impulse to kill him?'

'Father decided. I wanted to perform a miracle.'

'Did you?' Derek asks.

I don't say anything.

'Did you perform a miracle?'

'Of course.'

'What was it?'

'You, silly. You were the miracle.'

'Robin, you're making my head hurt. You mean the miracle was that I saved you?'

'I made you save me.'

'Hey, don't I get any credit for that?'

What does he expect? That he did it on his own? I can't help laughing. Derek laughs, too. I don't know what he's laughing at.

'You know I hitchhiked forty miles to come to see you,' Derek says. 'Forty miles. You think you caused that?'

'No,' I say. 'You have freedom to do as you wish.'

'Well, thank you. I'm glad you give me that much credit.' He looks out the bus window. 'Listen,' Derek says. 'We've got to get off this bus. You have any money?'

'Why?'

'I want us to get on a bus to Berkshire.'

'Fat chance.'

'Why? Where did you expect to go? Didn't you tell me you'd see me on Tuesday, back at Berkshire?'

I think for a while. 'The lord works in mysterious ways.'

'Geesh. Robin, *do* you have any money?'

I put my hand in my blue satin sash, come up empty. 'No.'

'I've got ten dollars. See how far that gets us.' He pulls the cord. 'We're getting off.'

I get up, I don't know why, and follow him down the aisle. The bus pulls over to the curb and stops with a whoosh. We step off.

'You said you didn't care for Max any more,' he says all of a sudden.

'Lied,' I say, turning away. Don't want to talk to Derek any more.

I don't know where my energy went. I feel like a rag doll. Derek is pulling me all over town. He asks directions of a lady with blue hair, and we start walking to the bus station. Derek's grumbling that he should have asked the driver. The bus would have gone there eventually, but now we have to walk fourteen blocks in the dark. I just follow along. I have no more will. Back to Berkshire. Is that what I wanted? I thought I'd be in Max's arms by now, looking out the rear window of a limousine festooned with ribbons and tin cans.

Father? I ask. Father? Damn. He's off to Peru. He figures it's all over. I performed my miracle, and I should be satisfied. Satisfied? I'm on my way back to where I started.

'I'm cold,' I say every few blocks.

'Walk faster,' Derek answers, and sprints away. It's all I can do to keep up with him, but it does keep me warm. Derek is pretty smart, really. I bet if he weren't bipolar, he could really be something.

'Here we are,' he announces, and I look up to see a low building surrounded by a swarm of buses. There are signs on top of each gate that say London, Kitchener, Toronto. Derek heads for the ticket office, dragging me behind.

'Two for Compton,' Derek says into the little hole in the window.

Two tickets shoot out the bottom. 'That will be $12.72,' a voice says.

'Shit, I don't have that much.' Derek starts fumbling in his pockets. 'You sure you don't have anything, Robin?'

'Nope,' I say, showing him my open palms, one of which has a gash. Nothing in this hand. Nothing in that hand.

'Never mind,' he says to me. 'What's the closest we can get to Compton with ten dollars?' he asks the window, shoving the two tickets back in.

'Brampton,' the window says. 'That will be $9.76.' Another two tickets shoot out.

Derek slides his ten-dollar bill through the space at the bottom of the window, and change jangles into the metal cup.

'That bus will be leaving in ten minutes,' the window says. 'You better hurry. Gate 7.'

Derek grabs the tickets, and we run to Gate 7, me dragging behind in my blue silk pumps. Get with the program, I can hear Melissa saying.

The bus at Gate 7 can't seem to make up its mind where it's going. Above the windshield, an electric sign scrolls through electric place names: Guelph, Fergus, Orangeville. On and on it scrolls, like a wheel of fortune, where it stops, nobody knows. Brampton, it flashes, and stops.

'We win,' I say.

'Let's go,' Derek says, and ushers me up the steps. We drop into a seat in the back.

'Robin,' Derek says. 'Do you have any of your medications with you?'

'Nope,' I say, showing him my open palms again. Nothing up my sleeve. In fact, no sleeve. Hey, who needs them? I feel pretty good, except for the voices, which are drowning out everything else.

'How's your hand?' he asks, taking it in his, turning it over so he can see the gash.

'It's okay. It's got a scab.'

'We'll get the nurse to look at it,' Derek says, pulling a plastic vial out of his inside pocket, and throwing one pill down his throat, gagging a little. 'So, one of us will be able to function, at least,' he explains.

'That's nice,' I say and smile.

The driver gets in and closes the door, starts the motor. We pull out of the station.

'We'll hitchhike from Brampton,' Derek informs me.

'Okay,' I say.

The bus moves out into traffic, onto a ramp and out on the highway. Cars and trucks sail along on either side of us. Along the road, we can't see anything in the dark. I'd bet anything if it were light, all you could see would be scrubby bushes, tree branches bare except for little bumps of green, scattered patches of yellow forsythia. But you can't even see that, because it's dark outside. All I can see is my reflection in the window.

Derek's got his eyes closed, his head resting on the back of the seat.

'You think they're married?' I ask him.

'They both said, "I do," ' Derek says, eyes closed.

'So, you think they're married.'

'Yes.'

'We left before Max gave her the ring.'

'They must have finished the ceremony,' Derek says, opening his eyes.

'They didn't have a wineglass to smash.'

'I think you did that for them,' Derek laughs.

I laugh, too. At least I wrecked their ceremony.

'Think they're still going to have the dinner?'

'Beats me,' Derek replies, closes his eyes again. 'They're probably looking for us.'

I picture Howard, red in the face, sputtering on the phone to the police. 'I bet,' I say.

We lie back and rest for a while. Then Derek opens his eyes and looks at me.

'You're pretty, but very crazy, Robin,' he says.

'Yeah, you, too,' I answer.

'I still love you.'

I think about it for a few seconds. 'I love you, too.'

I must have fallen asleep. When I wake up, the bus has stopped. The sign outside says Georgetown. I elbow Derek, who wakes with a grunt.

'Are we here?'

'I don't think so,' I say.

Derek peers out the window, sees the sign. 'Oh, probably the next one, then.'

The bus lets out three passengers and the driver closes the door. The motor revs and we start out again. 'Brampton, next,' the driver shouts.

'Good,' Derek says.

Berkshire. We're going back to Berkshire. Whitecoat and Martin and Alex, Roz and Beverly. 'Why are we going back to Berkshire?' I ask.

'You need treatment.'

'I'm just fine. I'm hunky-dory,' I say.

'You're not. You threatened Max with a broken glass, for God's sake.'

'I did it for Father.'

'That's just what I mean.'

'What are you talking about?'

'Robin, your father's dead! He's been dead since you were a baby.'

A few people turn around to look at us, but I don't care.

'So? He talks to me.'

'It's not your father who's talking to you,' Derek whispers. 'It's your own thoughts. Your own desires.'

'You sound just like Whitecoat,' I say.

'He's not real!' Derek whispers.

'Whitecoat isn't real?'

'Your father,' Derek says through his teeth.

'He's as real as you are.'

'Have it your own way.'

'I do. It's my world. I'm all-powerful.'

'Right. You're God,' Derek says and laughs.

'I am, although I don't use that name.'

Derek has stopped laughing. He's staring at me. Like he never knew this stuff. Why does he think he survived falling from the Dairy Queen?

'Oh, God, Robin.'

'Just call me Robin.'

Derek begins to talk, looking at the floor. 'I remember when I thought I was all-powerful. I remember the feeling. It was great. The world in my grasp. I could hear what people were thinking. I could transmit my thoughts to them. But I was wrong. Mankiewicz made me see that.'

'Of course. It's not your world. It's mine. I create it by looking at it.'

Derek looks up, takes his hands and puts them on my shoulders. 'Robin,' he says. 'You are not God.'

'Then call me Robin.'

'Robin,' he says again, his hands having moved to either side of my face. He's looking at me like my mother does, with too much concern. I don't like this. 'When you get your medication, it'll be all right,' he says.

'It's all right now,' I say and smile at him, but he doesn't smile back.

'It'll be all right,' Derek says, but he's not talking to me. He's talking to himself.

He's crazy, that boy.

We sit there for a few minutes not talking. Then Derek says, 'How long have I been at Berkshire? Seven months? Eight months?'

He's looking at me, but I don't answer, because he's not asking me. He's asking himself.

'Something like that,' he says. 'I know it's still not under control. I know that. But I have some insight now at least.'

I'm not going to say anything. Let him have his catharsis. It's still my world.

'Eight and a half months ago, I was absolutely manic,' Derek says. 'School had just ended, and my father wanted me to come into the business with him for the summer. The family business my mother's father started, Murdock's. Investment and a lot of other things. Bonds, options, insurance. A lot of stuff I really didn't know about. But Dad wanted it, so I went to work with him.

'At first, it was terrible. I didn't know my right foot from my left. Then, gradually, I started learning the ins and outs. I had luck with my investments, but it seemed to me it wasn't luck: it was that I understood how the whole thing worked. I did a little of my own trading on the side, and it worked out all right. Then I did a little more, and made some more. I had my fingers in a lot of things. It was like I was the puppet master, and I was just pulling the strings. Master of the Universe, you know. But then I lost some money. So, I bought some more to cover the loss, but the market did a nose-dive, and I lost more. But it was no problem. I just bought some more. I stole Dad's password, and now I had unlimited funds, so I just kept trading and losing and trading and losing.'

I like listening to Derek; he's got a mellifluous voice. The sound of his words are like waves on the beach, ebbing and flowing, trading and losing.

'And finally Dad figures it all out,' Derek is saying, 'and takes me into his office. He's holding this printout, and asking me what was this? He's pushing the paper in my face. It's so close, I can't even see the print on it. But, of course, I knew what it is. But it's not worrying me. Nothing's worrying me, even though Dad throws me out of the office, and tells me I better find something else in my life to do, because I'm certainly never going to work here again. Hey, it should have thrown me into a tailspin, but no. Already, I've got this new idea. I'm going to go into business on my own. Trade out of the house. Start an online information service.'

Trading and losing, trading and losing.

'I go home,' Derek goes on, 'but Dad's cut off the modem, so I can't trade. By this time, though, I'm really strung out. I think I can trade through the air. I don't need a modem. I don't need a computer. I can do it all by myself, waving my arms in space, conducting the universe. So, I go up to the attic and climb up on the roof, all the better to feel the patterns in the air. It feels good. I can see for miles. I rule the universe. I'm all-powerful!'

I'd like to stay like this, listening to him for the rest of our lives.

'My mother,' Derek is saying, 'who's every bit the nut case that I am, but depressed, not manic, sees me standing on the roof and shouts for me to come down.

'"No," I say. "I'm trading. Don't bother me."

'"You can't trade on a roof," she cries. "I'm calling Dr Mankiewicz. He helped me."

'So, she calls him, and half an hour later he appears. By this time, I think I can fly and am ready to take my fledgling steps off the roof. Dr Mankiewicz comes out the attic door to the roof, sits down next to me and talks me down.'

'Nice story,' I say. 'I enjoyed hearing it.'

'Do you understand what I'm telling you?' Derek asks.

I look at him and smile. 'Yeah. Dr Mankiewicz saved your life.'

'Well, yes. But also that I thought I was all-powerful. I was sure of it. But I wasn't.'

'You aren't. But I am,' I say.

'Robin,' Derek says. He seems upset.

'But it was a nice story,' I tell him. I don't want him to feel bad.

'Brampton!' the driver announces. The bus pulls into the gate and stops, and we get off.

'We've got to get on a main road,' Derek says. 'We'll never find a ride if we don't.'

'Okay,' I answer.

We leave the bus station and go back to the main street. It's gotten really cold, and I guess I'm shivering. Derek takes off his blazer and makes me put it on. Derek's not really big for a guy, but he's a lot bigger than me. I wonder what I look like in blue taffeta and a man's blazer, but there's no time to worry about it. I've got to catch up to Derek, who's ten paces ahead of me in the dark.

By the time I reach him, he's already gotten a car to stop. He opens the door and motions me to get in, too. I slide in and shut the door.

'Where to?' a middle-aged guy asks from the front seat.

'Berkshire. In Compton. You going anywhere near there?' Derek asks.

'Hell, no,' the guy growls. 'I don't go anywhere near there. You better get out.'

'Uh,' Derek says.

'Get out,' the guy repeats.

'You've got the wrong idea,' Derek is saying, but he's already leaning over me to open the door. 'We better go,' he says to me.

'Why?' I ask, staring at the guy. 'What did we do?'

'I don't want any loonies in my car,' the guy says.

Loonies. He calls us loonies. Who's he to call us loonies?

He thinks you'll kill him and take his car, a voice says.

'Oh, I get it,' I say. 'You think maybe we'll kill you and take your car.'

'Out!' he shouts. 'Out!'

Kill him, says the voice.

'Well, maybe we will!' I shout back.

Derek pushes me out of the car, and we tumble onto the pavement, my right shoe landing in a mud puddle.

'Don't ever say anything like that to people,' Derek whispers as the car roars off. 'They'll think you mean it.'

'I was just doing what the man said,' I reply, putting my shoe back on.

'What man?'

'The guy who said to kill him and take his car.'

'Stop it, Robin,' Derek says, but he's already looking down the road for the next hitch.

We both put our thumbs out, but the cars just whiz past in the dark. This goes on for twenty minutes or so. By this time, Derek's face is blue, he's so cold. I can see little icicles dripping off his arms. Finally, a green Volvo pulls over to the curb. The window rolls down, and an old lady looks out.

'You look cold,' she says. 'Get in.'

As we get in, Derek whispers to me, 'Let me talk.'

'Where are you two coming from?' the lady is asking. 'A wedding?'

'My sister's wedding,' I answer, laughing.

'Let me talk,' Derek whispers through the side of his mouth.

'Well, you don't look like your normal hitchhikers,' the driver says. 'Did you miss your ride?'

'That's exactly what happened,' Derek says. 'Thanks for picking us up.'

The woman must be sixty. She's not really old-old, but her hair's grey. She looks kind. I almost like her.

'Where are you two going?' she asks, turning her head to look at us, not just looking into the rear-view mirror, like the other guy did.

'Berkshire,' I say.

'Actually, just down the road from there,' Derek says quickly. 'You know the riding academy on Willow Road in Compton?'

'Sure. I don't live too far away.'

'Well, if you could let us off there, we'd appreciate it.'

The lady is looking at us a with a funny smile on her lips. 'You're not exactly dressed for riding,' she says.

'Oh, this,' Derek says. 'It's our family who owns the place.'

'The Malones!' the woman says.

'Uh, yeah. We're their … cousins,' Derek answers.

'Really,' the woman says, and turns back to the road. 'Didn't know they had any relatives at all.'

'They do,' Derek says, giving me a sidelong glance, just in case I wanted to say something.

'Was Jimmy Malone the one who left without you?' the kind old lady asks as she drives.

'Uh,' Derek says.

'Sure,' I say. 'Jimmy was supposed to wait for us, but by the time we got out, he was gone. I just don't know where Jimmy went!'

'Shut up,' Derek whispers.

'Was it a nice wedding?' The woman asks.

Derek looks at me, like he's going to bore through my head with lightening eyes.

'Very nice, thank you,' he says.

We drive a few minutes.

'What's your family's last name?' she asks me in the mirror. 'Maybe I know them.'

'Farber,' I say.

'Malone,' Derek says. Then, 'She's my second cousin once removed.'

This is actually getting to be fun. I start to open my mouth, but Derek glares at me, and I stop. We drive the rest of the way in silence.

She lets us off at the riding academy about a mile past Berkshire. We see Berkshire come and go, but Derek puts his finger to his lips, and that means shut up. Derek thanks her and she says she hopes we just don't get sick. She'll have to admonish Jimmy about leaving us stranded like that. Derek says, 'Yeah, well, I'll be sure to tell him that himself,' and she leaves, waving. We watch as the car gets smaller and smaller.

'Okay, let's go,' Derek says.

We start to walk down the side of the road, Derek without his jacket, and me in my blue silk pumps with the mud on one side. We walk and we walk, and it's so cold, and it's dark, and I try to give Derek back his jacket, but he won't have it. Finally, we see the light on the gate off in the distance. We get closer, and we see the big letter 'V' on the gate, the one for Vanderfeller. We wave to the guard in the little house, and he comes closer, sticks his nose through the gate.

'Well, look who's here,' he says, pushing a button. There's an electric buzz, and each side of the gate pulls back, parting the waters of the Nile. Derek and I walk through, and the gate closes, drowning the Egyptians. We walk the long walk back to the building.

Whitecoat went home long ago, but the nurse on duty tells us she's calling him back, that Derek's parents know he's missing, and a Mr Applebaum has been calling every hour since six o'clock.

'Who?' Derek asks.

'Howard,' I say. 'Howard Applebaum.'

Then we both begin to laugh.

'I don't see anything to laugh about,' the nurse says, dialling. 'Dr Mankiewicz is coming, and he's going to straighten all this out. Stay here. Don't move from this spot until he comes.'

Suddenly, this is all funny as hell, and the two of us keep laughing and laughing. The nurse tries to shush us, but it's no use, and we laugh and laugh till she gives up. Then we stop, because it's no fun any more. I give Derek his jacket back, and I take off my sorry shoes, worn down and mud splattered. We go sit down in the chairs in the lobby and wait for All-High Master of the Universe.

It feels like I've been gone forever, but it's only been a day and a half. I've never been in the lobby at night. It's quiet except for the clock, which is ticking like a bomb; the sconces throw ghostly shadows on the walls, and evil spirits call down to me from the dark above the chandelier. Suddenly, I don't feel good. My voices, which have been noisy but gay the whole time I was gone, turn dark.

The girl was bad. She was very bad.

Didn't take her meds. Now she's gonna pay.

The phone rings, and the nurse picks up. 'Okay, I'll tell them,' she says, and hangs up. 'He's coming through the gate now.'

A minute later, the front door opens, and here he is, a little worse for wear, dark circles around his eyes. Whitecoat takes off his coat and hangs it on the coat rack by the front door, removes his hat and hangs that on the top rung. Slowly turns toward us.

'Come with me,' he says, crooking his finger to us as he proceeds down the hall toward his office. Dum de dum dum. We both get up and follow him.

Whitecoat flips the switch on the overhead lights in his office, and sits down. He motions for us to do the same. I push my chair closer to Derek.

'You know I'm trying to help you both,' he says, his hands forming into a steeple on the desk.

Derek slumps in his chair like a deflated balloon, his mania all run out. He doesn't even look up, just sits there staring at the floor.

'I don't believe you,' I say. 'You're on their side.'

Whitecoat sighs. 'Robin, I'm not your enemy. I'm your friend.'

Don't listen to him, a voice says.

'Shut up,' I say out loud.

'You haven't been taking your medications, have you, Robin?'

I just sit there. Anything I say will incriminate me.

'Your mother told me six pills are missing from the bottle, so she assumes you took them.'

He looks at me. 'But judging from your behaviour, I'd say you tossed them into the toilet, is that correct?'

I still don't say anything. He already thinks I'm guilty.

'At least no one was hurt,' Whitecoat says.

'Are they married?' I ask.

'Yes,' Whitecoat says. 'They completed the ceremony. But you single-handedly ruined the reception that your stepfather paid a lot of money for.'

Yippee, shouts a voice.

'Robin, your mother and stepfather have been frantic. I hope you appreciate that. You've hurt your sister deeply, you ruined her wedding, and then you ran away. Why?'

'She stole my boyfriend,' I answer.

'You have a new boyfriend,' Whitecoat says, gesturing to Derek, who looks up.

'I'm not her boyfriend. She still loves Max,' Derek says.

'I don't think Robin knows how she feels about anyone. That's part of the problem. But I'm not going to get into that right now. Derek, I'm afraid I was forced to call your parents when you disappeared this morning, and after all of this –' Whitecoat says, waving his hands in front of him – 'meshugas,' he continues, 'your father has decided to pull you out of Berkshire.'

Meshugas, a voice says. There's a lot of that in this place.

Derek straightens up in his chair. 'But he can't, Dr Mankiewicz! You're the only one who can help me. You can't let him do it.'

'I don't have any power over this, Derek. You're not twenty-one yet, and your father is paying your bills. I spent a long time on the phone with him earlier, trying to convince him he's making a big mistake, but he has his mind made up.'

'Couldn't we have another family session?' Derek asks.

'I broached the topic. I told him you were making progress, but that some of your issues needed to be resolved with him. But he wouldn't hear of it. In fact, he said some nasty things about Berkshire.'

'He's always saying nasty things,' Derek says. 'I bet he said some nasty things about me, too.'

'He was justifiably angry that you took off the way you did without telling anyone where you were going.'

'So, he did say bad things about me.'

'Never mind what he said.'

'He hates me.'

'Derek, we've been all over this. He doesn't hate you. He wants the best for you.'

'Bullshit,' I say.

'Robin, stay out of this. In fact, I think you should go up to your room. Alex will be up there in a few minutes to give you your meds. I'll have a session with you tomorrow.'

'Robin!' Derek cries out. 'I won't see you again!'

'You'll see her tomorrow morning, Derek. Let her go.'

'I have nothing to live for,' Derek says, slumping back in his chair.

'Robin, please go up to your room.'

I stand up, but I don't leave yet. Instead, I go over to Derek and kiss his cheek. He looks up, and I can see that his eyes are wet. 'I love you, Robin,' he says.

Before I can say anything back Whitecoat says, 'Good night, Robin.' So I leave.

I think they drugged me last night. I wake up to bright sunlight; the clock says 10:30, and Beverly's not in bed. I rush to get dressed, and run all the way to Derek's room. The door is open, and I walk in, but there's no one there. I look in his closet, but it's cleaned out. I look in the bathroom, but there's nothing in the cabinet. There's nothing in the goddamned room.

I run down the staircase and all the way to Whitecoat's office, even though it's ten to eleven, and my session doesn't start till eleven. Facing Whitecoat and his big desk, sit Derek and his father. They turn toward me as I come in, because it's not like I'm trying to be quiet.

'Robin!' Derek calls.

'Get her out of here,' Mr Wineker says.

'Robin, please,' Whitecoat says. 'You're interrupting.'

'You're not taking him,' I shout, coming closer. 'I won't let you.'

Mr Wineker stands up. He's a really muscular man, and by just standing up kind of stops me in my tracks. 'Young woman,' he says. 'I don't want to ever see you again.'

Shit. Dreck. Turd. Doodoo, a voice says.

Whitecoat pushes a button on his phone, talks into it quietly.

'It was all my fault,' I say.

'That's probably true,' Derek's father replies. 'I know you threatened somebody with a piece of broken glass.'

'Derek saved me,' I tell him.

'And who saved the poor guy from the piece of glass?' he asks.

'Derek saved him, too. I would have killed him.'

'And this is the girl you proposed to?' Mr Wineker asks his son.

Shit. Dreck. Turd. Doodoo, the voice says.

Derek is just staring straight ahead, not defending me, not defending himself.

'We're in love,' I say.

Mr Wineker laughs. 'Derek will find someone more suitable. You're a bad influence on him.'

Shit. Dreck. Turd. Doodoo, the voice says.

I look over at Derek, who's still not saying anything. Suddenly, Martin comes in.

'It's you,' he says, but he comes toward me just the same. I'm kicking and biting, and I think I got him in the shin, with a good bite on his arm, but Martin manages to get a grip on my arms and pin them behind my back. Then he drags me out.

'You'll pay for this,' I yell at him, as he half carries me into the next room.

'I am already,' Martin says.

Through the wall, I can hear chairs scraping, Whitecoat's voice, and footsteps down the hall. I want to get out of here, talk to Derek one last time, tell him I'm sorry about what happened. Tell him Max is history, and Derek is now. That I shouldn't have broken the glass, but Father made me. That Max isn't my destiny after all. That we all make mistakes, especially me. I'm not God, I only think I am sometimes.

But Martin is standing by the door. I could throw myself at him, but he's a big, wide target, and I wouldn't get far. In the distance, I hear a door slamming. A car engine revving. The sound of Derek driving away.

Chapter Seven

I wake up, strapped to the bed, my last memory the sound of Derek driving away. From then to now, there's nothing in my head. Someone transported me to this bed and strapped me down, but who and when and why? The screen is blank. The film broke; the guy upstairs changed reels in the dark, and here we are in the next scene. And yet. I have to watch the world to make it real. Does it disappear when I'm asleep?

The windows are black, Beverly lying like a lump in the other bed. Everything is dead still except for the wheels of a cart approaching from way down the hall. Bits and pieces of things go through my mind. Derek and I on the bus, his voice rising and falling like a rolling wave. Walking down the aisle with three hundred pairs of eyes upon me. Broken glass edging toward Max's throat. Melissa standing with her hands on her hips. Max sitting on the end of the couch. No special order. Time is no object.

The voices are hushed; I couldn't raise them if I tried. Father? I ask. No response. Whitecoat tells me what I hear is an illusion. Derek said Father doesn't exist. But if it's all an illusion, why should I listen to them? They're illusions, too: just characters in a book. I make them up, and they tell me what's what. Watch out for the others, they say: they're illusions, but I'm real. Next thing you know, they'll tell me I'm the illusion.

Who's to know who is real and who isn't? What's in my head and what's outside? Where I end and the world begins? Tell me that, illusion, and I'll grant you reality.

Alex sticks his head in, back-lit against the light of the hallway.

'Here we go again,' he says softly, seeing me spread-eagled across the bed.

'Yeah.'

He comes toward me softly.

'You drug me again?' I ask.

'Shhh. Martin had to keep you quiet. You bit him.'

'He deserved it. He blocked the door. I'll never see Derek again.'

'Why you do that, girl?' Alex whispers, untying my left leg. 'You jes' make things harder on yourself.'

I kick the leg, just to show myself I can.

'Hey,' Alex yelps, backing away. 'Do that, and I'll leave the rest of you tied up.'

'Sorry.'

He begins on the right leg. 'Heard Derek Wineker went home.'

'Yeah. His stupid father took him.'

'Anything to do with you?' Alex whispers.

'Yeah,' I say after a few seconds. 'It's my fault.'

'How?' he whispers, untying my right arm.

'I made it happen.'

'You wanted him to leave?'

'No.' Give them freedom, and shit happens.

'Then why ...' Alex says, his hands still moving. The hands continue, while the mind stops.

That's it. When God is sleeping, the world goes on. I have given them life, and now they lead their own lives.

'Forget it,' Alex says, shaking his head. 'Jes' do me a favour, Robin girl. Don't make any more trouble for yourself.' He takes the cart and wheels it out, thinking, poor loony thing; I wish she'd get some sense.

I have infinite sense, but go tell him that. I lie there for a while. I'm feeling better, not so disembodied. But not exactly bodied, either. I can wiggle my toes.

Sense. Nonsense. Inno-sense. Two times I lost my innocence: once, in the back of Max's red Infiniti, and once ... well, once when Max told me about Schrödinger's cat. The cat that was dead and alive until I killed it by looking.

Giants are big. If they weren't big, they wouldn't be giants, right? Gold is gold, what else? Apples are red ... or green, or yellow for that matter. But they are *something*, for heaven's sake. A banana isn't blue. If it were, how could it be a banana? You want to believe that things are constant. They don't change from yellow to blue when you look away. They have certain properties you can't take away from them, or else they wouldn't be what they are. Or are they? It just blew my mind, and Max was no help. He really got off on the basic uncertainty of everything.

In fact, I think he did it all on purpose. Of course, he did it on purpose. I have my destiny, and I have to know these things. I had to unfold into the proper number of dimensions, or else God wouldn't be God. Hmmmm. Wouldn't I be God in any number of dimensions? Change me from yellow to blue, and wouldn't I still be God? A riddle. Does uncertainty apply to Me?

Anyway, Max always said that properties aren't owned by objects, after all. They belong to the observer, and only apply to other external objects after they've been observed. Then he told me the paradox of Schrödinger's cat.

'Schrödinger?' I asked.

'Erwin Schrödinger, great quantum physicist,' Max said. 'Schrödinger wrote, suppose you put a cat in a box, along with a radioactive atom. Fifty-fifty chance that the atom decays, and if it does, and the Geiger counter detects an alpha particle, the hammer hits a flask of poison, breaking it.'

'Killing the cat,' I said.

'Not necessarily,' Max answered. 'Maybe the atom decayed. Maybe it didn't. Before the observer opens the box, the cat's fate is tied to the wave function of the atom, which is in a superposition of states.'

'Super-what?' I asked.

'One state composed of some mixture of states. In this case, it's the state of being decayed AND undecayed. Until he looks, the atom acts like a wave. We don't know if it's decayed or undecayed. It's the state of all possible destinies,' Max said, smiling.

Decayed AND undecayed. How can a state be a little of this, a little of that? How can a thing be part this, part that? Here AND there. Heads AND Tails. Yes AND no.

'What state's the cat in, then?' I asked suddenly.

'Dead AND alive,' Max answered.

I was afraid he would say that.

'Until we look,' Max added.

'Open the box,' I cried. 'Find out.'

'You do that,' Max warned, 'and you may kill the cat.'

Next day, as I walk into Whitecoat's office, I see the two wing chairs pulled close around the desk, the backs of two heads just visible, one blond pouf, and one shiny crown. Mother and Howard. They both turn as I enter the room.

'Hello, dear,' Mother says.

They'll take you, too, if you're not careful, says a voice.

'Come in, Robin,' Whitecoat says, since it looks like I've gotten stuck in the threshold. I take one step out of the room.

'Come in!' Whitecoat says again, and this is not an invitation. I move one foot, then the other, cross the room, and sit down in my usual seat.

Howard's face is no earthly colour. Maybe a shade of greenish purple: they don't have a crayon in this colour. He's trying to look at me and to look away at the same time.

'Your mother has some things she wants to say to you,' Whitecoat says.

'What happened?' she starts at me. 'How could you do that?'

Mother's not asking me questions. She's telling me how upset she is, and she's sticking question marks at the end.

I shrug.

Don't ask, don't tell, says a voice.

'Robin,' Whitecoat interjects, 'answer the question, please.'

She won't understand, the voice warns.

I look around the room at three expectant faces. 'Father told me to do it,' I say at last.

'Father?' Mother gasps, thinking, she can't mean that. She must mean … 'Howard?' she asks.

She was right the first time, it says.

'Not Howard. Father. He talks to me. He told me to kill Max, then myself, so we could be together for eternity.'

Howard has turned more purple than green. 'Oh, my God, Robin, you didn't really …'

My God Robin, the voice says.

I don't bother answering. I know Howard, and he is already upset enough. Any more and he'd turn black and fall on the floor.

Now they've got the whole story, the voice says. The big enchilada. The whole nine yards. The full Monty.

'I didn't know … I didn't realize …' Mother is saying. 'How long has this … delusion … been going on, Doctor?'

'What do you have to say to this, Robin?' Whitecoat asks. He doesn't want to betray confidences. He wants me to betray my own.

'How was the rest of the wedding?' I ask brightly.

'The rest of …' Howard says, looking up. 'Ghastly, that's what. You ruined it.'

'Now, Howard,' Mother says. 'She isn't responsible …'

Too many voices. Inside, outside. I can't distinguish one from the other.

'Not responsible? Then who is? Fifteen thousand dollars wasted.' He turns to me. 'You told me you were okay with the wedding. You said you were happy for them.'

You said it, the voice says. And then you flushed it down the toilet.

'Howard, no one was hurt, really,' Mother says, playing the peace maker.

'No one ... Melissa crying her eyes out wasn't hurt? Max almost ... I don't want to think about it.'

Fighting, yelling, shouting, doubting. Don't listen!

'I'm not excusing her, Howard. I'm just saying ...'

'She doesn't deserve to be here! I'm not paying for this place any more.'

Max Max Bo-bax. Banana-fana-fo-fax. Mi-my-mo Merrick. Derek.

'Mr Applebaum,' Whitecoat interrupts. 'Robin is ill. You can't hold her responsible as you would a normal person.'

As you would a normal person, the voice says.

Make them stop, Father. Make them stop shouting.

No, it's me who's shouting. Flailing and falling. It's me.

'Sshhh,' Mother says.

I am dimly aware of three people hovering over me as I lie on White-coat's rug: Mother stroking my face, Whitecoat holding a paper cup of water to my lips, and Howard, pale and serious, standing alone in the corner.

'Too much stress,' Whitecoat is whispering.

Howard's voice: 'I didn't mean what I said. Of course, I'll pay for her treatment.'

Mother's: 'I'm sure she didn't mean to hurt Max.'

Howard's again: 'If I have to go into hock, I'll pay. She's as much my daughter as yours, Donna.'

Mother's: 'Thank God, everyone is all right.'

Whitecoat's: 'These things take time. Give me another year.'

Father's: Hi, Robin. Back from Peru! I'm really sorry about how it all turned out. I didn't mean to hurt you or Max. That's the last thing I would have wanted.

Whitecoat upped my dosage, but it still feels like I'm being assaulted from all sides, the way it is at a children's birthday party, with twenty-six children under the age of five all running amok: screaming, laughing, climbing onto coffee tables. That's my life, and there's no way to pack the children off for home.

I seesaw back and forth between knowing I'm insane and thinking that I'm the lord of the universe. Right now, I'm insane. And depressed. Given the circumstances, who in their right mind wouldn't be depressed? It makes a case for not being in one's right mind.

Mother and Howard went home. They had their catharsis; they're feeling better. Good for them. I'm left with myself, can't get away from Me. Right now it's lunchtime, and I'm poking along the hallway to the cafeteria.

The corridors in Berkshire seem quiet and sad, echoing my mood. Or maybe it's my mood that's echoing the corridors. I still can't detach myself from my surroundings. Most people think they know who they are: inside is Me. Outside is Not Me. I'm not so sure where Me ends and Not Me begins. It's all Me. Me thinking, Me seeing. It's all Me, because I'm the filter, I'm the creator. Me changes the stuff out there into what I perceive. The world isn't red and green and blue, it's Me making sense of it, making wave lengths into feelings. So, I get it wrong sometimes. So, sue me.

Shit, this is depressing. Why do they paint institutional walls green? I mean, not just green but some off-shade green with notes of vomit and slime? Is it to punish us for being ill, or is it to make us feel so ill that we'll do anything to get out of here?

I round the bend, and all of a sudden, I can smell what they're cooking today: overcooked broccoli. Mmmmmm. Through the doors, I see Roz at *our* table. No Derek but same old Roz. She puts down her fork and waves, mouths, 'Hi, Robin,' with something in her mouth. I go pick up a plate, some glop and sit down across from her.

'Where's Derek?' she asks.

'He went home, didn't you hear?'

'No,' Roz answers, stabbing a piece of potato. 'Why?'

I don't want to tell her the whole story, I really don't. 'He's cured,' I say.

'Wow,' she says. 'Wish it were me.'

We stuff our mouths for a minute or two.

'Roz,' I say, putting my fork down. 'Do you ever think we'll get out of here?'

She looks up at me, meditatively chewing. 'Sure. I'm gonna be a teacher.'

I pick up my fork, punching at a cooked carrot. 'I'm depressed.'

'Don't be,' Roz says.

'Yeah. Thanks.'

We sit in silence, eating. Roz is a good friend. She's always there; she bucks you up when you're down; you can depend upon her to be no more, no less ... Roz. Whitecoat could do a whole session on depression. Roz hits it right on the head: don't be. What else is there to say?

One side of the cafeteria is all windows. Hey, they're all reinforced glass, and we're on the first floor, so what harm is there? I look outside, at the green grass and the budding trees and a couple of wild-looking forsythias and think spring, a new beginning. Give me another year, Whitecoat said. One more year.

This mood goes on for a few weeks. Whitecoat's been fiddling with my meds and thinks I'm better, but really I'm just not overtly insane. He's drained it out of me, along with my personality. It makes him happy, it makes me sad. I'm almost at the point of throwing my pills into the toilet again.

Does Whitecoat actually understand what his patients feel, or is he just concerned with our behaviour? What he aims for is getting rid of the big positive symptoms like delusions. The negative ones: not feeling, not processing, not caring, those I have to deal with myself. He can't get into our heads; all he does is stand on the sidelines and watch. Even in our sessions, he just asks and listens; there's no way to get inside. Whitecoat makes educated guesses, but that's all. If he felt what I feel, he'd know what to do about it. But then he'd be insane himself, and no one would listen to him.

'Come in, Robin,' he says today.

I walk in, sit down, look up. One more year.

'How are you today?' he asks.

I look at him but don't say anything. What's there to say?

'Depressed?' Whitecoat asks.

'What do you think?'

'Maybe we should add an anti-depressant,' he suggests.

'Maybe. One more pill shouldn't make a difference.'

He sighs like I'm not cooperating. 'What is it, Robin? I can't read your mind, you know.'

'You can't?' I ask, with an edge. I remember when I could.

'No,' he says. 'You have to talk to me.'

'How's Rachel Ellen?' I ask.

'That's not what I mean, but she's fine. Sleeping through the night.'

'You're feeling well?' I ask.

'Yes. Much better. But this isn't what we're here for, is it, Robin?'

I slump down in my little hard seat. 'How's Derek?'

'I haven't heard from him. His father said he was taking away his laptop.'

I picture Derek on his roof, conducting the universe. Now, he can't even send an e-mail using the proper channels. 'Poor Derek,' I say.

'Let's stick to you,' Whitecoat says. 'Your delusions are gone.'

I shrug.

'I know you're depressed. It's natural at this stage, but you've come out of the acute stage, Robin, and that's progress.'

'I feel like shit. Sometimes I want to kill myself, but I don't have enough energy.'

Whitecoat says nothing for a minute. Maybe he's thinking. Maybe he's sleeping. I don't know any more. I used to be able to read his mind, but now I know that it was a delusion. So, I'm left with nothing. No delusions, and nothing to put in their place.

'You have to go through the withdrawal, the depression. I'm sorry it's not more pleasant, but you have to consolidate your gains. At this stage, you're particularly vulnerable to symptom exacerbation under stress.'

'Symptom what?'

'Stress could bring out the full-blown syndrome again.'

'The voices, the delusions?'

'Yes.'

'I could start hallucinating again if something bad happens?'

'Yes. But that's not going to happen. You're going to improve. Believe it.'

Positive thinking from a depressed person, good luck.

'Any dreams?' he asks.

'No. Yes,' I say.

'Tell me.'

'Something about Derek and my sister. I don't remember.'

'You're still angry with Melissa.'

'I don't even think about her.'

'You're dreaming about her. What are you feeling?'

'Nothing. I'm not feeling anything.'

'Are you feeling that she took Derek away from you, too?'

'I'm not talking to you.'

'Why, because I'm getting too close to the truth?'

I'm trying not to listen. Whitecoat is always on about feelings. What if you don't have any? What if you really don't care what your bitch of a sister is up to?

'You never resolved anything with Melissa. You ran away.'

Here I am, already depressed, and Whitecoat seems to think it's time to hit me with an umbrella.

'Damn you,' I say. 'What's there to resolve about Melissa? She's got Max, she's got a job. Mother says she's probably pregnant. She missed her period this month.'

'You're angry at her, because she has all those things you would like.'

Well, sure. I guess. 'Duh,' I say. Like he has to have a degree for this.

'And you're angry that Derek went away.'

'He didn't go away. His father took him away.'

'You think that Melissa made you lose Derek.'

Damn this guy. He's so persistent. 'If you say so.'

'Melissa didn't have anything to do with that, Robin.'

'He ran off to meet me at the wedding, and his father got angry and took him away.'

'That wasn't Melissa's fault.'

'Everything is Melissa's fault!' I shout.

'Good. You're letting out your anger.'

'She gets everything, and she's such a bitch!'

'Good.'

I start to cry. 'And I don't have anything! I want a life! I don't want to stay here forever!'

'Good,' Whitecoat says. 'You have to feel something before we can start working on what to do about it.'

Whitecoat looks at his watch: end of session. I get up and go up to my room. Beverly is not there, as usual. The room is my empty soul.

Sitting on my bed, all of a sudden I have the familiar feeling in my teeth: buzz, buzz, buzz. Incoming message. It's got the familiar flavour of Derek.

Robin, I miss you. Am alone. No way to get out. Father confiscated my laptop. Derek.

I send him a blast of good will, through my teeth and on into the atmosphere. Whitecoat says I cannot do this, that it's not real, and I cannot send good will to anyone. But didn't I just get a message from Derek? Wish we could be together, I say. Miss you a lot. They've put another person in your room, and it's just not the same. Robin.

Buzz, buzz. Got your message. Thanks for the good will. It warmed the cockles of my heart. Thinking of you. Love you, Derek.

I lie on my bed, remembering our two hot bodies under the bush, Derek grabbing me and tearing off my panties, me warming his cockles. I get into it so much, I get under the covers and start warming my own cockles.

'Meds,' I hear from the hall, and Martin stalks in, takes a good look at what I'm doing.

'I'll just leave them here,' he says, his arm reaching out, and placing the little cup on the bedside table. Martin's arm's got bite marks in two symmetrical places now: I've got good taste, even if he doesn't taste so good. Then he leaves, not bothering to check whether I take them or not.

Buzz, buzz. Robin, it's the pills that are making you depressed. I know, they did the same to me. Martin's just daring you to throw them down the toilet. Derek.

Funny, I don't remember Derek ever saying that his pills made him depressed. It doesn't sound like him. It sounds more like me. But I think twice about throwing the pills down the toilet: it's so very tempting. Sometimes I want that old craziness, the power and the glory. But, no, not this time, thanks.

Derek, I say. Think I'll keep taking them. I don't want to be a crazy forever. Thanks anyway. Robin.

A couple of weeks go by, me still taking my pills. Whitecoat says I'm making baby steps, but in the right direction. There's not much to do here. I walk around outside, under the trees. Daffodils and tulips are out, and lilies of the valley. You can sit on a lawn chair and watch the flowers grow. It gives you patience, watching something so slow. I am a flower, I tell myself.

Whitecoat tells me I should reach out to people, not withdraw like I usually do, but it's hard. It's really hard to approach someone who's only half there. Lots of people walk around aimlessly here: in their own world, Whitecoat says. Which is funny, because I always thought it was my world, but he says everyone has his own.

So, I asked Roz if she wants to walk with me, and we've been walking round and round the yard every afternoon. Mostly we don't talk, but this way, I'm not withdrawing. Three times around, and we stop, sit in lawn chairs. Then another three times around. Goal oriented, like we're preparing for a marathon. Goals are important, Whitecoat says, so I guess we're establishing goals. Baby goals.

'You're going to be a teacher?' I ask on the fourth lap.

'Sure,' Roz says. 'When I get out, I'm going to go to teacher's college.'

'You ever finish high school?'

Roz thinks for a minute. 'No.' She stops to smell a tulip.

'Whitecoat's been talking about me going to a group home,' I say.

'Can I come, too?' Roz asks.

'Yeah, sure. When you're ready. Abigail knows where.'

'Do you get your own bedroom?'

'I think you have a roommate. I don't know.'

'I'll be your roommate.'

'Sure.'

I feel the familiar buzzing in my teeth. 'Wait,' I tell Roz. 'I've got a message from Derek.'

We stop where we are, standing on the grass, while I focus on decoding the buzzes. It's not easy; you have to know the code. Three long buzzes spells Robin. Three short buzzes is a curse. If you get it wrong, it doesn't make sense, but, of course, I know how. Yes, it's Derek.

Hi, Robin. How are you? I haven't gotten out of bed in two days. Father isn't talking to me. I miss you. Derek.

Derek, I say. I'm walking with Roz, so I'll make this short. You have to get out of bed. I'm trying, you have to try, too. Talk to you later. Robin.

I tell Roz what he said and what I said. She thinks it's really nice we're keeping up this correspondence. She's the only one who knows. I don't dare tell Whitecoat; he'll just tell me it's all an illusion.

Then we start walking again and walk two more laps, each back in our own world.

I wonder if everyone has her own world, whether the worlds are the same. Are some of them in black and white? Do animals have their own worlds, where they speak animal? I picture each person walking around in her own private bubble of a world. When I talk to Roz, is it in my world or hers, or do the two bubbles touch in a kind of plastic balloony sound, a little window opening up in the wall where they meet? Hello, how are you, then the bubbles spring back, *suck-boing!,* to separate worlds. And does Melissa's baby have its own balloon world, and is it inside Melissa's: two circles, one a subset of the other? Somehow, all this seems a lot more complicated than me as God of the one and only one universe, and I was always taught that the best explanation is a simple one. I wonder whether Whitecoat could be wrong. He acts like he know everything, but then he would be God, and he says that's impossible; he's an atheist. Then he laughs. I think Whitecoat still doesn't take me all that seriously. That makes me angry, but he says that feeling angry is good, too.

There, we're finished. Roz is panting, she's so out of shape. I tell her we're done, and she nods her head and pants a few more times. The last lap leads us right up to the stairs. Roz can't make it, so I take her arm and help her up. I'm doing just what Whitecoat told me – reaching out to people.

'You're a good friend, Robin,' she says.

'Thank you, Roz,' I say, and we climb the stairs arm in arm.

Inside, Abigail rushes up to me.

'Robin! We've got you a place in the group home!'

'Oh.' I don't know what I feel. Whitecoat will want to know what I feel.

'What?' Roz asks.

'Robin will be moving out at the end of the week,' Abigail tells her.

'I want to go, too,' Roz says.

'Soon,' Abigail replies, placing her hand on her shoulder. 'Soon.'

'I don't want her to go,' Roz says. Abigail pats her on the shoulder. This feels like home. I don't know what I feel.

'Robin will be coming back three times a week for her sessions with Dr Mankiewicz. You'll see her then.'

'No, I won't,' Roz mutters, turning her back on us. 'I don't want to see her ever again.'

'Roz,' I say. 'You're my best friend.'

'Some friend,' she grumbles over her shoulder.

'She'll get over it,' Abigail says, leading me down the hall to her office.

I watch Roz walk away. That's what you get for reaching out to people.

'C'mon,' Abigail calls. 'We have some details we have to work out.'

We enter her office, and sit down.

'Aren't you excited?' she asks. 'You should be excited.'

'Should I?' I don't know what I feel.

'The home is right on the bus line.'

I picture Derek and myself on the bus to Brampton. Eyes closed, Derek telling me the story of his life.

'We'll get you a monthly ticket,' Abigail is saying, 'and you'll come here three times a week.'

The sound of his voice rising and falling like the waves.

'Do I have a choice?' I ask.

Abigail is looking at me. I wish I could read her mind like I used to. She's probably thinking, no, you don't have any choice. Nothing. Nada. Zilch. Gornisht. That's what she's probably thinking, but I really don't know any more. I miss those crazy times when I knew everything.

'Well,' she says, her fingers straightening some papers. 'Of course, you have a choice.' She pauses, moving a pile from one side of her desk to the other. What a coward. Even on medication, I know she's just delaying. 'But this would be very good for you, Robin. It's time. Dr Mankiewicz says you're at the stage of your treatment where you should start being a little independent, reaching out.'

Reaching out, I know. Suddenly, I feel the buzzing in my teeth.

Not now, Derek. I'm busy.

Buzz, buzz. Hi, Robin. Can you talk now?

No, Derek, I'm busy.

'Robin?' I hear. Abigail is looking at me like my mother does.

Who're you with? Derek buzzes.

Abigail. Talk to you later.

What's it about?

Dammit, Derek. It's about a group home. They're having me go into a group home.

That's great, Robin. Then I can visit you. I may not have a laptop, but I've got wheels. Say yes. Derek.

Bye, I tell him. 'Yes,' I say to Abigail. 'I'll do it.'

She lets out a sigh of relief. 'Oh, you were thinking. I wasn't sure....'

'Yeah. When do I go?'

'Maybe you want to take a look, first?'

Suddenly, I'm ready.

'No, it's all right. Just tell me when.'

'Friday, if I can arrange it. I'll call your mother for you, if you like.'

Cut the cord; say goodbye.

'Yeah, call her.'

'Good. I'll ask her if your stepfather can pick you up Friday.'

Auf Wiedersehen, Berkshire.

Fast-forward to Friday. Howard got special dispensation to park his car in the circle out front, and comes upstairs to help me bring down my life: two suitcases and a black garbage bag.

Yeah, I said goodbye to Roz. She didn't want to talk to me. She said I was a big traitor and no friend, and I could have taken her with me, but I didn't want to. No sense telling her I didn't have anything to do with it. She still thinks I can do anything.

Didn't have to say goodbye to Whitecoat; I'm coming back Monday morning. Said goodbye to Alex, and he gave me a kiss. Martin stood at the door, wished me the best, and looked relieved.

Howard is carrying the two suitcases. I heave the garbage bag over to my left side and place my right hand on the banister, letting it slide down one last time, straight, straight, till it reaches the snail at the bottom, where my fingers go round and round till they stop dead bang in the centre. I wave goodbye to the receptionist, then follow Howard out to the car and dump the bag in the trunk. Goodbye, Berkshire.

What do I feel? Whitecoat will ask. What do I feel? Like I'm leaving the womb, being pushed out, whether I want it or not. Do I want it? What does it matter? No one asks the baby if she wants to be born.

Howard opens the passenger door for me, waits for me to pull my legs in, then closes it. Not that I can't do it myself, it's just the way Howard is. I used to think it was my due as God, but now I realize it's just his way.

'Ready?' he asks before he starts the motor. Give me a break. If I say, 'No,' do we reverse the whole process? I picture me with my garbage bag, tracing the banister snail from inside out, walking backward upstairs, backwards down the hall, getting undressed and going back to bed. Yeah, sure.

'Sure.'

Howard starts the engine, and we pull away from the curb, my eyes fixed on the rear window. Berkshire grows smaller and smaller till Howard makes a turn; then it vanishes completely. Roz, Beverly, Martin, all gone. Me and Howard in a separate universe, a point moving along an unknown trajectory. Our past is as far as I can see through the rear window. Our present is Howard and me sitting on leatherette bench seats in an emerald mist Buick. Our future is the foggy road in front of us. Mine is not to reason why. Mine is but to do or die.

'You sure you wouldn't rather just live at home, Robin?'

One last chance, he's saying. You don't have to go if you don't want to.

'No, thank you,' I say through a closed throat.

'All right. I just thought you might be more comfortable at home.'

'I'm okay.'

'Well, you can always change your mind, you know.'

Don't say that. Please don't say that. I don't want choices. I want answers.

We sit in silence, trees whizzing by on either side, the future rushing to meet us. Howard turns off the main road and onto a side road, turns one more time, and pulls into a driveway.

'This is it.'

It's a little brick house framed with azalea bushes and a postage stamp lawn.

'Your mother and I came to look yesterday. It's nice inside,' Howard says, not looking at me. 'Six residents.'

He pops the trunk and we get out of the car. Howard hands me the garbage bag, a squint in his eyes and a little curl to his lips; he grabs the two suitcases and hoists them out, slamming the trunk hard.

'Let's go,' he says.

So, we walk up the cement path to the front door, and Howard rings the bell. A fat fortyish woman opens the door, and gives us a big smile.

'Robin! I'm Debbie. Welcome to the Forrester's Group Home.' She makes room for us in the doorway, and we haul our things in.

Inside is a girl in a wheelchair, an older man watching television.

'Louise, Ray, this is Robin.'

The girl in the wheelchair smiles; the man doesn't seem to know we're here.

'The others are at work,' Debbie says, 'but we all get together for dinner every night.'

I look around. It's warm and cozy, a little shabby. There's a shelf of books on the far wall. A soupy smell is coming from the back of the house. The staircase has a chair attached to the railing with gears and pulleys.

Debbie leads us upstairs to a big room with two beds, one covered with Grandma's quilt.

'We thought it would make things familiar for you,' Howard says, dropping the two suitcases by its side.

'Can you dispense your own medication?' Debbie asks me.

I picture myself dispensing it all into the toilet, but I nod, 'Yes.'

Debbie explains the rules of the place: everyone has her weekly duties. Look at the roster downstairs. Make your bed every day. No visitors after nine. No unrelated males in your room. Lights out at eleven. I nod at the end of every sentence. Fine, fine, fine. Okay. At the end of each fine, I feel worse. If this place is the answer, what was the question?

Howard is busy checking out the closet, opening up my suitcase, dragging his finger along the window sill for dust. He seems in his element, substituting things for people.

My heart is pounding. I thought I'd be all right; I didn't expect this fear. Whitecoat got me to feel: he said it is good to feel, but if it's good, then why does it feel so bad? Father? I ask.

I hear nothing back. Debbie's going on about mealtimes, and I'm nodding. Fine, fine, fine. Okay.

Father? I ask again, and suddenly I hear that familiar voice.

Robin, dear. I'm here.

'You take your own towels from the laundry room.'

Don't leave me, Father.

Wherever you go, I'll be there. You're my flesh and blood.

'We prefer you supply most of your coat hangers. You'll see there are a few wire hangers in the closet, but probably not enough.'

Why am I doing this? I ask.

Things change, Robin, dear. It's the nature of life.

But you'll stay with me awhile?

I'm back and forth. You can't anchor me in one place.

'There's a phone in the hall. I've already given the number to your parents. Well, that's about it.' Debbie smiles.

Leave already, Father says.

'Anything else, don't be afraid to ask,' Debbie adds, and disappears down the stairs.

I'm afraid, I tell him.

Howard has finished checking out the closet, exploring the window sill, arranging my toiletries on the top of my bureau, and he's now advancing with extended arms. 'Okay,' Howard is saying in a choked-up voice. 'I guess it's time to say goodbye.' I let him wrap me in his arms and kiss the top of my head, and I sit on my bed until he walks out.

'Your mother will call tonight,' Howard shouts from the hall.

You can do it, Father says.

I'm not really alone. I've got a whole group here to keep me company. So why am I feeling like I'm the only person left in the universe? Stop thinking that; it's not true. Remember when Max taught me that everything's connected to everything else: that we're all made of star stuff, each little particle of our being, entangled with every other particle? 'Entanglement,' Max called it. *Verschrankung*, really, because Schrödinger was German.

Just as one atom can be in more than one state at once, Max would say, separate objects can become so entangled with each other, that neither one possesses a state of its own.

'Oh, no you don't,' I said. I didn't know where Max was going, but I sure didn't want to go there. Where would this stop? I already had a dead cat on my conscience.

'You can entangle two atoms with light,' Max said, 'so that they have one state between them: zero. If one points UP, the other atom must point DOWN, cancelling the other out. Measure the first, and you know the state of the second. It has to add up to zero. A single state for both.'

'But they're opposite,' I protested. 'It's not the same state for them both.'

'A single state for both,' Max repeated. 'Besides,' he added, smiling. 'Opposites attract.'

The meaning was right there in his dark eyes. Opposites, schmopposites; they're entangled just the same. Only opposites are so right together. Yin and yang makes one. Two yangs don't make a right. Then he kissed me, and we didn't talk for a long time.

'Quantum teleportation,' he whispered as we came up for air. 'Information sent at the speed of light. Think of it,' Max said. 'Entangle two particles and send them off to opposite ends of the universe. Measure one, and know the other, instantaneously. If one particle is moving at the speed of light and relatively younger, measure its stationary partner to know its future.'

I could see the potential. INSTANTANEOUSLY — FASTER THAN

THE SPEED OF LIGHT. KNOW THE FUTURE BEFORE IT'S HERE! Hurry, Hurry, Hurry, Folks. Just send a few bits of information HERE, and, ipso facto, hocus pocus, read the future from THERE.

'You could send a message to the future,' Max said.

'Or, receive a message from the past,' I mused.

'Yeah, you could talk to your dead father,' Max said.

I didn't know it then, but that was the beginning.

Debbie says I don't have any duties today, since it's my first day. She helped me to make my bed and showed me how to make hospital corners by lifting up a triangle of blanket and sheet together, then left me to put all my stuff away. I haven't done it. Putting your stuff away is so final. It means you're staying. It means acceptance of your fate, even if this fate isn't anything like what you pictured. It means choices I don't like, and decisions I don't want to make. So, my suitcases stand at attention beside my bed, a sign to everyone that I'm ready to be off at any minute. You can't anchor a sailor.

But I've made my bed, so I'm lying in it, talking quietly to Father ever since lunch. Then suddenly this quiet tableau is interrupted by Roommate, who has just come in from her job at a shoe store. She tried to sneak in and not talk to me, which is just fine with me. So, we're both lying on our beds, and she doesn't know my name. Which is very fine with me. I go on talking to Father, out loud now.

'Who're you talking to?' Roommate says. 'There's no one there.'

'He's invisible,' I answer.

'Who is it, Harvey the Rabbit?' she asks, laughing.

'No, my father.'

'There's no one there.'

'Go to hell,' I say.

That should start our relationship off on the right foot.

'Hey, you!' Roommate says, jumping up. 'This is my room. You can't just come in here and tell me to go to hell.'

'I just did,' I say and snicker.

That gets to her and she runs out of the room. All this makes me feel much better, and I jump up and begin to unpack my bags. Suddenly, Roommate is back, with Debbie half a dozen paces in back of her. Debbie sits down on my bed, which sags under the weight, and looks at me.

'Jill, this is your new roommate, Robin. Robin, Jill tells me you just told her to go to hell. We don't use those words here, Robin.'

I sit down on the floor and fold my arms across my chest. I haven't taken my lunch pills or my dinner pills, and Father is telling me I'm being stubborn and uncooperative and either I sink or I swim – it's my choice, and now I've got three against one, and I haven't even unpacked yet. 'Go to hell,' I say again.

'See?' Jill cries. 'Go to hell, yourself!'

Debbie stands up, a mountain of fat in a white smock, and puts her hands out like a traffic cop. 'Now, Robin, I know this is your first day here, and you're probably a little upset, and you don't know all the rules, but we don't allow that language in this house. Is that understood? Now, I want you two to shake hands and be friends.'

Neither of us move.

'Now!' Debbie says.

I inch forward on my butt and extend my hand. Jill stretches her body till her right hand touches mine for a second before we both pull away.

'Now,' Debbie says. 'Come down for dinner. It's lasagna.'

Jill gets up and follows Debbie out. I sit on the floor a few more minutes.

Father? I ask.

I'm going off to Croatia, he says. You are not behaving yourself, Robin. Take your pills.

And he's gone, just like that. I call him a few times, but he won't answer. So, I'm on my own. I get up and take my pills, washed down with a cup of water from the plastic cup in the bathroom. I'm feeling sorry for myself: orphaned and abandoned. Father, Max, Derek, all gone. Mother, Howard, far away. Melissa, who cares. Damn the world and everything in it: maybe I'll do away with myself and they'll be sorry.

The smell of lasagna wafts upstairs. But I'll have dinner first.

I tramp downstairs to find the dining room full of people. There's Debbie, and Jill, and Louise, the girl in the wheelchair, and Ray, the guy who stares into space. A fiftyish black guy is just coming out of the kitchen, and a woman with wild grey hair halfway down her back is sitting down at the dining table. Jill is carrying out a big bowl of salad; Louise is folding napkins; Ray is still watching TV.

'Ray, it's dinnertime. Please shut off the television,' Debbie calls.

Ray continues to watch. Either he has amazing powers of concentration, or he's a space cadet.

'Ray,' Debbie calls again. 'Shut off the television and come to the table, please.'

He continues to watch.

'Or you'll get no dinner.'

At this, Ray picks up the remote and zaps the picture. He gets up and moves unsteadily toward the table. Apparently, he's not a total space cadet. He just lacks the proper motivation.

'Thank you,' Debbie says.

Debbie bows her head, and everyone follows, except me. 'For this food we thank you, Lord.'

Jill gets up and goes into the kitchen; comes back out with a big tray of lasagna and sets it right in front of me.

'La-sag-na,' says Ray.

'Good for you, Ray,' Debbie says. She looks over at me. 'Robin, will you serve?'

'Me?'

'Everyone participates at Forrester.'

Bart, the black guy, offers me the spatula, and a knife, and shows me what to do. I start to make a mess of it, cutting the lasagna into uneven pieces, mashing it, slopping it, lasagna toppling onto the plate. As I said, I've always been clean-up crew: serving takes talents I don't have. Bart takes over and shows me how it's done.

'It's easy when you know how,' he says, smiling, handing me a plate. I put it down in front of me.

'Pass it around,' Jill says. 'You're not the only one here.'

'This is a group home, Robin,' Debbie explains. 'Everyone here is a respected member of the group.'

Group, schmoop. What about me? I picture everyone in this house stuck together into one big blob, fourteen arms sticking out, higgledy-piggledy, a monstrosity jumping around on fourteen legs. I pass the plate.

Bart cuts another piece, and hands me the plate, which I pass. Three more plates, which I pass. The fourth, I try to give back to Bart, who's the only other person without lasagna, but he says it's mine. Hallelujah!

You can't even pick who you eat with here. You just eat with the whole damn group, whether you want to or not. I watch them all. Ray has the best technique: he's shovelling it in faster than anyone else. Bart's the most civilized. Jill talks only to Louise. Margaret has some sort of tremor. Who are these people, and why am I one of them?

Debbie starts the dinner-table conversation by asking each resident how her day was. I know she's going to get to me, and I don't know what to say. I come from the loony bin, I talk to my dead father, I had a fight with my roommate. Leave me alone! I want to shout. Just pretend I'm not here.

'You have good lasagna here,' I finally say.

'Bart made the las-ag-na,' Ray announces between bites.

'Good, Ray,' Debbie says.

'What's your name?' asks Margaret.

'Robin.'

'You schizophrenic?'

'Yeah.'

'Me, too,' says Margaret. 'But Clozaril gave me agranulocytosis, so I'm back to Thorazine. That's why I shake.'

'Nice to meet you,' I say.

'They had to put me into isolation for five weeks,' Margaret adds.

'Robin talks to her dead father,' Jill volunteers. 'She's loony.'

'Everyone's loony here,' Margaret says.

'We don't use that word, Margaret,' Debbie scolds.

'Screwy,' Margaret corrects herself.

'Screwy isn't very nice, either.'

'They're just words,' Bart says, looking down at me, smiling. He's got a nice face: it's kind of gaunt and his hair is grizzled, but, I don't know, I like the look of him. Like he's lived for a long time and he doesn't worry about anything, any more. And he makes good lasagna.

But the others, no. They're loony and screwy, and I don't like any of them.

I finish out the meal, my eyes not moving from my plate. Not looking, maybe I can make them not exist. A bowl of chocolate pudding gets put in front of me, and I eat it. A cup of coffee, I drink it. They don't exist if I don't let them. I finally get up, go to my room and get into bed.

In the morning, I'm woken up by Jill, who's kneading my shoulder.

'Get up. You're supposed to set the breakfast table.'

I look at her with sleepy eyes. Who is this?

Jill gives my shoulder another shove. 'C'mon, Debbie doesn't like it when we're late.'

'What?'

'You didn't look at the roster, did you?' she says, peering into my face.

I sit up slowly, Jill still three inches from my face.

'I'm up.'

'Good,' she says, going out the door. 'I'm going to tell Debbie you'll be right down.'

I sit on the edge of the bed, scratching my head. Debbie? Where's Beverly?

I remember now. I'm in Hell. I stand up and grab some underwear from my gaping suitcase.

Forrester, the forests of Hell. Hissing and crackling from the open pits of Hell.

I pull on some pants and a sweater, go into the bathroom to brush my teeth. Father? I call.

Nothing. He's on a task force in Croatia.

I put on my shoes.

Damn him. I thought he loved me. First, he says he'll always be there, that I'm his flesh and blood. Then he tells me, sink or swim, it's your choice, and leaves.

That's no choice. I swallow my pills and go downstairs to set the table.

Downstairs, I see the roster. Saturday, April 2, Breakfast. Robin Farber: table setting duty.

Debbie points out the dishes in the cabinet, the cutlery drawer, the napkins on the counter. 'Seven place settings,' she says. 'It's Saturday.'

I set the table in an unbroken sequence, plate, fork, plate, glass, knife, spoon, plate, fork, plate, glass, knife, spoon ad infinitum, around the table. Then I break the symmetry by leaving a broken fork at Jill's place. Hallelujah!

People start filing in: Ray, with his pants backward, Louise in her wheelchair. I sit down, wait. Bart comes over, pulls out his chair and smiles at me, a good, friendly smile. There's something empty about those eyes, I can't figure out what, but I like him. This is going to work.

Margaret is serving. She carries in a plate of scrambled eggs, the tremor in her hands making the eggs quiver in the dish. I picture the platter dropping, smashing on the floor, eggs bouncing up and down on the floor. Don't drop it; don't drop it, I pray, then worry that my thoughts will make it happen. But no, Whitecoat says I am not responsible for the universe.

I watch with bated breath until Margaret sets the platter down squarely on the table. There. All's well with the world.

Margaret goes back in, returning with a platter of bacon, which jump and jitter until she puts them down. Then, some trembling toast, whose plate does a little dance on the table. This is too much. I jump up and bring in the pitcher of orange juice, to save myself the worry.

'Thank you, Robin,' Margaret says.

'You're welcome, Margaret.' This is going to work.

'This fork is broken,' I hear from Jill's side of the table. A beat or two, while she looks over at me. I can feel her gaze, but I am too busy eating bacon and eggs to look up. Innocent until proven guilty, haha.

'De-li-cious,' Ray mumbles.

'Good, Ray.'

Louise leans over to tell me that Ray only talks about food. But this is good, because till last year he didn't talk at all.

There's a ringing somewhere. I check my teeth, but the ringing continues.

'Jill, will you get the telephone, please?'

Jill gets up and runs to the living room. I hear her voice, a pause, then, 'It's for Robin. He says his name is Derek.'

Derek Derek Bo Berrick! I run to the phone.

'Derek?!'

'Hey, Robin! How's my girl doing?'

He sounds happy.

'I'm okay. How did you get this number?'

'I figured how many Howard Applebaums can there be in Hamilton?'

'How many?'

'Two.'

'Really.'

'I called them both. Asked each one if they knew a Robin Farber.'

'And?'

'Your mother answered on the second try. I told her I was an old friend from high school, and I really wanted to see you again. Piece of cake,' Derek says and laughs uproariously for a few seconds.

'How are you?' I ask, but I know the answer. Good.

'Good,' he says. 'Really good.'

'Whitecoat said your father took your laptop.'

'Yeah, but I bought another one. And I got another e-mail account.'

'I e-mailed you over and over. Why didn't you e-mail me back?'

There's a pause. 'You have a computer there?' Derek finally asks.

'No. I ...' It was through my teeth. Whitecoat says I can't do that. 'Never mind.'

From the dining room I hear, 'Robin, please don't tie up the lines too long. There are other people here, you know.'

'Okay,' I call back.

'I want to see you,' Derek says.

'I want to see you, too.'

'I have wheels,' he says. 'A sweet little Miata.'

'Your father got it for you?'

'My mother. My father wouldn't buy me anything, if his life depended on it.' He laughs again.

'Oh,' I say.

'I'm coming,' Derek says. 'Tomorrow.'

'Okay. You know how to get here?'

'Yeah, sure. I looked it up on Map Blast on the internet.'

'Robin!' Debbie calls, louder than before.

'I've got to get off.'

'Tomorrow. One o'clock. Remember.'

'Okay,' I whisper. 'Bye.'

Derek Derek Bo-berrick. Banana-fana-fo Ferek. Mi-my-mo Merek. My Derek.

I make my way back to the table, a smile on my face. The table is half empty, Ray carrying dishes back and forth to the kitchen. Jill and Debbie stand around finishing their coffee.

'Robin's got a boyfriend,' Jill says in sing song.

'So what?' I respond.

Jill shrugs. 'You can't have men in the rooms,' she says.

'We're going out. He's going to take me for a ride in his Mi-a-ta.'

'My father has a Lexus,' Jill replies.

'Big deal.'

'Your father is dead.'

'Girls, girls!' Debbie scolds. 'Can't you two just be friends?'

'I wouldn't be her friend if she were the last person on earth,' I mutter and turn to go upstairs.

Take that, Jill Jill Banana Pill. She thinks she's so great. I tramp up the stairs and sit on my bed, picking up the corner of Grandma's quilt and rubbing it against my cheek. There, there, I hear Grandma saying. I sit like that for a long time in the dark, feeling sorry for myself, then I climb under the quilt. I feel so small: not a whole person, just a part of the group. A sprocket, or a ratchet, something that doesn't exist except in relation to something else. A nut, a screw, a nail. A fragment.

Chapter Eight

I wake up to the sun shining in the window. Roommate is still sleeping. I get up, fully dressed, because I never took my clothes off in the first place, and tiptoe downstairs. The roster is hanging on the kitchen door: Sunday, April 3. I take my finger and trace down the entries. Robin Farber. Table setting, breakfast, again. Kitchen help for dinner.

All the cobwebs in my head are gone. The sun is shining, and Derek is coming. I feel good. Yeah, good.

I stop and listen, but I don't hear a thing. Everybody's asleep. I go into the kitchen and take out the plates, the cutlery, the napkins, and set the table. Then I go upstairs, and unpack my bags. Jill makes a few jerky movements when I open the drawers, but I stop what I'm doing, and she goes back to sleep. I unpack everything and stow the bags under my bed, take a shower and get dressed in something nice. Then I go back downstairs and sit down on the couch.

Louise comes in first, gives me a small smile, checks the roster. Louise McLaughlin. Kitchen duty, breakfast. She wheels herself through the door, and soon I hear her banging around. I go in, myself.

Louise is having trouble reaching a pot in the upper cabinet.

'Anything I can do?' I ask.

'The pot,' she points.

I get it down for her.

'Anything else?'

'Thanks, I can do the rest,' Louise says in a small voice. She wheels herself over to the refrigerator, pulls out some milk and juice with difficulty.

I'm busy looking at her, and she notices.

'Multiple sclerosis,' she explains.

'It's always something,' I say and laugh.

Louise looks at me like I'm crazy, which I am. I guess she thinks I'm laughing at her.

'I didn't mean anything,' I say.

'Forget it. You want to bring the juice to the table?'

My new job: official juice carrier. I carry out the pitcher and come back. Louise is slicing a banana.

'Bart's nice,' I say.

Louise lifts her eyebrow, then smiles. 'Yeah, he is.'

'What's he doing here?'

She looks around to see if anyone's watching. 'He had a frontal lobotomy.'

This sounds like a front end lube job. 'A what?'

'They operated on his brain,' Louise says, cutting a strawberry. She's holding the knife in her fist, and pushing down; strawberry juice oozes out like blood.

'You want me to do that?' I ask.

'No, thank you.' She continues cutting with her fist. 'It was a long time ago. They don't do lobotomies, any more.'

'Why not?'

'Would you want someone to cut your thinking centre off from the rest of your brain?'

Sometimes I think that's what happened to me. 'No.'

'Well, there you are,' Louise says. 'You mind bringing the cereals out to the table?'

There I am. I lift half a dozen cereal boxes, carry them through the kitchen door and plunk them down on the table. Where am I?

'I don't understand,' I say when I return. 'Bart seems smart. He knows how to cook. He showed me how to cut up the lasagna.'

'It's subtle,' Louise says. 'You'll see.'

What will I see? I don't want to see. I just thought Bart was nice. I excuse myself and go sit on the couch in the living room.

Everyone comes in separately today, because it's Sunday. They just sit down at the table, take what they want, and leave. Bart comes down after a while. I can't seem to stop looking at him. He sits down and pours himself some juice, grabs a bowl and Cheerios, throws in some banana and milk and begins to eat.

'Hi, Robin,' he says.

I don't know. Something in the eyes, I guess. It's subtle, Louise said. I can't stop looking at him.

'Have a nice day,' he says as he gets up.

'You, too,' I answer. Whitecoat's right. This can't be my world. If I were God, I wouldn't have frontal lobotomies or schizophrenia. In my world,

Louise would walk; Max would be married to me, and Bart would be just a nice guy who made lasagna. I don't understand the point of suffering.

I'm not on duty for lunch, so I just eat and run. Derek is coming. I wait near the front window, and watch every car that drives by. Suddenly, a little red sports car zooms past, backs up at warp speed, and pulls into the driveway. The driver revs the engine one last time, and gets out. I open the door before he even comes up the path.

'Robin!' Derek cries and lifts me up, swings me around. He's so strong for a short guy. I probably weigh as much as he does.

'You're looking good!' he says, when he puts me down.

Boy, is he happy. He's got a racing cap on backwards, and a big smile on his face. He gives me a big sloppy kiss on the lips.

'What a great place!' he shouts. 'Wait!' He runs back to the car and pulls out a camera. 'Cheese!' he cries, and clicks a couple hundred pictures of me in front of the house.

The camera has all sorts of attachments, buttons, stuff. 'Nice camera,' I say.

'I just bought it. It's a Nikon digital. I can send you the pictures in an e-mail.'

Behind us, someone opens the door. Derek goes up to whoever it is, introduces himself, and asks the person to take a picture of the two of us. I turn around to see: it's Bart.

'Well, I ...' Bart says, but takes the camera in hand. Derek shows him how to do it, and steps back with me, framed by the house.

Bart dithers for a few minutes, then a few more, until it's obvious he isn't ever going to take our picture. Derek thanks him and takes the camera back.

'Who is that guy?' he whispers.

'Bart,' I say. Somehow I don't want to tell him.

Meanwhile, Bart is still standing there. 'Could you take a picture of Robin and me?' he asks.

Derek looks at him curiously. 'Sure,' he says.

Bart and I line up against the house; Derek clicks away. 'Great,' Derek says.

'Here, I'll take you,' I say to Derek. 'Show me how.'

Derek shows me what to push, and goes to stand in front of the door. Bart moves in closer and I take them both.

'Thanks, Bart,' I say.

'Glad I could help,' he answers and finally turns back to the house.

'I'll just edit him out,' Derek says to me, after Bart leaves. 'Then I'll put you and me together in one picture.'

I bring him in, show him around. Derek starts to go upstairs.

'No men allowed in our room,' I tell him.

'Oh, please!' Derek says and lopes upstairs.

'Don't!' I shout, but he's halfway there. By the time I get upstairs, he's busy peeping into every room.

I walk straight to mine, checking first to make sure Jill isn't there. 'Coast is clear,' I say, and Derek runs in.

'Hey, this isn't so bad.' He's starts looking at Jill's stuff, examining her perfume, opening a letter.

'Don't do that!' I cry.

'Close the door,' Derek whispers.

Someone is saying, Watch out.

We close the door and lock it. Derek lies down on one side of the bed and crooks his finger for me; I get in. We start out kissing, but Derek's like a maniac today. In minutes, he's got me pinned down on Grandma's quilt with my pants down, and he's pounding me like a machine. The bed is jumping all over the room. Bang. Bang. Bang. Slam-bang in the bed, and bang bang out of the bed, and there's panting and crying and heavy breathing.

And suddenly, I hear this loud rapping at the door. I guess we were making so much noise, we didn't hear it before.

'Robin!' It's Jill's voice. 'What are you doing in there? Let me in!'

'Uh-oh,' Derek says, and goes to unlock the door, his pants down and a smile on his face.

'No!' I shout, but it's too late. Jill is standing in the doorway, her eyes going every which way, finally settling on Derek's thing. She stands there half a minute, her mouth open, then she turns around and shouts, 'Debbie!' and runs down the stairs.

'Do these windows open?' Derek whispers to me, grabbing his clothes.

I shrug, but he's already lifting up the sash and climbing out.

'Meet you outside,' he says and ducks his head.

I look out and down. Derek's shinnying down the drain pipe. 'Close the window,' he mouths.

I shut the window, put on my clothes and lie down. Things are beginning to whirl around me all of a sudden, and the voices are back, telling me bad things about myself, that I never should have let him in, that I'm going to be hurt. I hear Whitecoat's voice telling me I have to consolidate my gains and Father's to sink or swim, it's my choice. I lie there, my eyes closed, breathing in and out for half a minute, waiting for the worst. Then, kerbam! Jill bursts in, with Debbie, panting, just behind.

'See, he's …' Jill is saying, wide-eyed, crazy.

'What? Debbie asks.

'I …' Jill looks around the room. 'I …'

'Jill, I've warned you before. You convinced us that time with Martha, but I really don't believe it any more.' Debbie turns to me.

'Robin,' she says. 'Jill says you had a man in your room …'

I try to look sleepy. 'I was just taking a nap.'

'And they were having sex,' Jill adds.

'I don't see anything, Jill,' Debbie says, 'Nothing.'

Jill looks under my bed, under her bed, in the closet.

'I just wish you girls would get along,' Debbie says.

'Out the window!' Jill shouts. Debbie goes over to the window, looks down, shakes her head.

'Jill, you do this again to me, and I'll …' Debbie says, walking to the door. 'I'm too old, and too fat, to be running upstairs all the time.'

Jill glares at me and goes out. I get up and go carefully downstairs. I can hear yelling, but I'm not sure if it's in the kitchen or in my head. I tiptoe across the living room.

Trouble, a voice says. But there's no one there.

I run out the front door. The Miata is behind a bush halfway down the street: the door is open, and Derek is beckoning me in. Run, run, get in. Derek revs the motor softly and away we go.

I'm huffing and puffing, and I can't catch my breath.

Derek is roaring with laughter and driving at the speed of light. 'Pretty neat getaway, don't you think?' he asks.

But it's not neat. Yeah, it's neat, but it's not. Derek is acting like he doesn't have a care in the world. Teflon man, he thinks he is. Me, I've got people telling me I shouldn't have done it, that they're going to punish me bad, and send me to jail.

'I'm going to be punished,' I say.

'Nah!' Derek answers. 'You worry way too much, Robin. They can't prove anything.'

He cuts off another car and merges into traffic.

'Please don't drive so fast,' I plead.

'I know what I'm doing.'

Derek passes someone on the right and speeds up.

'Let's go someplace and have a cup of coffee,' I suggest, huddling in my seat.

'Yeah, sure,' Derek says. 'Anyplace special?'

'Anyplace,' I answer. Anyplace that's not moving.

Derek cuts over two lanes to the ramp on his right, coming to a screeching halt at the light at the bottom of the hill. 'There's a place,' he says, and swerves over to an empty parking spot.

He's more than happy, says a voice. He's manic.

'You going for treatment?' I ask him, as we go into the tavern. It's a dark little place with red vinyl booths and framed pictures of men in high boots dangling dead fish, on the walls. There must be six people there.

'No, been there, done that.' Derek waves to the waitress. 'He said I was a failure.'

'Who?'

'My father.'

Not good, not good, says a voice.

'But Whitecoat said you improved.'

'Will you please stop calling him Whitecoat?' Derek barks. He waves to the waitress again, more urgently.

'Sorry.'

'Well, my father said he didn't see the improvement, and Dr Mankiewicz had had me for nine months. It was enough to create a whole new human being, my father said.'

'What does that mean?'

'What does what mean?' Derek gets up and strides over to the waitress, who is talking to another customer. I watch him talk, then her, then he turns his back on her, walks back and drops into the booth. The waitress gives him a dirty look.

'She said she'll be right here. Jeesh.'

Not good, not good, says the voice.

'Are you taking your medicine?' I ask.

'Hey, you on my case, too?'

No, the voice says. No.

The waitress saunters over, a pencil behind her ear, two menus in her hand.

'Whacha want?' she asks, setting down the menus on the table.

'A cup of coffee,' I say.

'You have banana splits?' Derek asks.

'Yeah,' the waitress says, writing on her pad. 'That whacha want?'

'Yes,' Derek enunciates. 'That is what I want.' He turns to me. 'You don't want a piece of pie or anything?'

'I'm too fat already,' I say.

'What do you mean? You're just right!' Derek laughs. 'Have a piece of pie.'

'Go ahead, honey. Have a piece of pie,' the waitress urges.

'Okay, a piece of pie.'

'Apple, blueberry, cherry. Which one?'

'Cherry.'

'That all?'

'Yeah,' Derek says, waving her away. 'Now, where was I?'

'I don't remember.'

'Well, it couldn't have been too important, then, could it?' Derek says and laughs. 'So what about you, kiddo? How's the group home?'

This is a new Derek. I've seen him high but not this high.

'It's okay.'

'Just okay?'

'I'm supposed to be part of the group,' I say, just as the waitress comes over and dumps coffee, pie, and one banana split on the table. Derek pulls the sundae over and digs with in his spoon. I cut a smidge of pie with my fork, put it in my mouth, picture Father asking for a taste.

The waitress is still standing there. 'You want cream?'

'Okay,' I say, and she grabs a bowl full of little containers from the next table and plunks it down in front of me.

'You were saying?' Derek asks after the waitress leaves.

'I don't remember.'

'You don't like being part of the group,' he says between spoonfuls of ice cream.

I think about this a minute, sipping coffee. 'Yeah. Then I'm no one.'

'You're still you.'

'Sometimes it's hard to tell who I am.'

'You're the woman I love.'

I look up and it's like I'm seeing Derek for the first time. I see this crazy guy with the backwards racing cap and the goofy smile, and I suddenly remember what got to me the first time: the way he looks at me. Not too hot and not too cold, not too hard and not too soft. Just right. Whoosh! I'm not in Kansas any more.

'Hey, you. Give me that banana,' I say, pointing with my fork to the lone banana slice remaining on Derek's dish.

Derek grins at me and takes the fork, impales the banana on it. I take it in my mouth and offer him one-half, just sticking out of my lips. We kiss, like Lady and the Tramp, over the banana slice.

From across the room we hear the waitress laugh, half a dozen people clapping.

Derek stands up on the red vinyl seat and takes a deep bow. More clapping.

Not good, not good, says the voice.

Oh, shut up, I tell it. Just shut up.

'Robin, do you love me?' Derek asks all of a sudden.

I look into his eyes, and Max is really history. 'Yes,' I say.

'I know you're not ready, and all that, but I want to get married. Father is never going to agree, but I could get the money from my trust fund next year. It doesn't matter what he thinks.'

Don't do it, the voice says.

Shut up, I tell it. To Derek, I say, 'I'm ready.'

Derek gives a little whoop. 'Great! Now let me get you home before anybody notices you're missing.'

Ray was the only one in the living room when I got back. I crossed straight into the kitchen and asked what I needed to do for dinner. Debbie put me to work chopping onions for the chile con carne. It was like I had never left. I think I was on borrowed energy all Sunday; I was a little mouse running on a wheel, a perpetual motion machine. The voices were there, telling me what to do, what not to do, how they would punish me if I married Derek, but I was running so fast, they couldn't catch up.

Until this morning. The alarm clock drills me awake, but I am a sack of cement. I turn slowly toward Jill's empty bed, then rotate my neck toward the clock, which is t-i-c-k-i-n-g with little mincing steps. I watch each nanosecond as it clicks into place: 9:00:57. 9:00:58. 9:00:59. 9:01:00.

Click and clack and click and clack, a digital heartbeat, so regular it puts me back to sleep. I am busy savouring the delicious memory of Derek and me kissing over a banana slice, when Debbie looks in, panting, from the doorway. 'Robin, get up. You have a session with Dr Mankiewicz at eleven.'

'Yeah,' I say. Can't get out of bed.

'Come on,' she says, entering the room. 'It's not my job to get you out of bed every morning. I'm just doing it today. There's a bus at ten, which should bring you right to the door by 10:40.'

The clock ticks: 9:02:47. 9:02:48. So much time, no need to rush.

'Robin.'

I pick one leg up and throw it over the side.

'I expect you down to breakfast in twenty minutes,' Debbie says, and leaves.

The other leg. Push myself up on one elbow. 9:03:59. Push up with the other hand. 9:04:31. Feet on the cold floor. 9:06:02.

I pad into the bathroom and take my morning pills. I've been trying to be a good girl, taking them every day. They keep me sane, or as sane as I'll ever be. Whitecoat says I've made progress. If I work hard, I can get a job, marry Derek, be normal. Whatever that is.

I brush my teeth, grab some underwear, pull on the pants and shirt that I left on the floor last night. The clock says 9:18:32. I go downstairs. Weekdays, it's every man for himself for breakfast. I grab Cheerios, milk, and have myself breakfast on the kitchen counter. Roster says I serve dinner.

Debbie walks me to the bus stop, gives me my monthly bus pass and waits with me till the bus comes. She tells the driver where I'm supposed to get off and repeats to me for the sixteenth time that I should pick up the bus at the place it lets me off. I wave goodbye through the window like it's my first day at school.

What would it be like if I were normal, I think as the bus pulls away from the curb. I know, but I don't want to think about it. Max is history, anyway.

But Derek is today. I think of our banana kiss, and all's right with the world. Sun comes through the bus window and kick-starts my metabolism, which has been cold like a lizard. Azaleas and dogwood pass by, then green-leafed trees, and country roads.

'Berkshire!' the driver calls, and the bus slows to a stop. I shuffle to the front, and climb down the stairs.

'Back so soon?' the guard asks, as he opens the gates. It's been three days, but it seems like three years. I walk down Roz's long circular path, past Derek's bush. I climb the stairs, wave to the receptionist and have all but approached Whitecoat's office, when he tells me to come in. Home sweet home.

To his back, I say, 'Hello.' Whitecoat swivels to face me. He looks the same. Nothing's changed for him.

'Good morning, Robin. How is the group home?'

I shrug. 'Okay.'

'Abigail says it's a nice place.'

'Yeah.'

'You don't feel like talking?'

I wanted to the whole time I was in the bus. Now that I'm here, I don't. 'No.'

'Okay, we'll just sit here till you do.'

We sit and sit and the clock on the wall goes from 11:02 to 11:34. I watch the second hand run round and round the face.

'I saw Derek yesterday,' I finally say.

'Oh? How is he?'

'Manic.'

'Is he getting treatment?'

'No.'

Whitecoat wipes his brow. 'That's what I was afraid of.'

We sit for another minute.

'Tell me about the group home, Robin.'

What's there to tell? 'I don't like my roommate. They won't let men in our rooms. We have to do chores.'

'It sounds like you don't like it.'

I shrug. 'Debbie says I have to be part of the group.'

'Is that bad?'

'I'm a screw or a widget. A piece of a big machine.'

'No, you're not. Being a member of a group doesn't make you less than a person. You're still Robin, whatever group you belong to.'

'That's what Derek says.'

'Well, he's right.'

'Derek wants us to get married.'

'Does he?' Whitecoat says.

Sometimes I wonder about this guy. I just said he did. 'Yeah,' I say again.

'That would make you part of a couple,' Whitecoat says, smiling.

What's he smiling about? I hate it when he smiles. 'No, it wouldn't. We'd just be Derek and me.'

'Marriage is an important step. You have to love someone enough to want to share yourself with him.'

I can't help but laugh. 'How do I share myself? You want me to cut my arm off or something?'

Whitecoat sighs. 'No, Robin. Nothing that drastic.'

He looks at the clock. 'I think the two of you better think about this for a while. Derek acts too much on impulse. And you, Robin, ... well, you don't always know what you're getting into. For the present, why don't you just work on being part of the group?'

'The group,' I say, and picture the big blob again: a pincushion with fourteen arms, fourteen legs, and my head.

It's Saturday, and Mother and Howard are here at Forrester. Mother is going around talking to everyone. She likes Bart, especially; he's so cheerful, she said. Anyway, Debbie asked them to stay for lunch, and Bart made mushroom soup, and now they're fast friends, because that's her favourite. She even managed to say a few words to Ray, though all he answered was 'Mushroom soup.'

So, Mother is converted to this place, thinks it's the best thing. Howard thinks it's good, but not as good as home. But he's being very nice. He hasn't said anything this time about maybe, since I seem so improved, I'm ready to live at home and get a job. He hasn't said that. Sometimes I'm sure he wants to, but I don't read minds, so who knows what he's thinking?

After lunch, they come upstairs and sit on the bed and talk to me about Melissa and Max and the baby that's coming in six months. If I figure from February, that's just right. Almost too right, and I wonder whether the baby went down the aisle with the rest of us. I don't care any more. I told Mother that. I don't care what they do. They can have six babies for all I care. But Mother keeps saying, the baby is part of the family, and you're a member of the family, and you're related, for heaven's sake. You're the aunt, Robin, don't you want to see it, and hold it? No, thank you. Not Melissa's baby. I want to vomit my disgust into the toilet.

I didn't tell them that Derek was here, but Derek sent an attachment of a hundred million pictures to Howard's e-mail address, so they know he was. Howard doesn't have a printer, though, and I don't have a computer, so Howard put it all on a floppy and went to PhotoLab and had the best one printed: a five-by-seven glossy of Derek and me in front of the house, all done up in a frame from All-mart. He hands it to me ceremoniously, and I laugh. Then I have to tell him why, because he's hurt and he's gone all purple and green in the face.

The picture shows Derek on the left and Robin on the right, and Bart, nowhere to be seen. Don't believe everything you see, I tell him. Maybe Derek wasn't really here at all.

Jill comes in and sits on her bed, and Mother moves over to her side of the room, and in no time, she and Jill are chatting like old friends. I wonder why Mother can talk to everyone else better than she can with me. We never could talk. She'd like to go around picking lint off my collar, or rubbing a smudge from my cheek with a finger that she stuck in her mouth, but do we talk? No.

Jill, too. We're hello/goodbye friends. That's all we say. I'd like to talk to her the way Mother is talking, but when I do, my voice gets stuck in my throat, and in the end, all I say are nasty things. Jill's got blond hair and has a diagnosis of personality disorder, so maybe I think she's Melissa. I don't know. People are sure a lot of trouble.

You know, I'm watching Jill talk to Mother, and though I can't hear their words, I could swear that Jill is telling her about Derek and me in my bed with the locked door. Debbie never did believe her, so now she's working on my relatives. Every once in a while, I hear Jill calling her Donna, and that worries me. Maybe Mother will want to exchange me for her. But Whitecoat says I can't read minds or send e-mails through my teeth, that it's just my own thoughts talking to themselves. I don't know. I'm watching them talking, and Jill is leaning in to Mother, and telling her something in all seriousness, and Mother is looking worried. Now she's looking over at me with her corrugated look. Damn, she's said it, and, of course, Mother believes her. Guilty till proven innocent.

Here comes Mother, over to my side of the room. Jill is a Cheshire cat sitting on her bed. 'Robin, dear, what's this that Jill is telling me about how she came up to your room, and the door was locked, and that some-one was in the room with you?'

It's just another of Mother's worries with a question mark at the end.

'I was sleeping,' I say.

Mother looks at me with her trademark concern. 'Really?' she asks.

'I locked the door, so I wouldn't be disturbed.' It could have happened that way.

Now she doesn't know what to do. Believe the roommate who has never lied to her as far as she knows, or believe her own flesh and blood, whom she doesn't believe and never has believed, so help her God?

'Well, you shouldn't have locked the door,' Mother says after a minute. 'Jill couldn't get in.'

'Sorry, Jill,' I say.

Howard is looking at his watch. 'Well, it's about time.'

Mother gives me a big kiss, as if she never doubted me: how could she, her own flesh and blood? Howard gives me a quick peck on the cheek, and they leave. Jill goes with Mother, still talking in her ear, but I stay back. I had enough of them. I want a little peace and quiet.

Derek Derek Bo Berrick comes over after lunch the next day. His father plays golf, and his mother is busy cooking Sunday dinner, and he says he just has to get out, anyway. He takes me out Sundays in the Miata, and we go anywhere we like. Today we go to a pond nearby, which the Canada geese have overrun. Derek's brought bread to feed them, but they're vicious, and they practically grab the slices out of our hands. We make our way carefully through the goose doodoo to find a place on the grass to put down Derek's blanket.

'You tell your father?' I ask.

'Not yet,' Derek says.

I don't want to push him. Derek has this thing with his father, like I have with Melissa. You can't reason with them, and you can't win, so that's why Derek doesn't want to tell him we're getting married.

A big goose walks straight up to me and sticks her beak out. Like, here I am. Feed me. Sitting down, I'm half her size. 'Here!' I shout and throw a piece of bread as far as I can.

The goose looks at me in contempt. Me chase a piece of bread? Instead, she takes a dump on the corner of the blanket. This is too much. Derek stands up, yelling and and waving his arms.

'Scat! Get out of here!'

The goose takes one look at Derek and decides it's not worth fighting over a lousy piece of bread.

He's still hyper. His mother has been getting medication for him on the sly, but it's not working. Whitecoat was always adding and subtracting, trying this, trying that, and even then he couldn't stabilize Derek, so how's he going to manage with whatever his mother brings home for him? I want to tell Derek he's afraid of his father, and he has to start standing up to him, except I can't do that. I just can't do that to him. He needs someone on his side, and that someone can't be like my mother who keeps needling and needling, all the time acting like she's just the sweetest person this side of the Atlantic. No, Derek needs loyal support. No say-this-and-do-that sort of thing.

Goose is back, and this time she doesn't take no for an answer, so we take our blanket with doodoo on the corner and leave. Derek is muttering something about Ontario ponds and Canada geese, and swinging the blanket at whatever geese get in his way. He gets angry a lot these days. I think it's his father he's really angry at, but right now he's taking it out on the geese. Derek takes one more swipe, then throws the blanket in the trash can. I have to run to catch up with him, he's walking so fast.

We get into the Miata, and he speeds away. He gets this kind of smirk on his face when he drives fast, and I don't know whether he's happy or angry. I just can't read anyone any more. Now I know what Deanna Troi on *Star Trek* felt like when she lost her empathic powers.

'I'm going to talk to him tonight,' he says all of a sudden, and I know. Angry.

'Who?' I ask, just to make sure I'm not wrong.

'Who do you think?' he barks at me. 'My father. I'm getting my trust funds, and I'm telling him about you. They don't like it, they can lump it.'

I don't say anything. Derek's not listening, anyway.

We get back to Forrester in record time, and Derek gives me a kiss with the motor running, so I know I just better get out and let him get home. He's been kind of ranting and raving during the trip back, and I know he wants to get it out of his system. I want to say good luck or take it easy or something nice, but everything I think of sounds like a warning, so I just say, 'See ya,' and wave. Derek backs out of the driveway at about seventy miles an hour, then revs his motor and he's gone in a blur of red. I walk inside with a queasy feeling in the pit of my stomach.

Ray is watching television as usual. 'Chicken cutlets,' he says to me.

'Hi, Ray,' I answer. 'How are you?'

'Delicious,' he says.

I go over and check the roster. Robin Farber, serving dinner.

I go on into the kitchen, where Jill and Bart are preparing dinner. I grab the plates, the napkins, the cutlery, lug them out to the dining room and lay them out. Seven place settings. Always seven. What would it be like to have two, with a candelabra in between? I picture two wineglasses and Derek's face on the other side of the table.

'My father went for it,' he says. 'He's giving me everything in my trust funds, and they're insisting on paying for the whole wedding.'

I nod at the vision. 'I knew it would be okay.'

'Bye,' Derek says, and disappears with a pop.

This little scene cheers me up immensely. I go back into the kitchen and help Jill and Bart with the vegetables. I'm even nice to Jill. They're paying for the wedding. Wow.

We sit down to dinner and Debbie asks Louise to say grace. She recites 'Thank you Lord for our daily bread' in a vanishingly little voice, so little that we have to strain our ears to hear. Then we pass around the food. No one talks too much.

Just as I'm bringing in the applesauce, the phone rings. Jill runs over to the living room. I hear, 'Hello?' then a shouted 'Robin, it's your boyfriend!'

I drop the bowl of applesauce in the centre of the table and run out.

'Boy, is he ever upset!' Jill tells me with a Melissa smile as she passes me the phone.

Oh, no. I pick up the phone, say, 'Derek?' in a voice as small as Louise's.

The words are just running on and on. It's like he never even heard me. Maybe he thought I was still Jill.

'Derek!' I shout into the phone. 'It's me, Robin!'

'Yeah, I know it's you. I've just been talking to you,' he babbles.

'Start again. Tell me what happened.'

'I just told you. Father said no. Not over his dead body will he give me my trust funds early. Told me that all I had ever proved to him is that I'm not ready to spend my money. Then he gave me a few more shots about how my judgment is poor, and to remember that time when I thought I was controlling the universe from the roof of the house. I tried to tell him I was sick, and now I'm better, even though that isn't really true, because he's dead set against my getting any more treatment, so how could I improve? Anyway, he says he doesn't see any improvement, and no, he's not giving in to my getting married, what do I think he is, an idiot? Then he said some bad things about you, but I'm not going to tell you what they are …'

'Derek!' I shout into the phone. 'Slow down.'

I don't think he hears me, because he just rambles on. 'And then I said that I was, too, going to marry you. That you were the best thing that had ever happened to me, and he says then I can do it with my own money, that if I marry you, I will never get another cent from him. I say, it's Mother's money, but he says, "I'm the one around here who manages the money." Fine, I say. I don't want your stinking money, and I left.'

'Where are you, Derek?'

'I'm in the car. I'm almost there. Wait for me outside.'

'Okay,' I say. 'Just calm down. Don't speed.'

'Yeah, yeah,' he says, and the phone cuts out.

By now everyone has finished their applesauce and is waiting with bated breath for me to finish the story that Jill has begun. I go back to the table and ask that I be excused.

'You want to talk?' Louise squeaks.

'No, thank you. I'm going to wait for Derek outside.'

'Ten o'clock curfew,' Jill calls, as I cross to the door.

'Take a jacket,' Debbie says.

So this is what a group is. Not a pin cushion, but something warm and fuzzy, like a blanket.

I run out into the night without a jacket. It's early May, but it's still cool at night. I stand there shivering for a few minutes, staring up at a flock of geese silhouetted against a full moon. Honk, honk, honk, I hear after they pass. The sound comes after the light, like thunder follows lightning. Suddenly, the door opens, and Jill comes out with my white sweater.

'Thanks,' I try to tell her, but my voice doesn't come out.

She pats me on the shoulder, and goes back in.

Derek Derek. Please let him be okay. Banana-fana Fo Ferrick. I'll do anything. Please Please. I'll take my pills forever. Mi-my-mo Merrick. Derek.

All at once, I see a blur of red screeching around the corner, racing down the road, dashing up the driveway where it stops with a lurch.

'Robin!' Derek shouts and jumps out. He's got that angry, happy smirk on his face.

'Robin,' he says, grabbing me in his arms. 'Robin,' he says again, his lips starting at my lips, then wandering all the way down my neck. 'Robin.'

A shivery feeling goes all the way down my spine. It doesn't matter what his father said. Everything is all right. Let everything be all right.

'Let's get in the car,' Derek says. 'It's cold out here.'

I think we're just going to sit in the driveway and talk, but the moment we get in, Derek starts the motor.

'Where are we going?' I ask.

'Anywhere,' he answers, revving the motor. 'Nowhere.'

'I want us to talk,' I say.

'There's been enough talk,' Derek says, pulling out of the driveway.

The car seems to drive itself, up one street, down another, gliding down dark streets till we reach the pond. In the moonlight, it looks romantic, not the goose-infested swamp it is. Derek pulls the car under a tree, and shuts off the motor. In a minute, he has my blouse off and my bra unhooked. It's hard making love in the bucket seats of a Miata, but it happens fast and urgent, and, I don't know, maybe it's the extra element of pain from the gearshift digging into our backs, but we reach a moment I never reached with Derek before. He's got me pinned down in the seat, Derek in me so deep, it's like he's going to come out the other side. The two of us at exactly the same infinitesimal point in space, smaller than the head of a pin: a zero-point energy field where everything shrinks to a vanishing point, and there's no telling where I stop and where Derek begins.

Suddenly, *part of a couple* makes sense. Once you've both been to that same infinitesimal place, you're back before the Big Bang, and there's only one thing. There's no two or sixty or five thousand. You're one and the same. You're parts of the same whole. I am he and he is me, and now, no matter what comes of us after that: dead or alive, here or there, up or down, top or bottom, charmed or strange, we're connected.

We sit under the honking moon and Derek tells me he doesn't care about anyone else but me, and that he's moving out as soon as he can get his stuff together, and then we'll get married, and drive off someplace exotic and buy a hardware store and name it Robin and Derek's. Finally, he takes me back to Forrester's, where he gives me one last kiss, and drives away at a million miles an hour.

Chapter Nine

Debbie is shaking me, yelling, 'Telephone! Telephone!' in my ear. It's one of those dreams where nothing makes any sense, so I'm not going to be tricked. I try to turn over, but the sunlight is seeping in under my eyes, and when I open one to check, Debbie really is standing there, yelling, 'Telephone! Telephone!'

She hands me the portable phone before I'm even awake, and leaves the room. Derek's voice comes loud and clear out of the receiver.

'Derek?' I say. What time is it? Why is he calling two minutes after I said goodbye?

'I had an accident,' Derek's voice says.

'What?' I ask. I picture the Miata lying smashed by the side of the road.

'I totalled the Miata.'

'Oh, no!' The dead Miata upsets me so much, I don't think to ask how he is.

'I'm pretty much okay.'

'I'm glad you're okay.'

'I broke my leg and spit out a few teeth.'

'No!'

A voice I haven't heard for a long time says, Yes.

'But they set my leg in the hospital, and I'm home,' he says.

'You're not moving out then.'

'Not for six weeks, anyway.'

I can hear something in his voice. Not in the words, just the voice. 'You okay?'

'Yeah, sure.'

'Don't kid me.' Feels like some of my powers are coming back.

'I'm all right … just a little depressed.'

'Uh-oh,' I say.

'Robin, don't you think it's natural to be low if you total your car?'

'I don't want to hear you're depressed. Take your pills.'

'What pills?' Derek asks.

'Didn't your mother get you some pills?'

Derek snickers. 'Those? They're long gone.'

Long gone, says the voice.

'Someone's here. Gotta go,' Derek says. 'Love you. Bye.'

'Love you. Bye.'

I'm on my way to Berkshire. I look out the window, but instead of seeing trees and flowers, I see dead Miatas and broken legs. Debbie asked me what was wrong. I told her Derek had been in an accident, but he's all right. She said he seems like a very wild guy, and that he's lucky to be alive. I told her that he's not a wild guy, he's just bipolar and to mind her own business.

Calm down, calm down, calm down. Don't think, don't think, don't think. You took your pills. You'll be all right.

Will you? asks a voice.

Shut up, you don't even exist, I tell it.

For the moment, that stops it, but I have a feeling it will be back.

'Berkshire!' the driver shouts.

I stand up and move toward the front. Down the stairs. Down the path. Past the bush. Don't think, don't think. You'll be all right.

Whitecoat's reading a newspaper. He folds it up when I come in.

'Derek was in an car accident,' I tell him before I even sit down.

'No! Is he all right?'

'Yes. He broke his leg.'

'That's all?'

'He says he's depressed.'

'I'm glad you told me, Robin. I'll see if I can call his mother.'

I knew she wouldn't last, I hear.

She'll be in and out from now on.

'What?' I can't hear him so well against the hum of voices.

'I said I'll see if I can call his mother,' Whitecoat says. He leans in closer. 'Are you all right?'

She'll probably end up back here.

'They're saying bad things about me,' I say.

Whitecoat jots down something on his pad. 'What are they saying?'

'That I won't last. I'll end up back in Berkshire.'

'It's the stress of Derek being in the accident. That's all it is.' He takes out his prescription pad and writes something on it.

Is that all it is? the voice says.

'They won't shut up. Make them shut up.'

'Robin, calm down. I'm writing you out a prescription. We'll just up your dosage.'

'Now they're laughing at me,' I say.

Whitecoat rips off the top sheet and hands it to me. 'I want you to give this to the administrator at your home to have filled.'

'Debbie,' I say, taking the sheet and stuffing it into my mini-pak.

'Okay, remember to give it to Debbie,' Whitecoat says.

She won't remember, the voice laughs.

'I will!' I say out loud.

'Who are you talking to, Robin?' Whitecoat asks.

'Him.'

'Well, go ahead and tell him that you are going to ignore him from now on.'

'He'll punish me.'

'There's nothing he can do to you, remember that.'

I'll punish Derek, the voice says.

Whitecoat is looking at me with my mother's look. 'Will you be all right on the bus today, Robin?'

'Yeah. All right,' I say.

'Then go straight home, and ask Debbie to get the prescription filled.'

'Okay.'

Whitecoat walks me to the door, squeezes my hand. 'Go straight home.'

'I want to stay here,' I wail.

'You're just feeling the stress of Derek's accident,' Whitecoat says. 'You don't need Berkshire any more.'

I'm going to hurt Derek, says the voice.

Derek doesn't call me any more, but he e-mails me through my teeth. Maybe his Father cut off the phone. He's a big jerk; he doesn't know how connected we are. It started in the bus on the way home. Right from the moment I climbed the stairs, I could hear him loud and clear, straight from his bedroom.

Buzz, buzz, buzz. Hey, Robin! I'm fine. The leg's in a big cast, and I can't move around, but Mankiewicz called me this very morning, and says he'll be coming to me, starting tomorrow. So, hey! Don't worry about me. I'll be all right. Derek.

This comes as a great relief. I can't tell you how worried I was for him. I pictured him getting into that fetal thing he does, all scrunched up except for his leg, which, of course, can't be scrunched right now, and going lower and lower and lower. But Derek's okay, so I don't have to worry any more.

By the time I got back, I realized that I didn't need the extra prescription. The voices haven't gone away, but since Derek told me he's okay, they're being nice to me again, so I really don't see why I should medicate myself to the point of stupor. I hate that stuff. So, I took the prescription and crumpled it up and threw it in the trash can at the bus station.

Debbie took one look at me when I came in, and saw that I was all right.

'Feeling better?' she asked.

'Yeah,' I said.

'Sorry what I said about your friend. I didn't know he was bipolar. Next time he comes, ask him to dinner. Bart always makes too much, anyway.'

'Thanks,' I said, walked up to my room, lay down on Grandma's quilt. Just in time.

Buzz, buzz, buzz. Hi, Robin. Just got home? It's really boring here. Mother went out to get me a computer game. Well, really, a head game. I mean, I don't need a computer any more, do I? Haha. Love, Derek.

Dear Derek, How do you play the game? Be careful shooting aliens in your head. Love, Robin.

Buzz, buzz, buzz. You're right. I shot an alien in my head, and almost exploded my cerebellum, haha. By the way, Mother says not to worry. Almost all the property is in her name, and when my leg is healed, she's going to mortgage the house and give me the proceeds to pay for our wedding. So, don't worry, everything is copacetic! Love, Derek.

Dear Derek, Your mother is great. I'd ask my mother to help me arrange the wedding, except she's a little funny that way. I don't think she believes we can talk like this. So, I'll have to wait until I see you, and then we can do the guest list. What do you think of an all-black colour scheme?

Love, Robin.

* * *

The next two weeks are good, really good. Whitecoat didn't even ask me whether I had had the prescription filled. He just took one look at me and saw I was happy, and assumed I had. Bad assumption. Told him the voices were still there but no problem, and he assumed (ha) that it was the medication. Whitecoat really has delusions of grandeur. Physician, heal thyself!

Four weeks to go until Derek gets his cast off. I can't wait.

I don't dare tell him about airmailing Derek. I know what his reaction would be, and I really don't see why I should have to deal with Whitecoat's singular lack of imagination. I mean, where's the problem here? Derek and I have powers he can't even imagine. We're so connected, that one of us thinks one thing, and the other automatically knows what it is. It's simple quantum mechanics, but go try to explain that to Whitecoat.

Mother and Howard are here today. They can't seem to get over how much better I am.

'Robin, I've really been thinking this over for a long time,' Howard says. 'And I think it's time you got a job. Jill has been working for quite a while, haven't you, Jill?'

Jill is sitting on her bed, pretending to read a book, but it's just totally obvious she's listening, because she looks up the moment her name is mentioned. 'A year and a half,' she says.

'Are there any positions open there?' Howard asks.

'No.'

Hey, I don't blame her. I wouldn't want to work with her, either.

'What about All-mart?' Howard asks me. Without waiting for an answer, he adds, 'I'm sure Melissa could put in a good word for you.'

'I don't want to work with Melissa,' I say.

'She's leaving in four months,' Howard reminds me.

'Yeah, well.' I fiddle with a loose thread in Grandma's quilt.

'Think about it,' Howard says, being magnanimous. Then he can't help himself and says, 'But not too long.'

'Okay, I'll think about it,' I tell Howard, and he's happy.

You know, it's really not so hard to make people happy. It takes a little extra effort, not much. The thing to remember is that everyone has something he wants. Let them think that you're doing that, and they'll go away happy. Mankiewicz wants me to take my pills. My mother wants me to be friends with everyone. Howard wants me to come home and get a job. No one wants to hear that Derek and I communicate faster-than-the-speed-of-light. No one *ever* wants to know that Father talks to me from beyond the grave. Tell them it's all just quantum mechanics, and they'll look at you as if you're the crazy one. I say, let them believe what they want to believe. Then they're happy.

'How's Derek?' Mother asks. Debbie told her what happened.

'He's okay. He gets the cast off in four weeks.'

'Good. I have nothing against him. I'm glad he's going to be all right,' she says. Then, a minute later she says, 'But don't ever get in a car with that boy again, Robin. He's a menace.'

'Yes, Mother.'

I let them leave with smiles on their faces, and go down to help prepare lasagna with Bart. He shows me how to cook the noodles and lay them out in the pan, layer them with ground beef in sauce, and mozzarella cheese. It's not hard if you know how to do it. Bart tells me he was a cook in a restaurant before he had the lobotomy, that he can still cook all those things he used to cook. That he's still the same, really, better, maybe. He used to have all these violent rages, but now, they're gone. So, he doesn't know what people are all going on about. His sister cries whenever she sees him. Bart shrugs. He's fine. Maybe it's the other people who aren't.

I tell him I know just what he means. There's nothing wrong with me. It's all the other people in the world who think there is. And that's their problem.

Bart nods and sprinkles the lasagna with parmesan cheese. 'I hear ya,' he says.

'Have you seen Derek?' I ask Whitecoat two days later. He should have seen him half a dozen times by now.

'No,' Whitecoat replies. 'But I talked to his mother earlier this week.'

'How is he?' I'm asking a leading question. I know he's fine. I wonder, though, why Whitecoat didn't see him when he was supposed to.

Whitecoat hasn't even opened his mouth, yet. Finally, he says, 'He's not well, Robin.'

'What do you mean?' I yell. 'He's fine. He told me, himself.'

'You talked to him?' Whitecoat asks in surprise.

'Well, I …' I can't say this, I can't say that. 'Last week.'

'Well, maybe he was better that day. His mother says he's severely depressed.'

'But …' I don't know what to say, really. It doesn't matter, because Whitecoat is not finished.

'Ever since the accident, he's been unable to get himself out of bed.'

'I thought he was playing video games.'

'Where did you get that idea, Robin? He can't even telephone.'

'But why aren't you seeing him?'

'His mother says Derek's father forbids it, and she won't go against his wishes.'

'But if you talked to Derek …'

'I left word that he should call me. He hasn't.'

This is totally puzzling. I don't understand it. Why would Derek lie to me like that? He loves me. We're going to get married. Why would he lie to me? I suddenly picture Derek in my room that one time, reading Jill's letters and smelling her perfume. Maybe he loves Jill, not me. I can't stand it. I've got to talk to him.

'I've got to go,' I say, standing up.

'But you haven't had your session,' Whitecoat protests.

'I've got to go.'

Whitecoat gets this funny expression on his face. 'Robin, I hope you're not going to Derek's house.'

'How could I?' I say. 'I don't know where it is.'

'Good. Then tell me what it is you're feeling.'

Feelings. He's always going on about feelings. 'No.'

'Robin, I don't like what I'm hearing.'

'So, don't listen,' I say.

'Robin.' It's like he's threatening me, but he doesn't have anything to threaten me with.

'I'm just going to talk to him. That's all.'

'He won't answer the phone.'

'I'll get through.'

Whitecoat looks at me curiously. 'If you get through, tell me how he is,' he finally says. 'His mother told me not to call any more.'

'Why?' I ask. What's wrong with her? His mother was going to mortgage her house to pay for our wedding.

'Derek doesn't want to talk to me,' Whitecoat said, swivelling to face away from me.

'That's what *she* says.'

'That's what *she* says. I don't know what Derek says. I can't get through to him.'

'It'll be okay,' I assure him. Now, I'm the doctor.

'I hope so,' Whitecoat says, swivelling back.

'I've got to go,' I announce, and leave before he can say anything else.

Outside, I contact Derek right away.

Derek, what's going on? Whitecoat says you're depressed. That he hasn't been seeing you at all. Are you lying to me?

Buzz,buzz. No, of course not. I'm okay. He doesn't need to come. It's as simple as that.

Derek.

He says your mother told him not to call any more. That you don't want to talk to him. Robin.

Buzz. What are you talking about? Tell you what. I'll call him. That should take care of this whole misunderstanding. Derek.

Good, do that. He wants to hear from you. Love, Robin

There. I knew this was all Whitecoat's fault.

'Did you talk to him?' Whitecoat asks as soon as I sit down a couple of days later.

'Yes,' I say.

'His mother answered?'

'Uh, no. Derek called me, himself.'

'Really? Well, that's very good. How is he?'

'Better.'

'Did he say he was depressed?'

'He said, "Don't you think it's natural to be low if you total your car?"'

Whitecoat laughs. 'That sounds fine. I didn't even think he'd talk to you.'

We drop the subject of Derek and get back to me, which is what Howard is paying him to talk about. Whitecoat thinks the job is a good idea. He thinks I'm smart enough to do a job at All-mart with my eyes closed. 'But don't keep your eyes closed,' he says with a laugh. 'Look the people in the eye. Don't stare into the corner the way you do with me.'

'I'll think about it,' I say, staring into the corner.

Just about then, I get a buzzing in my teeth.

Not now, Derek, I'm talking to Whitecoat, I say.

Buzz,buzz, it continues. There's no voice, just an empty feeling.

Is that you, Derek? I ask.

Buzz, yes. Depressed.

Derek? I ask, but he's gone.

'Robin?' I hear. 'Robin?'

It sounds like Whitecoat. I look up.

'What was that?' he asks.

'What?'

'You were in your own world there for about five minutes.'

I shrug. 'Sorry.'

'Nothing to be sorry about. Who were you talking to?'

Damn, this guy knows me too well.

'Derek,' I say. I look him straight in the eye. 'I've got a bad feeling, Dr Mankiewicz.'

It may have been the 'Mankiewicz' that got to him, or the eye contact, I don't know which. But he starts dialling up Derek's number just like that. Like he believes me, for God's sake. It must be ringing four, five times by the way he's waiting, fingers drumming on the desk. Finally, Whitecoat hangs up. 'Just a phone message, saying they're not there right now.'

He's acting sheepish, because he suddenly realizes that he acted impulsively, exactly like one of his patients would have. And because he believed me. Me. The girl who talks through the air.

'So,' Whitecoat coughs. 'What were we saying?'

'I don't know.'

We both sit there for a few minutes, in silent prayer.

It's Sunday, and I'm feeling down. Derek hasn't been here for three weeks. I miss the coffee shop we went to where we kissed over a banana slice. I miss the pond with the goose that took a dump on our blanket. I miss the Miata, where we experienced the universe. I miss Derek, especially Derek. I haven't heard from him since Wednesday, not even in my teeth.

Suddenly, I can feel the telltale buzz. Buzz, buzz.

Yes, yes, hello? Derek?

I'm here.

Who? I ask. Father?

Yes, dear. How are you?

I'm okay. I thought you were Derek.

No. Are you disappointed?

No. Yes. I guess. I love you Father, but I'm a little worried about Derek.

I know. He totalled the Miata.

Yes, and I don't know whether he's depressed or not.

He *is* depressed. You better talk to him.

I'm trying! I'm trying! He won't call me back.

Try again, dear. It's getting late. Well, gotta go. Off to Zanzibar.

So soon?

Can't keep the crew waiting. Bye.

He's gone. I wallow in Derek sickness for a while. Why do men always leave?

Buzz, buzz in my teeth. Yes? Derek?

Robin. I love you. Derek.

Derek! Derek? Where are you? Derek!

Robin, I love you. I have to go. For eternity, Derek.

No! No! Don't go! Don't go! I love you, Derek. Where are you going?

There's a physical feeling of pain, then a release from pain. Then a feeling of wide-open space and an eternity of time. Then, whoosh, and end of connection. Empty air.

OhmyGod, I think. He did it. He's dead. Mi-my-mo Merrick. Derek.

All I can do is lie in bed. I'm on the roster for something, but no one can rouse me. Jill tries to get me up, but I hit her in the head. Debbie comes upstairs, panting, and can't do a thing with me. Go away. There's nothing to live for. Nothing. Nada. Zilch. Gornisht.

The next morning Debbie comes up again, sits on my bed.

'I want you to get up. You have an appointment with Dr Mankiewicz at eleven today. He'll help you.'

'No one can help me,' I whisper, eyes closed.

'But, why, Robin? What's wrong?'

'Derek's dead. I can feel it.'

She sighs, like she expected this. 'Robin, this is not true. You are ill. Sometimes you hear things and feel things that just aren't real. Your mother told me how you were so sure your sister's fiancé was going to marry you. It wasn't true, now, was it?'

Shock treatment. This may work on other people, but it doesn't work on me. 'That was different,' I say, opening my eyes.

'No, it isn't,' Debbie says. 'Robin, I want you to go to Dr Mankiewicz.'

Maybe she's right. Maybe I'm crazy like they all say, and Derek's sitting up in bed playing video games. 'I'm calling Derek first,' I say.

'Okay. You have the number?'

I sit up for the first time. 'In my drawer.'

Debbie hoists herself up, crosses to the desk. 'This?' she asks, waving a piece of paper.

'Yes.'

By now, I'm up. I grab the paper from her grasp. Still in my clothes from yesterday, I pad downstairs to the living room, Debbie way behind me. I dial the number slowly, and it rings. Rings again. Rings two more times, then a phone message in Derek's father's voice comes on saying this is the Wineker residence no one is there right now, please leave a message at the beep. Beep! 'Is anyone there?' I yell into the phone. 'This is Robin, is Derek all right?' Nothing. Nada. Zilch. Gornisht. The line cuts off.

'Go see Dr Mankiewicz,' Debbie says again, coming up behind me.

I drop onto the couch, put the pillow over my head. Derek! I shout to the universe, but the universe isn't talking.

Debbie comes back with a glass of orange juice in her right hand, her left a closed fist. 'Take these,' she says, opening her left hand to reveal my morning pills.

I take the pills, drink a little juice. 'Thank you,' I croak.

'You'll see. I'm sure Derek's all right.'

Debbie walks me to the bus station and puts me on the bus just like she did the first time.

The bus circles through its route. I sit like a lump in the seat, calling out to him in my head.

Derek? Derek? Where are you?

'Berkshire!' The driver announces and I get off. Down the path, past the bush, up stairs, and into the main building. Everything the same, and not the same. Just outside Whitecoat's office.

'Come in!' Whitecoat calls to me with a gravelly voice. He's facing the wall. Everything the same, but not the same.

To his back, I say, 'Hello.' Whitecoat swivels to face me. The moment I see his face, I know something is wrong. God, let it be Rachel Ellen. Martin. Abigail. I don't care. Not Derek.

'What?' I ask.

He doesn't say anything for a moment. I notice that his hands aren't doing that steeple-thing they used to do. They're gripping the desk, all white at the knuckles.

'Is it Rachel Ellen?' I ask.

Whitecoat shakes his head, swallows. 'Robin, I've got some bad news.'

I can read his mind, and he's saying loud and clear, that there's something wrong with Derek, it's very bad, it's so bad.

'Oh, my God, it's Derek,' I say.

He nods, swallows again.

'Yesterday,' I say.

'Yes.'

'It's bad?' I ask.

'Yes.' Whitecoat's struggling with something that he doesn't want to say. Don't tell me, then.

We sit there like that for half a minute, neither one of us talking, and the air sparkles with potentiality. Don't ask, don't tell. Derek's dead, but he's not dead, if I don't ask. Like Schrödinger's cat, he's dead and alive at the same time. Until I know for sure, Derek's alive. Don't tell me. Don't tell me. It's the telling that will make him dead.

Suddenly, Whitecoat takes a big breath and says, 'Last night, Derek crawled out on the roof in his parents' home and jumped off.'

'No!' I shout.

He continues, almost like I'm not there. 'He broke his neck on impact.'

'Dead,' I say, examining the minute patterns in the carpet.

Whitecoat nods, both hands gripping the desk.

'Why.'

'He left a note saying that he didn't want to live. He said he loved you, Robin.'

'The note.'

'His parents have it.'

'Bastards,' I say. 'You're all bastards.'

'You know how sorry I am,' Whitecoat rasps.

'No, you aren't!' I yell. He says he cares, but he doesn't care. All he does is talk and give us pills. And then he goes home to his precious Rachel Ellen. 'You don't care. You don't care. I hate you,' I shout as I fall off the little, hard seat onto the rug, burying my face in the old wool.

'Robin, I loved Derek as if he were my own son,' Whitecoat says, in a kind of choked voice. He stands up, like he's going to come over to me, but then he sits down again and covers his eyes. 'We're not supposed to get involved, but I always do. My wife tells me time and time again....'

Then he gives a little cry and swivels his chair toward the wall.

Damn Derek. Why did he have to do this to us?

I lift my head out of the pile and say, 'He didn't love me enough. If he loved me enough, he wouldn't have done it.'

'Love had nothing to do with it,' Whitecoat says, his back to me.

You caused it, a voice says.

'It's not my fault,' I say.

'Of course it's not your fault,' Whitecoat says.

'I told him not to come,' I answer from the floor.

'Not to come where?' Whitecoat asks, swivelling back. His eyes are red.

'The wedding. I told him not to come. His father took him. Not my fault.'

Whitecoat is looking at me funny from across the desk. 'Robin. I want you to calm down.'

'Calm down,' I say.

'Yes. Get up off the rug.'

I get up off the rug and sit down in the little seat, but my heart isn't in it. My heart is far away, wherever Derek is.

'Did you know this was going to happen?' he asks.

You knew it. You caused it, the same voice says.

Stop it. It wasn't my fault. It was Derek's own fault.

'Robin? Did you hear me?'

'No. Yes. He told me yesterday.'

'You called him?'

'Called him today. Wasn't home.'

Annoyance comes and goes on Whitecoat's face. 'When was the last time you talked to him, Robin?' he asks.

'Sunday. Told me goodbye.'

'Told you goodbye,' Whitecoat repeats. 'Then ... you knew?'

I look up, and I realize he doesn't have a clue. 'Not by phone. But I knew.'

Whitecoat looks at me dumbly. 'Oh, Robin,' he says, then, shaking his head. O'Robin.

We wait a few minutes, just sitting there.

'If it was anybody's fault, it was mine,' Whitecoat confesses. 'I shouldn't have let his father take him. I should have insisted he get continuing treatment.'

'His father said no.'

'I know. But I should have tried. Talked to his mother.'

Your fault, his fault, Derek's fault, the voice says.

'Stop it! Stop it! It's no one's fault!' I scream.

I don't know what I'm doing. I think I fell to the floor again. The voices are the little devils, the anti-matter of the universe. They keep picking at people, picking at them, until they break; they make bad things happen to good people. Oh, Derek? Why? Why?

Why not? the voice asks.

Goddamned devils. When you think how much energy it takes to keep the universe in good running order, and then they throw in a pinch of chaos, and ruin the whole thing.

Whitecoat is standing over me. He leans down and grabs my hands, holding them so tightly it hurts. 'It's no one's fault,' he says. 'It's just the way of the world.'

And that's the last thing I remember.

Chapter Ten

It's dark and I'm lying on a bed: not tied down, just lying on top. Thin strands of moonlight filter through the window, illuminating a lump in the next bed. The unoiled wheels of a cart: squeaky, squawky, Squeaky, Squawky, Squeaky, Squawky, come to a stop outside the room. The door opens with a blaze of light from the hall, and a dark silhouette pads towards me.

'Well, well. Couldn't stay away, could you?' He smiles, one tooth missing.

'Hello, Alex,' I whisper. 'What am I doing here?'

'Don't remember, do you? You blacked out in Dr Mankiewicz's office. Martin brought you here, back to your old room.'

'I didn't bite him, did I?'

'Who, Martin? I don't think so.'

'Good. I never really meant to hurt him. Martin isn't so bad.'

I point to the lump in the next bed. Beverly?'

'Yeah. He smiles again. 'Jes' like old times, isn't it?'

'Am I here to stay?'

'Till you're better, I guess.'

Beverly moans, turns over.

'Ssh,' Alex whispers. 'Just checking in on you. Go back to sleep.'

He pads out the door, closing it slowly, and the light retreats with him.

I remember coming into Whitecoat's office and falling on the rug. Can't remember any more. What the hell. I turn over and go back to sleep.

'I think you'd better stay here for a few days,' Whitecoat says the next day in his office. 'Till you feel well enough to go back to the group home.'

'I'm okay.'

'It was too much to take in in one day, even for a normal person.'

A normal person, a voice says.

'But you look better today,' Whitecoat adds.

'Yeah.' I feel a little bedraggled. Benighted. Bewitched, bothered, and bewildered. Like I was in a fight. There's something I'm supposed to remember but can't.

'The funeral is Thursday,' Whitecoat says.

Funeral, funeral. Ohmygod. Derek Derek Bo-berrick. Banana-fana-fo Ferek. Mi-my-mo Merek. Derek.

'I want to go,' I murmur.

'His father wants a very private affair. Just a few relatives,' Whitecoat says.

'I can't go?'

'No.'

'I *did* love Derek.'

'I know.'

Derek is history, a voice says.

Shut up, I tell it. 'I want to talk to my mother.'

'She's coming, Robin. I called her yesterday. She and your stepfather are coming today.'

'Why did Derek do it, Dr Mankiewicz?' I ask.

Whitecoat gives a little start at 'Mankiewicz', but I know that Derek would be pleased. He hated it when I called him 'Whitecoat'. Said it sounded like Frankenstein.

'He must have been in a lot of pain,' he says. 'And he couldn't see anything but pain in the future.'

'But it wouldn't have been just pain. It would have been him and me against the pain. We were a couple.'

Mankiewicz smiles at that. 'I'm sure Derek knew that, Robin.'

'Then why …?'

He shrugged. 'We'll never know.'

'Are you still hearing voices?' he asks after a moment.

There's a hum of voices throughout. They comment on Derek, on me, but Mankiewicz changed the medication, and they don't bother me much. They shut up when I tell them to.

'Yeah, but now I know who's real.'

'That's progress. Some things you may have to learn to live with.'

'Derek couldn't.'

'You can.'

We sit there for a few minutes in silence for Derek.

'Dr Mankiewicz, I think I want to go back to the group home today,' I finally say. 'Howard can drive me there. I'm not hurting your feelings?'

He laughs. 'Don't worry about my feelings. It's yours I'm worried about. You okay?'

'As sane as I'll ever be,' I reply.

Whitecoat smiles, gets up, walks me to the door. 'See you Wednesday.'

Later, Mother and Howard come to take me back.

'I'm sorry about Derek,' Howard says. 'After all, he did save Max, and he sent us all those pictures.' He gives me a peck on the cheek and backs up a few paces to stand against the wall.

'Oh, Howard,' Mother says, and puts her arms around me, crying a little herself. Now that she's here I don't have anything to say to her.

They take me back to Forrester in the car. Mother comes in while Howard stays in the car with the motor running. Bart says, 'Hello,' to both of us; Debbie comes over, looks at me hard to see how I've taken it.

'Okay,' I keep telling everyone. 'I'm okay.' I must look like shit, that everybody's staring so much.

Mother walks me upstairs to an empty room and has trouble saying goodbye. I know she wants to comfort me, but I don't know how to be comforted. It's been so long I've been comforting myself, I can't accept it from anyone else. Especially Mother, who's got a subtext underneath every consolation. How many times has she told me it's okay to lose? Failure *is* an option, that says to me. Her consolation is awarding me the consolation prize: the Biggest Loser Award. She's not comforting me; she's telling me she doesn't believe in me.

When she's finally gone, it feels good to be alone. I don't want to be with anyone but me. I'm not really okay: there's a big hole where Derek used to be, like the hole in your ear after the earring comes out. What's to put in it but another earring? But I don't have another earring, at least not one as brilliant and sparkly as Derek was. I'm not the same without Derek. The two of us made one thing, and now I'm only half. I want to be whole again.

Suddenly, I hear, 'Hey, Robin! How's my girl doing?' I look around, see nothing.

'How soon they forget,' the same voice says. The voice is like Derek's but with a metallic echo, like it's coming from a long tunnel.

'Derek?' I ask.

'Who else?'

'Where *are* you?'

'Well, that's a silly question coming from someone who said she was God.'

I smile, even though there's no one to see me do it. 'I'm not.'

'I know, but I love you anyway.'

'Then why did you do it, Derek?'

'Shit happens,' I hear, and he's gone with a whoosh.

I don't know if he's coming back or anything. There are so many things I had to say. I lie face down on Grandma's quilt and cry till there's a big wet spot on the poplin square under my face.

Later, I get a call from Melissa.

'How're you doing?' she announces, like nothing's happened since I last talked to her. No wedding, no Derek jumping off the roof.

'I'm okay,' I answer. 'How are you?'

'Fine.'

There's a silence on the line until Melissa finally decides to speak again.

'I heard about Derek.'

I'm getting so tired of this. 'Yeah, you and everyone.'

'Well, I wanted to know how you are.'

'I'm okay. I just told you that.'

A minute of silence, then, 'You know I'm pregnant.'

With Max's baby, I think. 'Mom told me.'

'You sound pretty good, Robby. Sad, but good.'

'Mankiewicz gave me some new pills.'

Another minute of silence, then, 'What are you doing with yourself?'

'Nothing. Thursday I see the doctor.'

'That's all?' Melissa asks.

'Yeah, I don't have your exciting life.'

Minute of silence. 'I don't think you should be sitting around like that, moping.'

'I'm not moping. I'm grieving.'

'Whatever. How about I see if I can get you an interview where I work?'

'All-mart?' I snicker.

'Well, it's not as if you can pick and choose, you know,' Melissa replies.

'All-mart,' I say, testing the syllables on my tongue.

'So, are you interested or not?'

Somehow, this sounds familiar. So, are you going to be my maid of honour or not? 'I don't know,' I murmur.

'Yes, or no. I don't have that much time.'

Yes no yes no yes no. 'Yes,' I say.

'Okay. I'll get back to you tonight. Bye.'

The phone goes dead.

That night, Melissa calls back.

'I've got you an interview tomorrow at two,' she says.

'Tomorrow!' I repeat.

'Howard is coming for you at one,' Melissa replies.

'But, tomorrow!' I say again.

'Is that all you can say, Robin? You know all the trouble I went to to get you this interview?'

I blubber something about not knowing what to do in an interview.

'She'll ask you questions about yourself. You answer them.'

'What's the job?' I ask.

'Display,' Melissa answers. 'You dress up dummies and make them look good.'

'Dress up dummies?' I repeat.

Melissa sounds exasperated. 'It's simple. It's like dressing a doll. You have anything to wear?'

'The black sleeveless dress,' I say.

'No! No! No!' Melissa cries. 'You think you're going to a cocktail party? No, wear a skirt with a matching blouse.'

I think I'm going to be sick. I can't even dress myself. How am I going to dress some dumb dummy?

None of this seems to occur to Melissa, who blithely goes on talking. 'I'll meet you at the entrance, quarter to two. Just be yourself. You'll be fine.'

'Fine,' I say, but I'm just repeating what my sister said.

Hey! a voice says, the moment I hang up. My heart jumps.

Derek? I ask.

You expecting someone else? the voice asks.

No, no, I say. How are you?

What, is this a phone call? Derek says. Hello, how are you? You know how I am. Dead.

Dead and alive, I can't help thinking. A superposition of states.

No, he says. Just dead.

I miss you, I say.

I'm not going anywhere. What's this about an interview?

Melissa got me one. At All-mart.

All-mart? Derek's voice says. You really want to work at All-mart?

Yeah, I've got to start somewhere.

Well, break a leg, Derek says.

That gets me thinking. Did your leg ever heal, Derek? You know, from the accident?

No. But it doesn't make any difference now. I'm feeling *no pain*, let me tell you.

I'm glad, I say. Good night, Derek.

Night, Robin.

Chapter Eleven

So, Howard picks me up at one. I come down dressed in my brown corduroy skirt, Jill's white silk blouse, and Margaret's brown and white scarf. Jill said I had to be accessorized, so here I am: a real-life display dummy.

Howard, in the driveway, whistles. 'Very nice,' he says as I climb into the Buick.

'Thank you,' I say. He starts the motor.

Howard tells me it's just luck that he can take today off, that if I get the job, I'll have to make other arrangements. He starts telling me some convoluted story about how he traded time with somebody else in the office, but I'm not listening. I'm lost in a fog of fear and dread. Interview? I hardly know you.

Suddenly, I hear,

You can do it, dear.

Father? I ask. It could be anybody, really. I'm like a big radio receiver. Turn my dial and receive Radio Zanzibar.

It's me. Who else would it be? Father asks.

Derek. I thought it might be Derek.

Ah. No, but I can get him for you, if you like.

No. That's all right, I tell him. I want to talk to you.

You don't want to talk to me? another voice interrupts.

Derek?

Yeah, it's me.

She said she didn't want to talk to you right now, Father says.

Well, *excuse* me. I heard my name.

This is all very confusing. Don't do this, I tell them. One at a time.

Okay, Derek says. I'll come back later. Whoosh.

I sigh. Fear and dread and too many people.

'You okay?' Howard asks.

'What?' I say, my head turning toward the sound.

'I just asked you if you were okay.'

'Yeah.'

Don't worry, Father says.

'Please!' I say out loud.

'Please what?' Howard asks, turning toward me.

'Please let's not talk,' I say in a small voice.

'Well, sure, if that's what you want,' Howard replies, hurt.

Well, if that's the way you want it, I'm going back to Bombay, Father says and disappears.

Silence for the rest of the trip.

We drive up to a huge building topped with four-foot electric letters spelling out ALL*MART. Howard pulls into a parking space and looks at his watch. 'Sixteen minutes to two,' he says, looking impatient.

We stare at the entrance. No Melissa.

Howard keeps checking his watch every minute. Fifteen to. Fourteen to. Thirteen to. Twelve ...

'You know, even when she was a little girl, Melissa was always la ... There she is!' Howard cries out and leans across me to open my door.

Melissa, in a little blue dress, is coming toward us. She doesn't *look* pregnant. Well, maybe a little. I get out of the car, waving.

Melissa gives me a kiss, leans inside the car to kiss Howard. I hear her say, 'She won't be long. You can come in, if you like.'

Howard doesn't move, so I guess he'll wait for me in the car. Melissa slams the door.

'Let's rock and roll,' she says, smiling.

I look at her as if she's crazy. She looks back the same way. 'You're seeing the merchandising manager,' she says. 'Mrs MacIntosh.'

'Mrs MacIntosh,' I repeat, not moving.

'Let's go,' Melissa says, taking my arm and trying to pull it off.

'Wait,' I say, resisting.

'Whaat?'

'Do I look okay?'

She looks me up and down. 'You'll do,' she says. 'The scarf is a nice touch.'

'Okay.'

We sprint back across the parking lot and into the store: a forest of shoes, VCRS and housewares. Melissa threads her way through an aisle of towels; I hurry along in back, afraid I'll lose sight of her blue dress and die of exposure, my decomposed body finally turning up across from the

Martha Stewart flannel sheets.

You okay to talk now, Robin? I hear.

Later, Derek. I'm running after my sister.

Later, later. It's always later. I thought you loved me.

Please, Derek. Oh, no. I think I've lost her.

No, Derek says. Look. She's right behind Women's Panties.

I run to catch up.

Talk to you later, Derek.

Later. Whoosh.

I follow my sister to the back of the store, where she stops in front of a closed door, looking at her watch.

'Let's go in. It's time.'

'Wait,' I say.

'What now, Robin?' Melissa asks, hands on hips.

'Mrs McGregor?' I ask.

'MacIntosh. Like the raincoat.'

There are voices, not as low as they used to be, telling me not to do this. Derek, I say in my head. Take care of them. I'm going in.

Okay, baby, Derek replies. Suddenly, the voices go down a notch.

I nod to Melissa, who opens the door.

It's a small room carved out of a dressing room. Racks of clothes line three mirrored walls; a woman at a desk sits against the fourth.

'My sister Robin,' Melissa announces, leading me across to the desk. I catch a glimpse in the mirror of a look Melissa used to give me when we were kids, something that says, 'You-better, or-else,' but she's not looking at me.

The woman stands up and extends her hand. She's wearing a suit with a contrasting scarf. 'Hello, Robin.'

'Hello.' I forgot her name. Mac. Raincoat.

'Thanks Melissa,' Mrs MacRaincoat says and motions to a chair. 'Sit down, Robin.'

Melissa slips out the back door. Come back! I want to shout. What's her name?

But Father is here with me. Don't worry, he says.

'Melissa says you've never had a job before,' Mrs MacRaincoat is saying.

'That's right, Mrs …'

MacIntosh, Derek whispers. Tell her you're smart and learn fast.

'MacIntosh. But I'm smart and learn fast.'

The woman smiles. 'Is there anything that leads you to think you'd be good at display work, Robin?'

My mind goes blank. 'Um,' I say.

Say, I was good in art, and I like to accessorize, Derek prompts.

'I was good in art, and I like to accessorize.'

Mrs MacIntosh, he adds.

'Mrs MacIntosh.'

'Well, that's a start.' She looks me over. 'I like your scarf.'

'Thank you. I like yours.'

This is basic suck-up stuff I remember from kindergarten, but Mrs MacIntosh smiles again.

Look her in the eye, Father says, so I do.

She asks me where I went to high school, what I was interested in, how I did. What I've been doing since.

OhmyGod. What I've been doing since.

Finding yourself, Derek prompts.

'I've been ... finding myself,' I say.

'Ah,' Mrs MacIntosh says, rolling her eyes toward the ceiling. 'I have a son like that. Three years he's been finding himself.' Then she turns back to the file on her desk.

Whaddya know, Derek says. She bought it.

'Well, what would you think of coming to work at All-mart, Robin?' she says when she looks up.

I gulp. 'Yes. I'd like that. Thank you, Mrs ...'

MacIntosh, Derek sighs.

'MacIntosh,' I say.

Melissa said she wasn't surprised at all I got the job. That it really would have been hard to screw this thing up, even for me, with all the trouble she had gone to setting it up, but that I did good. Really good. That Mrs MacIntosh said she might have hired me anyway, even if she didn't have to. I don't know what that meant, but I think she meant it as a compliment.

Howard was very happy for me. Kept saying this was the best thing, and, if now, I could only come home to live, it would be closer and much, much cheaper. Derek called Howard an idiot, but really, he's too hard on him.

Anyway, Derek was with me the whole time back in the car, gloating. He takes credit for the whole thing, and, after all, he's right. If it weren't for him, I'd probably have called her Mrs MacRaincoat and told her I've been living in an institution for the past year. Derek said I had a great career ahead of me, but that I needed him to manage me. No contract, he said. He trusted me.

I got back in time for dinner. My name was on the roster to serve, so I ran upstairs to change and came down just in time to bring out the dishes. Everyone's seated; Debbie's saying grace.

I slip into my seat quietly.

'How'd it go?' Jill asks when they're done.

'I got it.'

Applause and clinking of glasses. I go back into the kitchen for the meat loaf.

'When do you start?' Debbie asks when I come back. 'We'll have to work out the bus schedule.'

'Monday.'

I place the meat loaf on the table and begin to dole out the slices.

'How was the outfit?' Jill asks.

'She liked Margaret's scarf.'

Margaret smiles, knocks over her glass of iced tea, and I have to rush into the kitchen for paper towels. I sit down next to Ray. 'My compliments,' he says to me.

We all stare in astonishment that Ray would comment on anything other than food.

'On the meat loaf,' Ray finishes.

We eat in silence, interrupted by Jill who says she sold five pairs of shoes today, by Margaret who tells us she thinks she's coming down with something, and by Ray, who keeps asking for the ketchup.

I get up to clear the dishes and carry them back and forth from the table to the kitchen. At the counter, Ray is pulling off long ribbons of plastic wrap, happily tearing them against the serrated edge, scrunching it all into a wrinkled mess, which Debbie patiently re-stretches over plates of leftovers. Jill soaps and rinses the dishes, handing them down too fast for Louise to dry, one plate clattering to the linoleum floor where it bounces, whirls, and rolls into a corner. Hurray for plastic. The television burbles on, tuned to *Wheel of Fortune*, against a background of voices chattering in my ear. It's all as warm and fuzzy as the night before Christmas. We may be a family of misfits, but for the first time in my life I belong to a group.

Monday. Debbie's walked me to the bus station and put me on the Eatontown bus. I'm dressed in my corduroy skirt, Margaret's tan blouse, and a new pair of brown wedgies that Jill brought back for me from the shoe store. She said it's okay if I pay her next week. We're getting along pretty well these days, I don't know why. Jill says I've changed. That I used to be an argumentative bitch. I say she's changed: she used to be a lying, manipulative jerk. Then we get angry and stop talking to each other until we forget what it was we were arguing about. I still like Louise better.

The bus zooms along. The voices are really loud today, telling each other Robin's going to fail, that she's a stupid idiot who's never had a job. That she doesn't know anything about dressing herself, much less dressing dummies. That she *is* a dummy. They won't listen to me at all, but Derek finally tells them all to shut up, and they do. Men still have more authority when it comes to telling other people off.

OhmyGod. The sign says Eatontown with a big arrow turning right. Here we go. Shut up, you. No, I'm not a dummy. You are.

The bus keeps rolling down the street, despite my telling it to turn around and go back where it came from. It turns right, and pulls up to the curb. There it is: ALL*MART, right across the parking lot. I get up, pull the strap of my purse onto my shoulder and start down the aisle. I'm not listening to you. Shut up, I'm going in, anyway.

Dr Mankiewicz says the voices will go away when I make a life for myself. That until then the medications should make them low enough for me to function. That's what *he* says. Derek says Mankiewicz is full of shit. He's as real as anyone else, Derek says; he's not just a voice, and he's not going anywhere. That dead is not the opposite of real, and Mankiewicz doesn't have a clue how the universe works. Of course, that's not what Derek used to say, but he says he's learned a lot of new things since he's dead. By the way, Derek says to me, you're not God. God is male.

Melissa said I have to go through the back loading dock, whatever that is. I think I'll try the front door, instead.

'Robin!' I hear suddenly. Melissa is standing along the side of the store, pointing to the back.

'Yeah, I'm coming,' I say, and start to walk toward her.

'I told you the back loading dock,' she says as I reach her.

'I don't know what a back loading dock is.'

'*This* is the back loading dock,' she says. We turn a corner and there are a zillion trucks backed into a platform. We climb the stairs on the side and walk into this humungous space, where a dozen guys in baseball hats are unloading big cardboard boxes.

'Hey!' one of them shouts to Melissa. All the guys go for Melissa, even with a potbelly.

'Hey, Bob,' Melissa shouts back, smiling.

'Doesn't he know you're married?' I ask.

Melissa rubs her stomach like it's a magic lamp. 'Of course he does. Bob and I are just friends.'

Melissa always had *friends*, even when she was going steady. I'm not surprised that she still has *friends*. I just wonder if Max knows.

Melissa leads me across the warehouse to a door in the wall. Against the humungousness of the warehouse, this looks like a very little door, an Alice-in-Wonderland sort of door. You need a special key for this kind of door, but Melissa just grabs the doorknob, turns and opens it. Melissa always has the key. She goes inside, and I can see her going down the hallway: she hasn't turned into a white rabbit or anything, so I go, too.

'Close the door behind you!' Melissa shouts from the other end of the hallway. 'It's drafty.'

I close the door behind me.

Following Melissa is like following the white rabbit. Already, she's turning into another door down at the end of the hall, and I have to hurry and catch up with her.

'Come on, already,' I hear from the vicinity of Melissa's hand, waving from inside the threshold.

I walk through the doorway and bump into a dummy wearing a hat and a kilt. The floor is a minefield of shoes. A dozen bald and naked mannequins welcome me with open arms.

'Anybody home?' Melissa calls.

A guy in his mid-twenties, blond hair, black jeans, diamond stud in one ear, steps out from behind a torso. 'Yeah. Oh, hi, Melissa. This our new girl?' His eyes travel automatically from my brown wedgies to my tan blouse, while his mouth puckers.

'Yeah. My sister Robin. Treat her nice.'

'Hmmm. Can't say I see any family resemblance,' he remarks.

Melissa, halfway to the door, says, 'Yeah, well.'

Thanks for defending me, Melissa. 'We've got different genes,' I say.

He laughs, puts a limp hand out. 'Greg. Welcome to display, Robin.'

Do I shake this or kiss it? I shake it.

Melissa goes out.

'You ever work in display?' Greg asks.

I shake my head, no.

A slight roll of the eyes tells me Greg wouldn't have picked me for his assistant. Oh, well.

'C'mon,' he sighs. 'I'll show you the store.'

We retrace our steps out into the hallway, but go out the other side. The door opens into a Wonderland of children's clothes. Greg keeps going till the aisle, where a child mannequin is standing. 'Next week they're promoting back-to-school. We'll probably dress her in a corduroy skirt and white shirt.' He takes a look at me, and waits a beat. 'Like that.'

Robin, the geeky girl dummy.

Greg saunters around, waves to people and shouts their names. They wave and shout back.

'How long have you been here?' I ask.

'Year and a half,' he replies, looking morose.

'You don't like it here?'

He smiles, but it's one of Derek's angry smiles.

'Used to be at Hollenby's, but, well … management wasn't pleased with something I did.'

'Shit happens,' I suggest.

'It doesn't just happen,' Greg says.

We approach a dummy dressed in a red lace bra and panty set standing underneath a 'Women's Underwear' banner. Greg stands in front, sizing it up.

'We'll give this another week. The manager says she got a double shipment.'

We swing around to Young Men's where the dummy's wearing cargo shorts.

'I've tried to tell them how passé this look is, but they keep telling me, "Squeeze it dry." Oh, well.'

Finally, Greg leads me to a mannequin wearing a cheesy print dress.

'Sportswear's gotten in a shipment of fall merchandise, and wants us to do something special,' he says, shaking his head at the dummy. 'God, get that thing off of her. She looks like a bag lady.' Greg looks at me, a lightbulb going off. 'Robin, tell you what,' he says. 'Cynthia's yours.'

'Mine?' Does he want me to take her home?

But Greg is already headed back to the warehouse. What is it about these people? Where's the fire?

'I'll show you what they've gotten in,' he's saying. 'Play with it. See what you come up with. I'll be back in Display.'

'Okay,' I say. I think he wants me to dress the dummy.

Greg takes me over to a wall of boxes in the warehouse and disappears. What a place. I stand there staring up at the wall, wondering what I'm doing here. The voices are here big-time, telling me I'm a dressmaker's dummy, that I can't do this, that Greg thinks I'm wearing children's clothes.

Go away, I tell them, but it's not working.

Derek, I call.

Whoosh. Hey, how's my best girl?

How am I ever going to do this?

Hey, go crazy.

I am already.

No, I mean, just go with the flow. Open up all the boxes. Have fun.

Then, whoosh, he's gone.

Damn. I look up, up, up at the twenty-foot cardboard wall. 'Anybody here?' I call out, but suddenly, there's no one around.

Can't do anything, a voice says.

Shut up, I say. I walk round and around the wall of boxes. I don't know what I'm looking for. I just want to sit down in a corner and curl into a fetal position.

She'll never amount to anything, I hear.

Oh, yeah? I tell it, and push at a box about the height of my shoulder. Three giant boxes come cascading down, just missing my head.

What a dope, the voice says.

I push on another, and three more come down. Eventually, all of Women's Sportswear is at my feet. I stand there, staring at the boxes.

'Hey, you!' I hear behind me.

I turn around to see a silhouette of a tall, geeky guy with glasses. 'Max,' I cry.

'Max? No, it's Frank. Housewares.'

Yeah, now that I look at him closely, he's not that Max-like. Not that broad-shouldered, and his hair is receding. Kind of stupid-looking, actually. But I'm happy to see him, even if he isn't Max.

I hear myself saying, 'Robin. Display.' Wow. That's who I am. Robin from Display.

Robin from the Moon, the voice remarks.

I mean it, shut up.

Meanwhile, Frank has been surveying the damage on the warehouse floor. 'Tornado?' he asks.

I shrug. 'How do you open the boxes?'

He flips a box over, slips his hand under a joint in the plastic tape that secures the box and pulls. The tape breaks. 'Open sesame,' Frank says.

'I'll be okay, now,' I say. 'Thanks.' But Frank Housewares doesn't go away. He helps me to open each and every box and to select a handful of chic pieces for my dummy. With each piece, he writes the style number on a blank inventory sheet he just so happens to have in his pocket.

'Never can tell when you need an inventory sheet,' Frank says, reaching into a box, and, voilà! pulling out a vinyl bomber jacket.

'Yes, yes, the jacket,' I cry.

Frank hands it to me, but he's not done telling me about accounting practices. 'The department manager will kill you if you don't itemize what you took out,' he says. 'Remember. You don't want to piss off the department managers.'

I nod, my arms full of the height of All-mart fashion.

Escorting me back to the dummy in the stupid dress, Frank gives me the inventory sheet. 'Nice to meet you, Robin in Display,' he says, and leaves.

'Thanks,' I call out after a minute, but he's long gone.

I don't like that guy, I hear Derek say.

Frank's a nice guy, I tell him. He helped me.

Oh, it's Frank, now, is it?

Derek, leave me alone. I've got work to do.

No, he says. I'll never leave you alone.

With that, the voices come on strong, as if Derek is the foreman, and he can tell them when they can talk and when they can't.

What a dope, I hear again, and She can't do it.

I ignore them all, Derek included, and dress the dummy with the stuff I brought out. Cynthia looks back at me in a black T-shirt, red satin vest, bomber jacket and capri pants as if to say, 'Are you sure about this?' I turn my back on her and proceed to Women's Shoes. That's where I see Melissa.

'Hey, little sister,' Melissa calls out to me from behind my back. 'What are you up to?'

'Can I take these?' I ask, pointing to some red patent leather boots.

'Oh, I wouldn't, if I were you.'

'But can I take them?' I ask again. I can't even imagine Melissa being me.

'I've got to see this,' Melissa says, grabbing the boots and making as if to come with me.

We walk over to the mannequin.

'Hmmm,' Melissa says. 'Has Greg seen this?'

'No,' I say, tugging the boots onto her feet and lacing them up. I back away from the dummy and take one last look. 'Hmmmm,' I say, myself.

'Let's see what he says,' Melissa says, and off she goes to the back of the store.

I stand there looking at Cynthia, wondering if she would pick these clothes herself.

Not on your life, a voice says.

Three minutes later, both of them are back.

'Well?' Melissa prompts.

Greg looks at Cynthia, takes four steps backward, puts his hand to his chin, and laughs. He looks over at Melissa, then back at me.

'A little edgy, but ... I like it.'

So, it's been going okay. Greg had me do the glass display case in watches, and I got some dummy hands and painted them black before putting the watches on. Greg told me to watch the people watch the display, and that's what I've been doing. Most of the people do a little double-take when they see the black hands. Especially black people. The department manager says sales are up 25 per cent.

So, I get to do some good stuff. But half of Wednesday, I washed display cases. Greg says I can't expect to do creative work all the time. That's his job. I'm an apprentice.

The sorcerer's apprentice, a voice says.

The voices haven't stopped. I saw Mankiewicz Saturday morning, and he says that's to be expected. I'm under stress. That he can't give me more medication or else I won't be able to function. And Derek says I just have to keep it together.

Haven't told Mankiewicz that Derek is here almost all the time. He comes and goes just as he pleases. Whoosh, he's here. Whoosh, he's gone. Worse than Father. And he's so jealous of any guy who walks past. I can't reason with him. He tells me I'm still his, even though he's dead, and he doesn't want to see me flirting with any of the other employees, especially Frank. I was going to tell Mankiewicz, but Derek came on strong and told me I better not tell.

So I didn't.

I watch Melissa sometimes, and she's a real flirt, just the way she used to be. This Bob guy, she's always talking to him, and he's nowhere as good-looking as Max. I was going to say something, but ... I didn't.

So things are going all right, except for those things.

More display cases to wash.

'Robin from Display,' a voice calls in back of me. It could be that demon who keeps telling me I'm the sorcerer's apprentice. I turn anyway, and the water in the pail I'm carrying slops over the top onto the floor.

'Frank from Housewares,' I say.

'You spilled your water.'

'Yeah.'

Frank pulls a rag out of his pocket and mops up the water. 'Never can tell when you might need a rag,' he says.

'What else do you have in there?' I ask, peering into his pocket.

'You want to see?' he says with a fake leer.

Derek's voice is suddenly loud and clear. 'Stay away from that guy, Robin.'

'No,' I answer.

'Nothing to see, anyway. It's empty,' Frank admits. 'Hey, Robin, I could use your help. I've got a load of Revereware in yesterday. A real shit-load of stuff. Pots and pans, and tea kettles, and casseroles. They buyer says we're up against big figures from last year, and I need to sell.'

'I've got to wash some cases,' I say, lifting the bucket for emphasis. Water slops out again.

'Let me carry that,' Frank says, after wiping up the new puddle.

I give him the bucket, and he walks me over to Electronics. 'I'll be over after lunch,' I tell him. Already, I've got a great idea of what to do with pots and pans. Robin from Display. That's who I am.

'After lunch,' Frank says, putting down the bucket and going back to his department.

I try to keep my mind on the work, focusing on the glass. Dunk, squeeze, slosh, wipe. Dunk, squeeze, slosh, wipe. It's hard to keep your mind totally focused on such stupid work. It keeps slipping off onto Max or Derek or Melissa. Or Frank. But when that happens, Derek comes back with a whoosh. I've got to think of something else. I picture the mannequin in the red bra and panties bending over a big pot, stirring it with a spoon. By the time I've finished the cases, I've got the whole enchilada for the Housewares display. I don't even take lunch. Lunch is history. Housewares is now.

I just go on over to Lingerie and drag the dummy away.

'Just a sec,' I tell the sales associate who's standing there with her mouth open. 'I'll bring you back something that's just as good.'

Frank isn't there when I bring the mannequin over, but he's got his shitload of pots half unpacked in the back of the department. I empty the box and bring it out to the floor, cover it with white contact paper, arrange the pots on top, fill the big pot with red wrapping paper like sauce, and a big spoon sticking out. The dummy – Melissa I've called her – is bending over the pot in her red underwear and cooking mitts, making dinner. I'm working away at this, unaware even of the demons, and suddenly I hear a laugh.

'You'll never get away with this,' the voice says. 'But it's great.'

I turn around, and it's Frank. He's standing there, and the light is in back of him, and I can't really see his face. For a second, I think he's Derek, because Derek's in my head telling me to stay away, but it's not. It's Frank, and he's laughing. Not like Max's laugh, where he just threw his head back and let go, but nice. A nice laugh. I stand up and look at the display with Frank's eyes. Sexy dummy. Sexy Revereware.

'Sex sells,' Frank is saying. 'But you better run it by Greg first.'

I can see the sales associate in Lingerie straining her neck to see what I've done with Melissa.

'I have to do another display first,' I tell Frank and head for Lingerie. Miss Sales Associate is still staring over at Housewares.

'You've got something you have a lot of?' I ask, and she brings me out a cheesy black satin teddy set. I take this over to shoes and grab a pair of satin mules off the rack, marking down the department and the style numbers on Frank's inventory sheet. I take all this back to Display, slap a black wig onto the closest mannequin and dress her in the teddy set and slippers. I drag her out to the floor, stopping at Jewellery for a pair of tasteful pearl earrings.

'Hey,' I ask the woman in back of the counter. 'What's the department number for this?'

'You can't just take anything you like,' the girls says. 'This is my last pair.'

'Okay,' I say, giving it back. 'Give me something you want to sell.'

She hands me a pair of over-the-top dangling rhinestones and fills in the department and style numbers herself. 'You want any more?' she asks, indicating a whole caseful.

I shake my head no, drag the dummy back to Lingerie, and take a good look. Frederick's of Hollywood. A little edgy, but I like it.

Melissa the cooking dummy is a hit. Half the store has been milling around the display, smiling and pointing. The lingerie buyer came out and checked it out first thing, then told us it was her idea. Greg told her no, it was his idea.

Frank says that's all well and good, but if the housewares buyer sees it, there's going to be hell to pay. He knows what those people are like; he used to be just like them. They'll say sex doesn't belong in Housewares, and miss the whole point that sex sells everything – even housewares.

As we speak, a middle-aged man asks to buy a whole set of Revereware … for his wife.

Greg and I leave Melissa there, stirring the pot in her underwear, and walk back to the display room.

'Que sera sera,' Greg says as we walk down the hall. 'My bet is the buyers won't quibble with sales.'

I say nothing. The voices are doing all the talking, and I can barely hear anything else.

Derek, I call in my head.

Silence from the one voice I want to hear. If I know him, he's sulking.

Derek, I call again. Could you please get them to tone it down a little?

Nothing from Derek. Laughter from the rest.

All this time, Greg's been telling me the latest gossip: the store manager and the sales associate in Jewellery, Ronald in Hardware who's marrying his second cousin, Melissa and Bob. Wait a minute.

'Melissa, my sister?' I ask, stopping in my tracks.

He laughs, and starts to clear the table off of wigs and accessories.

'You know this for sure?' I ask after a couple of minutes.

'I shouldn't have mentioned it,' Greg says. 'Forget it.'

'How can I forget it?' I'm almost in tears, thinking of poor Max, and how Melissa is making a fool of him, of how Max is worth a hundred Melissas and never should have married her in the first place.

'Maybe I heard wrong,' Greg says, getting up and putting his arm around me. 'Sometimes it's just a rumour.'

I know the guy's gay, but I don't like him touching you, either, Derek says to me all of a sudden.

'Derek!' I whisper.

'What?' Greg says.

'I have to go to the ladies' room,' I tell him, and walk out the door, rush down the hall toward the staff bathroom and lock myself in a stall.

Derek! I've been trying to contact you all morning.

Well, I was busy, he says.

Melissa's been screwing around with this schmuck named Bob, I tell him. And the baby ...

Yeah, the baby may be his.

Yeah. I pull off a length of toilet paper and wipe my eyes.

Melissa is also a schmuck, Derek says.

Girls can't be schmucks, I say, throwing the paper into the toilet and spooling off some more.

I'm not going to quibble. She's a ... piece of shit. Dreck. Turd. Doodoo. Your own words.

Yeah, I say. What do I do, Derek?

Nothin', kiddo, he says. There's nothing you can do. You're not God, you know.

Then it's whoosh and he's gone, and I don't hear from him for the rest of the day.

Chapter Twelve

Last night Debbie showed me the article in the newspaper on Melissa the dummy stirring a Revereware pot. The headline runs, 'Sexy dummy sells pots,' and the article goes on to say there's been a run on Revereware at the local All-mart store. Along with the article is a picture of a smiling Frank, one arm around the mannequin, the other waving a frying pan in the air.

The moment I get in today, Frank tells me four housewares buyers are on their way. And the store manager wants to see all three of us, he says. Now.

We find Greg in the back and make our way up the escalator to the store manager's office. He tells us to sit down, so we do. My voices are going double time.

She's in for it now.

Heads will roll.

I focus the best I can on the three other people in the office.

'Whose idea was this, anyway?' Mr Caputo is asking.

'Well, it was kind of everybody's,' Frank is saying.

'Everybody's?' the manager says, his eyes going all squinty like my mother's.

'Robin Farber,' Greg says, his finger pointing straight at me. 'My new assistant.'

Mr Caputo looks at me for the first time.

'Did you do this on your own, Ms Farber?'

Come clean, Derek says.

'Yes, it was my fault.' My fault, his fault. It's no one's fault.

'Well, it's not your fault solely. Actually, I hold you all responsible,' he says, shifting his gaze to Greg and Frank. 'She's just an assistant.'

She's just a girl. You can't hold her responsible as a normal person, a voice says.

Greg and Frank hang their heads.

'Now,' he says, facing me. 'Normally I applaud originality, young lady, but this is just outside the envelope ...'

Tell him sales are up 25 per cent, Derek prompts.

'Sales …'

'But I'm going to reserve judgment until after I meet with the buyers …'

'Are up …'

'… I want you to remember what All-mart stands for.'

'Twenty-five per cent.'

'And I for one do not want to jeopardize our image for a few sales.'

Frank has his finger across his lips, but I'm done already.

'You understand that?' Mr Caputo asks.

'Yes sir,' we all answer.

'Good, I'll tell you what I decide after I meet with the buyers. Thank you.'

Frank and Greg stand up. I look at them stupidly, until Frank takes my arm and pulls me up.

Don't let him touch you, Derek says.

'Don't worry,' Greg is saying. 'Management never decides anything until they see the results. If it succeeds, you're a hero. If it fails, you're dead meat.' Somehow I have this feeling he's talking about himself.

Greg and I are standing discreetly behind a mirrored column across the aisle from Housewares, so we see the buyers come trooping in a little before ten. They stomp across the floor, carrying reams of computer sheets, spend ten minutes staring at the display, writing furiously in their notebooks, looking at each other, shaking their heads. Just as they start to make their way to the register, all hell breaks loose. A snake of customers rushes through the store, making a beeline for the housewares department. Soon, there's a mob of ladies fighting for pots and pans, pushing and shoving, holding copies of the newspaper article above their heads like stock options. Frank has to start ringing in along with two sales people, to keep up with the customers. One lady, holding a toaster oven, tries to get his attention.

'Is this Revereware?' she's shouting.

'Yes, yes,' he nods.

'I'll buy it,' she says, pushing to the head of the line.

'Frank!' I hear one of the buyers call out, as they watch the pots fly out of the store.

'I'll be right with you,' Frank calls, ringing up the lady with the toaster oven.

The buyers stand there for twenty minutes, and we stand there watching them. Finally, Frank comes over to them with a register tape in his hand. 'We just sold $15,000 worth of merchandise.'

'Can't argue with that,' one of the buyers says.

Another buyer flips open her cellphone to call the head office, and I hear her giving orders to set up sexy displays ASAP in every store that carries Revereware. 'Bra and panties,' she's shouting.

I'm still watching everything from behind the safety of the pole, but suddenly, it all gets to me: the commotion and the noise, buyers and customers, heroes and dead meat. Robin in Display. Is that who I am?

Good job, Derek says, and then everything goes black.

I wake up with Melissa cradling my head. 'It's okay. It's nothing,' she's telling everybody, shooing them away. 'I'm her sister.'

'Wow,' she says as I open my eyes.

'What?'

'The mob that ate Housewares,' she answers, helping me to sit up. Housewares, across the aisle, is a shambles.

'Sorry,' I say, thinking of the mess I made.

'What are you sorry about? The store is going to break sales records today.'

Funny, the voices are gone. There's silence inside my head. I'm not sure I like this.

Melissa is looking at me strangely. 'You okay?'

'Yeah.'

'You want to stand up?'

'Okay.' The two of us help me up.

I catch Frank watching me from in back of the register. He runs over. 'You okay now?' he asks.

'Yeah,' Melissa answers for me. 'She does this all the time.'

'Really?'

'It's nothing,' Melissa assures him, walking off. 'I'm getting some lunch.'

'You really pass out all the time?' Frank asks me.

'Only when there's too much excitement,' I say.

'Well, I better hold onto you, then. Mr Caputo says he's decided he likes what you did, and he wants you to do it again.'

* * *

So, two days later I'm back on the loading dock, staring at a gazillion boxes of v c r's and stereos. Make them sexy, Mr Caputo says. Yeah, right.

The pots and pans idea just came to me. It was fun, like Derek said it was supposed to be. Go crazy, he said, and I did. But I didn't know the whole world would go crazy. Crazy with crazy doesn't work.

Frank's been really good throughout this thing. He's been my port in the storm, a rock, something to hold onto that won't blow away. I guess he's a little like Howard that way: not showy or brilliant, just a real solid guy. Maybe I see why Mother was drawn to Howard, after all the romantic madness, the infatuation, the charisma, and finally, the frenzy and the lunacy, that she had with Father. Frank's like a concrete foundation to build a house on. Derek was the ground around the San Andreas fault, always waiting for the big one. Me, I'm a house built on sand. The slightest vibration and I tumble down. Build me a concrete foundation, and maybe I'll last.

But Derek doesn't like Frank. Tells me he's a jerk, and he doesn't know what I see in him. Then when that doesn't work, he just starts ordering me around, telling me I can't see him. Finally, when I don't listen, he threatens me with … what, he won't say. I don't know what to do or who to tell. Derek says I better not tell. Or else.

So, I'm standing here, staring at a load of very unsexy boxes. Caputo wants me to do the same thing. Dress a dummy in bra and panties and sell the damn merchandise. But I don't want to do that. I'm through with that. That puts me in the same box with the merchandise, selling the both of us.

No. I won't. No, I said.

So, what else is new? The voices are back. They were gone for about five minutes, that's all. It was really spooky with only me in my head. Is that what normal is: empty? It was like moving into a big house all by yourself. But, hey, there's nothing to worry about, because they're back. Everyone. All the devils, Father, Derek. And they're all giving advice. Do this. No, do that. No, for God's sake, Robin, don't do that! We're a bunch of monkeys all in the same monkey suit. An army of ticks all biting the same dog.

Still, I've got to admit it, all the chaos in my brain produces something unique, e.g., Cynthia the cooking dummy, a true Robin-inspired creation. From a mess of various parts and sundry voices emerges something unexpected, something good and useful. I let the whole thing stew and ferment, and out bubbles an idea. I'll get an idea about the stereo display. I'm not worried now. I'll go out to Electronics, and start checking out the space. I'm kind of thinking of having the stereos blasting 1950s rock and roll, some Dick Clark tapes on the VCR machine: I can see it now.

So, I'm on my way out of the warehouse, through the Alice-in-Wonderland door, down the hallway, my mind set on promotion! and merchandising! and I hear funny noises behind one door. Little squeals, whispers, grunts. I open the door, and the sounds stop. I can just distinguish two shapes in the dark.

'Get out!' a voice growls.

But I stand there in the threshold, the light behind me, trying to make out what I see. A baseball cap, a high-heeled shoe, a man's torso, a woman's breast.

'Shut the door, stupid!' Melissa's voice shouts. And now I know what I saw.

I slam the door, run into the display room and cry with the dummies.

The voices got really loud after that, and I took the bus and went home early. Right now, I'm sitting next to Ray and Bart watching television. It's a sitcom, but Ray looks like old stone face. Bart is laughing along with the studio audience. I'm moping.

'C'mon, Robin. It's funny,' Bart says.

'Yeah,' I say. 'I know.'

'Then why aren't you laughing?'

'I'm not in the mood,' I answer and get up to check the roster on the dining room wall: Dinner. Bart – cooking; Robin – table service.

'What are you making for dinner, Bart?' I call.

Bart is still laughing from the last stupid sitcom joke. 'Hahaha, lasagna,' he says.

I go into the kitchen and take out the plates, the spoons, the knives, the forks, the napkins, and whatnot. I shuffle out into the dining room, bringing plates one time, then back into the kitchen. Then I bring the spoons. Then the knives, then the forks, then the napkins, then the whatnot. The routine calms me: the back-and-forthness, the forth-and-backness. No thinking. I don't want to think. I hear Bart laughing in the living room, and smell lasagna cooking in the oven. The voices are there, telling me I'm dead meat, that Bart had a lobotomy, that Melissa is a shit, and Max is a dope. I let the two sides fight it out. Laughter and frontal lobotomy. Lasagna and dead meat. Melissa and dope. Max and shit. Nobody wins.

Mankiewicz is already bringing his hands together into a steeple in front of him: business mode. 'Have the voices changed in any way?'

'Yes,' I say.

'How?' Mankiewicz is asking. 'How have they changed?'

Don't say a word, Derek commands.

Suddenly, I'm afraid. 'I can't say,' I whisper.

'You can't say?' he says. 'Why can't you say?'

Don't you dare, Derek warns.

'Stop it!' I yell.

Mankiewicz recoils in his chair. 'What is it, Robin?'

'It's Derek,' I say in a small voice, waiting for the roof to cave in.

'Derek?' he asks, leaning over. 'Have you been hearing Derek's voice?'

'Yes. He's always talked to me. Always. But now, I don't know. He's jealous all the time. He's jealous when I say hello to a guy, any guy. He threatens me ...'

'Go on, Robin,' Mankiewicz prompts.

'I can't. My head hurts. I can't.'

'Robin, he's not real.'

'He says he's as real as any of us.' My head is bursting.

'Robin, Derek is dead. You've got to face that.'

'He called you a jerk.'

For the first time, Mankiewicz smiles. 'Now, you know and I know that Derek never would call me that.'

'I can't say any more,' I whisper. 'He'll punish me.'

'Oh, Robin,' Mankiewicz sighs. 'What can he possibly do?'

'No, Derek,' I shout. 'Don't!' But it's too late. The pain slices through my head and everything goes black.

Chapter Thirteen

I've been back at Berkshire for two days now. Mankiewicz tells me he knew this was coming, and he blames himself for leaving me to deal with it myself. I tell him not to blame himself, but I can tell he still does. Mankiewicz internalizes too much. Maybe he should see someone about that.

Anyway, he's changed my medications a little and increased our sessions to four times a week. Mankiewicz called Howard to make sure it was okay, and it is. Howard says he'll just take it out of my wedding money; then he laughs. It's a joke, he says. I don't get it.

So, I've been working with the good doctor, who keeps telling me I have to *give up* Derek.

'Give up?' I say. I wasn't the one who invited Derek into my head. I didn't ask for this, and I'm not the one who's holding on.

'Yes, you are,' Mankiewicz says. 'Derek isn't real. He's a figment of your imagination.'

Oh, we're back to that, Derek says to me.

Sometimes I just wish I could get the two of them to argue it out by themselves. Me, I'm pretty good these days. I feel good; there's nothing wrong with me. My only problem is Derek harassing me. I'm beginning to think I need an exorcist, not a psychiatrist.

Mankiewicz, of course, disagrees. The problem, dear Robin, he says, is not in our stars but in ourselves. He tells me I have to find myself. That in finding myself, the voices will fade away. I'm not lost, I tell him. Just convince Derek to go and haunt someone else.

Mankiewicz sighs. '*You* do it, Robin,' he says again. 'It's your need that forces you to create him.'

And on and on. Greg says they're keeping my job for me, but they can't hold it forever.

Forever, Derek says.

Five days, now. This place is so confining. I think I never realized it before, I was in such bad shape. But I'm better now, and I want out.

Oh, stop complaining, Derek says.

Beverly has gone on to a sicker place. They couldn't do anything with her, Alex told me; she was trying to hurt herself all the time. After she broke the mirror and slit her wrists with a jagged shard, they took her away. Beverly's bed is still empty, awaiting someone who's sick but not so sick. Sick but not so sick: a very select demographic. Berkshire doesn't just take anyone, you know. I took her pillow, but it's really no better than mine, after all those months of coveting it. It's the person I really want, not the pillow. I miss that crazy girl who was forever reading page 11 of *Vogue* magazine.

And Roz is just Roz. She keeps telling me that she's going to be my roommate real soon, but then she withdraws into her own little world and doesn't talk to me at all. I asked Mankiewicz about her, and he just shakes his head and says she's one sick girl. There's no one here to talk to except you-know-who, and he's no fun.

So, I was really happy when Frank (ouch!) came to visit, but the place got to him. He came, so jolly, with a box of candy and flowers, like I was in the hospital for a broken leg or something. Then he saw Roz and all the rest of them and turned into Howard before my very eyes, taking four steps away and saying that he'll see me back at the job. Greg called, too, but by then I didn't want to see anybody. Damn! Damn! Where is it I belong? I don't belong inside and Mankiewicz says I'm not ready to go back outside. I'm nowhere, no one. Where is Robin in Display? Where did she go?

Down the staircase, right turn at the bottom. 'Come on in, Robin,' Mankiewicz calls out before I get to the door. We've already had three sessions, and nothing is changed except now Derek is really pissed.

I walk in, sit down on the chair. Mankiewicz turns to face me. The doctor is in.

'Robin, I'd like to talk to Derek,' he says right off.

'But he's not real, you said.'

'Let's just assume his existence, then.'

Let's just assume *your* existence, you moron, Derek snaps.

'Tell me what he says, Robin,' Mankiewicz says.

'He's not saying anything.'

'Just repeat what Derek says, when he says it.'

Shit. Dreck. Turd. Doodoo, I hear.

I repeat every word.

'Is that what he said?'

Yes, you idiot.

'Derek said, "Yes, you idiot."'

'Angry, isn't he?'

'But you said you don't believe it's Derek.'

'It doesn't sound like him, no. Don't you think this person sounds angry?'

'Yes,' I agree. 'He's always angry lately.'

'Derek, why are you so angry?' Mankiewicz asks.

I'm angry at Robin, Derek says.

'What did I do?' I shout out loud.

You didn't stop me.

'I didn't know! It wasn't me, it was you. You didn't trust me enough!'

Trust you? *I'm really sorry about how it all turned out, Derek. That's the last thing I would have wanted. I didn't mean to hurt you.* Didn't you say those things?

'I never said those things.'

You were thinking them, then.

'I didn't know you could hear me.'

I heard you, you bitch. You were all set to trade me in for model Max, but he didn't love you.

'I said I'd marry you. I said I loved you.'

You didn't mean it. I killed myself because of you. I'm really angry at you, Robin.

'No, no!' I shriek. 'I'm angry at *you*. You left me. You killed yourself and left me, just like my Father did.'

At this, Dr Mankiewicz breaks in. 'Robin, did you just hear yourself?'

I look up at him foggily.

'You're angry at Derek for leaving you,' he says. 'And you're angry at yourself for not stopping him. And you're keeping the idea of Derek alive, because if he isn't really dead, than you don't have to deal with your feelings.'

'That's not true! You heard him, Dr Mankiewicz. He just said he's angry at me.'

'I didn't hear anyone but you, Robin. You stopped telling me what Derek said after the first three sentences.'

It's true, Derek says. You fucked up, you stupid bitch.

'Damn it, Derek,' I cry, and run out.

* * *

I've got the feeling that Mankiewicz is doing a scientific experiment. He wants to prove something. He's sure it can't be the real McCoy, the real Wineker, but, being a student of human behaviour, he knows there's this little bit of chaos in everything. Something he can't explain. Maybe that's why he went into psychology: the last frontier of reason, a para-science. Psychologists go into psychology not to prove scientific truths but to disprove them. They don't really want to find that the answer to life is cut and dried, i.e, the human brain is a random assortment of adaptive mutations, and that's all, folks. No, they want to find more mystery. Mystery upon mystery. An infinite Russian nesting doll of mystery. An impossibly knotted ball of DNA. A hopelessly complex and insoluable puzzle. They fear peeling the onion layer by layer all the way down to its centre, only to find … more onion. Mankiewicz is going into this thing ostensibly to prove Derek a fake, and hoping against all hope that he is real.

Never mind that he can't hear Derek's voice for himself, and that I am not to be believed. Am I a hopeless lunatic, or am I Idiot Savant, Portal to the Universe? Am I, Robin Farber, privy to knowledge that Mankiewicz, Lord High Commissioner of Psychology, can only dream of?

Shut up, Robin, Derek says. Let's get this over with.

'He says he wants to get started.'

'Well, Derek is going to have to wait his turn,' Mankiewicz says. 'I want to talk about your father, first, Robin.'

Not him again, Derek complains.

'Robin, do you remember your father when he was alive?'

'Of course,' I say. 'I remember when he strung himself up from a light bulb.'

'But, you were just a baby then. You never would have seen that.'

'Well, I can see it all. Maybe it was Father telling me.'

'Did you ever ask your mother about him?'

'She won't talk about him. She says he ruined her life.'

Mankiewicz just sits there waiting. We've been through this before.

'How can she say that to me?' I rant. 'It means she wishes I wasn't born.'

'Are you angry at your mother, Robin?'

'Angry? No.'

Mankiewicz makes a big show of disentangling his fingers from their steeple, stretching them, braiding them back. 'So, you only know what your father told you?' he finally asks.

'Yes.'

'I see. Does he love you, your father?'

'He tells me he loves me all the time, but he's here, he's there. He's always got somewhere to go to that's more important than me.'

Mankiewicz seems lost in thought. 'Robin,' he finally says. 'You've got to realize that you idealize the wrong people. Your father, for example. You never knew him. You don't know him. What you hear in your head is a father you wish you had. He's not really there. He was never there for you.'

'And Max,' he adds. 'He didn't love you. Max left you for your own sister. Derek was the one who loved you.'

'Max loved me.'

'I think not. You take all the people who love you for granted. Derek. Your mother, who was always there for you. Howard. Look at Howard, Robin,' Mankiewicz says. 'He has no genetic bond to you, but he's been as good and loving a father as anyone can want. Yet you tell me he's a fool.'

'You're right,' I admit. 'Howard's okay.'

'You obsess over the people who never cared for you, and take for granted the ones who do.'

That's exactly what I've been telling you, Derek remarks.

I don't bother repeating this.

Dammit, Robin, you're not telling him what I say. Don't ignore me!

I sigh. 'Derek says we're ignoring him.'

'Okay, Derek,' Mankiewicz says, a hint of a smile on his lips. 'Talk to me.'

I'm not angry. Robin just makes me mean to her, so she won't care anymore.

Me? I'm making *you* mean? I ask.

Don't change the subject. Tell him.

I clear my throat and repeat it out loud.

'Robin, listen to what you just said,' Mankiewicz says.

'I heard it. I just told it to you.'

'Listen to it.'

'I heard it. I heard it.'

'Who's the angry one, Derek?' Mankiewicz asks.

Robin. Robin is angry. She's angry that I left her. I'm sorry, Robin.

I repeat the words.

'What are you feeling, Robin?' Mankiewicz asks me, for the millionth time.

'Why are you always asking me what I'm feeling, godammit?' I shout at him. 'I don't feel anything!'

That isn't true, Derek says.

Something bubbles up inside me, exploding like a grenade.

'I'm pissed off!' I shout. 'Sick and tired of everyone always leaving me! Sick and tired of being so powerless!'

Suddenly, I'm sobbing, I don't know why. He comes out from behind the desk and puts his arms around me. I hold on tight for I don't know how long. When I let go, there's a big wet spot on his clean white shirt and a silence in my head.

Derek? I call. No answer. I didn't mean it, I tell him. Don't leave me, Derek. Father, where are you?

'Robin?' Mankiewicz says, breaking the silence. 'What's the matter?'

'I'm alone.'

'*I'm* here.'

'The voices are all gone.'

Mankiewicz just stands there studying my face. Finally, he says, 'How do you feel about that?' Good old Mankiewicz. It's nice to know some things never change.

'I don't know.' Exhilaration and terror are taking turns.

'The disappearance of the voices is a good sign, but probably only temporary.'

'You mean, Derek might be back?'

Mankiewicz sighs. 'As a voice only, Robin. You *must* come to terms with it. Derek's dead.'

'I don't want Derek dead.'

'You're going to have to learn to live without him. Finding yourself is giving up the others.'

'Not Derek.'

'It's the first step, Robin. Be brave.'

Suddenly, I'm angry again. Mankiewicz is doing it again, telling me what's good for me, ordering me around. What does he know of being left behind? 'What do you care?' I shout. 'No one's leaving you. You go home every night to your sexy wife and your precious Rachel Ellen.'

'What?' says Mankiewicz, blinking.

'You lock the door and go home. Leave us alone with our craziness. Drive away and leave us behind. What do you care?'

Mankiewicz is staring at me, like he's never seen me before. 'Robin.

It's true your father and Max and Derek have all left you. And you have a justifiable right to be angry about that. But you have no right to say I don't care. I've always been here for you.'

'Because Howard pays you to.'

Mankiewicz looks at me like I've hit him with a baseball bat. 'Robin, you've hurt me deeply.'

'I don't believe that,' I say. 'You're Teflon-coated. All hard and shiny and untouchable. All-knowing. Whitecoat, the All-High Master of the Universe.'

'Robin, that was never me. That was you.'

'No, no! It's you. I'm just a little powerless girl. Shut her away and throw away the key. No, You! You're Whitecoat the All-Powerful.'

'God knows I'm not all-powerful,' Mankiewicz says. 'Psychiatry is an art, not a science. Sometimes all we can do is to try to get the patient to heal herself.'

'Whitecoat,' I say, talking over him. 'The guy who makes us swallow pills whether we want them or not. Who keeps us locked away when we don't want to be or who calls our parents and makes them come and get us when we want to stay. Who rules our lives. Who ties us down. Who decides our goddamned lives for us. Who sits on a throne. You're God.'

'I'm sorry if you feel that way, Robin, but I'm surely not God. Yes, I'm too stiff. I don't relate as well to the patient as some of the younger doctors do. I can't help it. They trained us like that. Be detached. Don't get involved.'

'Whitecoat Whitecoat Bo-bitecoat Banana-fana-fo Fitecoat Mi-my-mo Mitecoat Whitecoat,' I sing as loud as I can, drowning out his voice.

'Robin, it's not me you're angry at,' Mankiewicz says. But his face is red and there's sweat on his upper lip.

I can see I'm getting to him, and I'm happy about it, because he's been the problem all along. I can't believe I didn't see it before. 'Yes it is. I'm angry at you. The All-Powerful Whitecoat.'

'All-Powerful,' he says, staring down at me, a smile on his lips but his eyes all black and sad. 'Robin, do you have any idea what it's like to have to care for people who never get well? To try every treatment available, and to make no difference? To do all these things and fail? Day after day to watch and listen and not to be able to help?'

But I'm not even listening I'm so mad. 'You!' I shout. 'You're the one who killed Derek. Who let his father take him. You said yourself you should have gone to his mother, made him take treatment. You could have done all sorts of things. But you didn't.'

Mankiewicz takes a step backwards, catching himself on the desk. 'No, I didn't,' he says in a choked voice, grabbing the rim as he makes his way all around the desk. He drops down into his chair, and turns it toward the wall. Above the chair back, I see his shoulders heave. Poor stuffy Whitecoat. Always down to business: listening and listening and listening, being objective, never breaking down, never, never showing your feelings ... Not even Whitecoat is God. No one is God.

Suddenly, I'm not angry any more. I'm sorry. And I'm sad. Sad for the world and for all of us little powerless, caring creatures in it: Derek and Father and Roz, Mother and Howard. And Mankiewicz. I come round his desk and put my arms around him.

Acknowledgements

My profound thanks to Leon Rooke, who believed in this book, and without whom it might never have been published; to my editor, John Metcalf, whose enthusiasm and expert knowledge guided this book to its full potential; and to Tim Inkster and Jack Illingworth at the Porcupine's Quill for their professional support in its publication. Most of all, I thank my husband, Mordechai, for his perceptive feedback and constant love and support.

PETER G. BORG

Bonnie Rozanski currently resides in New Jersey, but has lived all over the United States and Canada. She has degrees from the University of Pennsylvania, Adelphi University and the University of Guelph, and worked in both academia and business before deciding to return to her first love, writing. She has written several books in which scientific issues inform the plots, as well as two prize-winning plays. *Banana Kiss* is her debut novel.